westside storeys

edited by Dotun Adebayo

The
X
Press

Published by
The X Press
PO Box 25694
London, N17 6FP
Tel: 020 8801 2100
Fax: 020 8885 1322
E-mail: vibes@xpress.co.uk
Web site: www.xpress.co.uk3

Printed by Cox & Wyman, Reading, UK

Distributed in UK by Turnaround Distribution
Unit 3, Olympia Trading Estate, Coburg Road, London N22 6TZ
Tel: 020 8829 3000
Fax: 020 8881 5088

ISBN 1-902934-23-7

'Ear Wot

London's not just full of storeys, it's full of storytellers. Everywhere you go, everywhere you look, somebody is spinning a story that will make you smile, cry, cuss and fuss. You're spoilt for choice of storeys and stories. There are so many good ones, it's a question of where to start.

Like the little boy of eight or nine or ten begging you 'a ten pound change' because he's somehow been untangled from his big sister and the only way he can get home is by taxi(don't laugh, he was bawling his eyes out at the time, crying me into submission — the little raas) and that if he didn't get home straight away his house would surely burn down because he had only just remembered that he had left a pan of boiling water on the gas stove. By the time you realise it's a good story, he's skipping away down Craven Park Road, laughing his head off at your gullibility, taunting you with the tenner gripped firmly in his clenched fist, blissfully unaware of his hidden literary talents. And what about that yarn that Babatunde, the rastaman who owns that bookshop down on the Grove is always spinning whenever you go in to collect your payment for books sold? You know the one, where he clutches his chest as if he's about to keel over and then starts wheezing his once upon a time about a bad heart and a doctor who insists that he must take it easy, and not allow anything to stress him, least of all money worries. Of course it's a yarn, and not a particularly good one (it would work better as a soap opera or a Benny Hill sketch) but you're not a yardie or a Kray so you've got to entertain the remote possibility that there's a twist to this story and you agree to defer the invoice until a later date. "Yeah, right," he agrees. Yeah, RIGHT!

So you wipe the bird shit off the top of your head and you flag down a 36B, but the driver doesn't like the look of you at that time of the night, so you're going to have to make your way south some other how. Now you're wishing that you had told Babatunde to give you your money and die. Remember dat?

Yeah, yeah, yeah, mo'fucker, you done your repetition, hesitation and literary alliteration, now tell us something we don't know, ho. Make the story flow with some descriptive narrative.

Somehow you make it south cross the river flow, into 'yo-man's' land, home of the best blow on the island. Past the Dog Star on Coldharbour where trendy liberals sit and discuss Marx and nuclear fission (with all a rustic's intuition), where once (in its pre-Dog days) sat villains of the past exchanging tabs and tips on how to duck and dive. But this ain't 1993 and Brixton ain't what it used to be. There's a time and a place for memory lane, but first you've got to walk the plank of Railton Road at this time of night, so you hold your breath, steel your resolve and inch your way cautiously past the old frontline, more tense now that operation eradication has cleaned up the area, than it used to be back when it was the first stop Bob Marley would make on arrival from Jamaica, just to see wha' ah gwan.

There you go with that old school revival business. You done already said that this wasn't the time and the place… Are you trying to win some literary prize or something?

So you're at the trendy liberal dinner party and you're telling the story about when you woz a kid in Tottenham, at school with Winston Silcott (that always grabs the attention — now they're sitting up, listening keenly, "Did he just say WINSTON SILCOTT!").

"Yeah, THAT Winston Silcott — Tottenham Riots, Broadwater Farm, 1985. The same Winston Silcott that never killed Blakelock. He did a lot of other shit though. But back then we woz just eight or nine or ten, and he was just a good footballer, and one of the hardest guys in school. No doubt. You see, his old man used to give him licks like my old man used to give us licks."

Okay, now you've got our attention mo'fucker, turn the page and tell us the rest of the fuckin' story. Suck me in quick else I'm flakin' out.

"In that case, I'll give you the last bit first and work backwards (you see how we versatile and coming with style after style after style). Put it this way, I'm locked up in a police cell at the age of twelve. In Welwyn Garden City (a long way from home) in the middle of the night. When they finally got hold of my old man, he was cussing bad word, not too happy about being woken up at three-fifteen in the morning. He told the cops to do whatever they wanted with me. So they locked me up. Said I had sent them on a wild goose chase. You see, before they woke my father up, they woke Mr Hadjiminas up. They had been trying for hours by phone, with no joy. That's why I had given Mr Hadjiminas's number, because I knew they slept tight in that household. No amount of ringing was going to wake them up. But I hadn't reckoned on the Welwyn Garden City cops requesting the Tottenham cops to go round and wake the town if they had to. And when the Tottenham cops told Mr Hadjiminas that they had his son thirty miles away at Welwyn Garden police station, Mr Hadjiminas assured them that they didn't. The Tottenham cops insisted that they did. Until finally Mr Hadjiminas obliged by going upstairs to his son's bedroom, to see that the real Stelios Hadjiminas was snoring away peacefully where he was supposed to be.

"You see, I figured I could get back to London before anyone realised I was missing. But the last train back to Finsbury Park was just leaving as I got to Stevenage station at midnight. That's how come a twelve year old black kid dressed in drainpipe trousers, brother creepers, a drape coat and a bootlace tie came to be hitch-hiking to London at that time of night. Got a lift to a hotel in the middle of nowhere. Walked into the bar and begged another ride. Got to Welwyn and just missed the last service train before dawn. I knew my old man was going to kill me. So I walked into the police station of my own accord, like they were a limousine service to drive me home.

Bill Haley and the Comets? They weren't even all that. The teds — old and new — turned out to hail him though. As usual, it was spot the black teddy boy. Amused and bemused, the old timers with their brylcreemed ducks arses and thinned-out greying quiffs couldn't figure out where I was coming from. Especially Sunglasses Ron, the self-appointed President of the Confederate States of America. Let's face it, he was apartheid through and through."

Okay, that's deep, but who the fuck are you? Introduce yourself. Tell us who your mother was, what your father does, and the rest of that David Copperfield shit. What makes a good story are the people who reside in those storeys. London's full of 'em.

"Meet Les. He was my flatmate (with Simon V. and that tosser Conk Smith, who had a huge nose and played excellent classical piano, but was such a snob he insisted on speaking in French all the time, especially regarding the revolutionary status of his sexual agnosticism — "Je suis un artiste. Je n'ai pas de sexe."). This was back when I was twenty storeys high in Kennington — Britannia Point — with a widescreen view of the Houses of Parliament out the two bedroom window. Now Les had a bad stammer. I mean, really bad. Once the stutter started, he was unable to proceed until he threw something up in the air and caught it. Then he was fine and he would deliver the next few sentences fluently before he would need to chuck something in the air again and catch it. Sometimes we would take the piss out of him, when he was desperately trying to tell us something important, by catching the matchbox or the set of keys in mid-air and withholding it. He would then start "F-f-f-f-f-f" and flapping around desperately for something not too heavy to throw up and if he couldn't find anything we would take pity on him and let him have the matchbox only to hear him splutter, 'F-f-f-fuck off, you cunts.' Anyway, on account of the flat being a two-bedroom flat and four guys, Les lived in the storage cupboard (I had one bedroom, Simon V. had the other and Conk Smith had the living room through which you had to walk to get to the kitchen). So I come home from work one evening and head straight for the kitchen and walk in on Les and his missus stark bollock naked on top of Conk's piano, playing it doggystylee. Les sees me, starts searching for a box of matches or his keys and reaches over for a set on top of the window sill. Needless to say, it tilted their precarious balancing act in favour of gravity and Les and his missus come crashing to the ground with a bang — so to speak. I'm standing there rolling around with laughter while Les is still grabbing for those keys. He tosses them up in the air and catches them and blurts out, "I'm on the fuckin' job, next time knock before you enter."

So you're full up of storeys and you've got a coupla stories, but how do they all link up? Where's the engine that keeps the motor tickin' over, page after page after page? I'm talking about the plot. Where's your page turner?

Well okay, here's the coup. Weird London stories. You know, the ones that make you think — "Weird!" Call it quirky or whatever, but something that will be a surprise whether you're up on the twentieth floor of Trellick Tower or down in the basement of a building earmarked for demolition to make way for the new King's Cross Channel Tunnel rail link. "Weird, you say? Well, this was back when we were all down in Deptford — Me, Conrad and Robert-fuckin'-Davis who couldn't tell the truth even if it dragged his balls across a set of dirty razor blades. So there we were smoking the best weed, to distract are thoughts from the impending eviction after a glorious couple of years of not paying rent, when we started wondering why we were paying so much to get high from our own supply and we started kicking around ideas of how we could bypass HM Customs with a ki or two of the stuff. You know, we ran through all the possible scenarios by air, sea and mail. None of us fancied rowing a boat, Con said something about sniffer dogs at the Post Office, and so we figured that the only thing left that was full proof was the carrier pigeon idea. Okay, they can't carry that much, but if you took them down to Amsterdam and loaded an ounce or two on their backs, they would surely find their way home. You've got to be pretty stoned to entertain such an idea and, like I said, Zebbie's Brixton Special Reserve cess was the best. Before we knew it, we had pulled out calculators and estimated how many carrier pigeons it would take for us to be millionaires by the end of the year. The only thing missing was the carrier pigeons. Robert-fuckin'-Davis lied as usual that he knew how to train carrier pigeons, all we had to do was find them. So there we were at Trafalgar

Square feeding the friggin' pigeons and trying to nab 'em on the sly. Fuck that cess really was the best. No lie, we woz buzzing. Robert-fuckin'-Davis only manages to capture one, doesn't he, stuffs it under his coat and we go, so cock-a-hoop about our smuggling operation that I grab him by the cheeks and kiss him on the lips (a government health warning against smoking high grade if ever I saw one) and say, "Yo Rob, you're my favourite white boy," not realising that we had kidnapped the pigeon queen.

"The next morning, I staggered out of my bed and got ready for work dreaming of the day when I could tell 'em to stuff it, which I would once the contraband started to come in regular. I opened the front door to what seemed like the whole neighbourhood. A camera flash went, and in the distance police sirens wailed their approach. All attention was focused on our roof, on which a thousand pigeons and more covered every available tile. Flashes of Alfred Hitchcock's 'The Birds' came to mind. I'm no stupid white man, when shit like that happens you don't hang around for the last reel of the film by which time you've had your eyes gouged out, you get the fuck out and find a quiet corner to buil' another spliff. I jumped on my motorcycle and rode off in the sunset, but I was unable to shake off the flock of pigeons above shitting on me wherever I go still to this day."

Of course, if that master storyteller Hitchcock was here he'd say it's not just the story, it's the way you tell 'em.

In chronological order, here are the heads that tell these *West Side Storeys:*

The Extremists — Jason Durant and Samar Durant, brothers from the south side, coming from a rap perspective and blowing up like nitro.

Jemima Gibbons, is an experienced television producer and media consultant, and a party animal by night. 'Hoxton Babylon' is her first published work.

Nick Barlay is the author of three novels (Curvy Lovebox, Crumple Zone and Hooky Gear) which form a loose trilogy of loose people mapping out the underbelly of contemporary London. He has written award-winning radio plays and works as a journalist, contributing to Time Out, The Guardian and other titles. Born in London to Hungarian refugee parents.

Barlay's London is more a state of mind than a real place, and there's a brutal poetry in the dialogue of his low-lifers.
(Time Out)
With his debut novel Curvy Lovebox, Barlay could do for Kilburn what Irvine Welsh did for Edinburgh.
(Evening Standard)

Francesca Beard, a rising star of the London literary scene, was born in Kuala Lumpur and spent the 70's growing up in Penang, an idyllic island paradise on the East coast of Malaysia. After a spell in real jobs, she gave it all up to become a fictional character and now exists as a London-based poet, performing 'spine-tingling' spoken word. She has a regular column in the Guardian Guide and writes fluent and thoughtful stories wrapped up in surreal comedy.

The Queen of British performance poetry
(London Metro)

Monica Grant hails from West London. Her first novel The Ragga and The Royal was published in 1995. She is a single mother of a young son and lives on the twelfth floor of a high-rise in Shepherd's Bush. Her West Side storey W10 Closer To Heaven Than W11 is based on a true story.

The Ragga & The Royal — a hilarious mick take of the
monarchy. Even the Queen would have to be amused.
(The Voice)

Vic Lambrusco is the author of the politically incorrect and in-yer-face verses that are published in two pamphlets: Oo Wants It?! and Vic Lambrusco Has It Large.

Awesome… funny as fuck
(John Cooper-Clarke)
Urban verse with a hard edge
(Observer)
The funniest thing I've seen for twenty years — and I'm only 29!
(audience member at Buzz Club, Manchester).

Kenny MacDonald has lived in a first floor flat on Ladbroke Grove for years. You can imagine the carnival parties that we had back in the day. From his balcony we watched and danced and sang as revellers, swept by the momentum of the parade, the steaming, and the police and thieves in the street, herded past. But Kenny doesn't have those parties any more. His flat is always locked up and deserted at carnival. He always goes away at that time. He says the last party he had was murder...

'The Gatecrasher' is his West Side storey.

Aoife Mannix was born in Sweden of Irish parents and grew up in Dublin and New York, and is now based in London. In 1998 she was awarded first prize in the Dr Marten's New Writers Competition. She is the general manager of the Royal Court Young Writers' Programme and a script editor for the BBC 1 series Holby City. Her debut collection The Trick of Foreign Words has just been published. Her West Side storeys are a bittersweet look at the chaos of life and love.

Michael Baker is an East End writer currently based in Coventry where he teaches kids in between the usual ducking and diving. He is the author of Guns of Acton.

Kieron Humphrey is a new author currently residing on the south side where he writes West Side storeys from back in the day when men were bold and the streets of the Big Smoke were never paved in gold.

Jared Louche, the thin white dude — unfiltered from stem to stern, fully mechanised with juices to burn — was the vocalist and front man for the machine-rock duo Chemlab, whose classic album, Burnout at the Hydrogen Bar, is a seminal work. After the breakup of the industrial duo in 1997, he found himself deep in debt, working as an investment banker on Wall Street with no outlet for his creativity, so he came to London to shake up the writing scene. Time we all realised, he is a fucking genius, maaaan.

Patrick Neate's storytelling has already won him the Whitbread Novel Prize (2002) for his second book Twelve Bar Blues. His first novel Musungu Jim and the Great Chief Toloko needs to get props too as one of the funniest stories in fiction. Right now he's in Zimbabwe (who knows where he'll be tomorrow) building a house in the bush when other white dudes are trying to get as far away from the Robert Mugabe experience as possible.

And **Dotun Adebayo** — yeah, you know me!

westside storeys

Life of Pain
THE EXTREMISTS
(Jason Durant/Samar Durant)

Raised in the eighties…

Who remembers Adidas Torsions, all the range in the 1000's, looking to make thousands in a black leather jacket bandanna an' cap-it, ready to jack-it with the double 00's and ratchets? It weren't fair but down at the fair we pat pockets, move in a gang, robbin' a man, hear him bawl out " 'Low it!" Go, tru' he's a chief and I'm a thief, so jus' gimme it. Yeah dem days were hectic.

On every level there's a rebel who remembers carnival. Eighty eight and eighty nine was rife with crime, we steamin' in lines looking for anything that shines to pop it. No joke that belcha and rope chain I got it. I even slashed for cash and lashed your tek and get some traveller's cheques from it. Cause that was the spirit from drinking beers and spirits, we woz lean from Thunderbirds and green, we flexed on the corner listening to Coxsone and Saxon Hi-Powa. Police waan lock off the set a lot earlier.

1

"Go weh!" crowd run 'em out the area. Sounds under the flyover. We congregate together under the slabs of concrete structure. Those days I remember, I was there as a teenager, in and out of danger. Listening to Ninja and Shabba, rolling up my C17s and Chippie jeans.

Who remembers wax Barbour jackets in blue and green?

Check the scene I'm on...

All I see is long Aqua-Scouton scarves last forever. Remember sheepskins and leather with mittens if you were dapper? Who remember tracksuits like Kappa, Taccini, Lacoste an' Fila? Remember coats like Duffer and jackets like parka and bomber, wearing Lois or Farrah, Adidas Gazelles or Somoa?

With so much memorabilia I could go on forever. But part two will come later...

Just to get paid, run a ram-raid in a Range Rover stolen from Dover. Reversed back through the shop window. Load it up, hooded up, hide your face from the camera. "Quick, we gotta dus' before the blue lights follow."

POLICE. CAMERA. STOP. ACTION. THRILLER.

Spy satellite in the sky — fly helicopter. I'm the getaway driver like Tanner. Police got me on their infra-red scanner. I had to bus' a sharp corner -"Quick, we gotta dus', I told you before, it's either dem or us..."

On the floor with the pedal flush.

"Hush, don't panic, we made it. I told you I'd do it."

Just to get paid I prayed before I made from escapades. Now many man bathe from them blade raids and stay engaged to the shotgun guage, to raise the cash they lash, stick the stash in the gash in the wall, then wait for Paul to call all interested.

But watch out for dem bwoy dat want us arrested, dem eye mussi infested with green. Envy. So don't blame me when I smoke the envy cause they're just weed to me. Nowhere near my potency. Cause you see, down here the money's my care cause I want new gear to wear. New gear to prepare for fiends who share. Spare a thought for fair and you've lost down here. We win. Living in sin it's just the system, bredrin. I'm crimmin', just to get paid again.

I was probably sixteen when I first kissed the tips of her lips green. She was introduced by nicotine to the team. Very keen I accepted. Now I'm addicted as predicted. My love for her is expected. Smoking sacred plants, my mind she enhances, I hold my stances on this. The natural herbalist. Always missed her company when she's not with me. I feel lost and lonely. Hear her calling 'Roll me'.

I build it quickly, smoke slowly, savour the memory, mainly because she doesn't weigh an oz for me. Usually I smoke ten pound B.A.Gees — even a drive to see me through my daily smoke screen. You see, my green queen keeps me lean on the scene, although I haven't always been so keen. I had an affair with the clean, whitewashed rock queen turned me into a fiend until I weaned myself off and got back with what I lost — so glad I never tossed my life away when I went astray.

Hey, pay attention!

3

She releases tension at any time! I'm alert on line, the formula for my rhyme, she's my wife through time. The two of us unwind. I find she opens my mind to see things sublime... sub-lime. You catch me on cloud nine — cloud 9. She's my green queen, green queen...

Dressed in different clothes (the selections I've chose), smelling sweet like a rose to my nose. In a blunt dutch masters or blue rizla rolled, sweet liquorice rizla I fold and stick quick, construct my spliff thick and stiff. When I spark you catch a whiff. Forget the myth. I remember, every bit of this, a member of the italist, raw ganja ritualist — seen!? The green mean more than it seems. Me, I deep sleep dream when I'm feeling lean, I gleam brightly and move lively, not suprisingly passed around my friends she's feisty, promiscuous maybe, but still my lady when they hate me. Do you blame me? Maybe not. Who cares? I won't stop . It's like food like crop, this herbal tea's hot. To hit the spot. From toe to top. I never wanna drop. I'm high at the top.

My green queen...

In all types of pipes we reach tall types of heights double-U double-E — D, delights me, except for the fights we've had, where I felt real bad — am I seeing too much of that green bag? My eyes sag and still I take another drag on the spliff.

Sometimes I wish I never got myself in this., Now I'm hooked like a fish on line, taking the piss with my mind. She's out of line. I'm off (cough) then I cough, "We can carry on but I'm the boss. Don't get me cross." She does that sometimes with the price she costs — to always be there is a must — is it love or lust? To see her pure is like gold dust, because now she mixes with other stuff — Blast! — how it happened, don't ask. She gets to my head sometimes and life' s a blur with her and now I'm having to think twice about the whole thing. This king may be abdicating, it may be bye-bye buzzing, but until then I'm still smoking. Eyes slick smiling... smiling. I'm green queening...

Dear Diary,

I need to control my fiery temper, still stinging like an emperor scorpion, opinion to life and death. Still spilling blood for love, guv, I've carved up clowns with cuts that slide down the talk of the town round my side, you hear the same, same sound. Sirens and rounds from revolvers unfound. Love this or not it's non-stop to the top, it's very hot but yet it's so cold. It's ice blocked stop. You can't knock the noc -turnal life I live rife for my slice with ice — I want the cherry on the top the whole lot. Look, I want cause I ain't got, and that's how I feel a lot of the time to commit crime and keep my enemies in line. Lay down or stay away from mine. This kind don't take too kindly to you and your crew — seen?! And that's what I'll say to all before they all fall.

Dear Diary, let me tell you how I've been lately. Since the last time I wrote I'm more keen to survive upstream.

Dear Diary, you're the only one who hears me fully. And I mean that sincerely.

Living a rife life of riley burning rubber on Kawasakis,

Honda CBRs and Ducatis.. phone calls received on hands-freeze, they're dealing 'B' to C.A.Ts. Money triple easily — free from VAT business is healthy. Him and his boys make plenty money out there, weather rainy or sunny don't care is their attitude. Sounds rude but don't get confused with the views of most youts who've used their skills in different fields, finding ways to surivve the kills, blood spills, starvation, poverty, bills. While many make mills, more of the poor feels. Given the choice, what appeals to you more — rich or poor? Be truthful and you'll be sure to score maximum points in this game show ghetto seen by all. Though not everyone wants to play though, they wanna play with dough, green plastecine morphine for more fiends, the dirty side they don't want seen, don't know where they've been. Needles infected, passed around, injected, blind in their mind just wanna get lifted out the ghetto. It's hell snow. Very cold, very cold, bro, in the ghetto. Living a rife life of Riley.

Throughout life we learn that practice makes perfectness. But God forbid that your lesson be strict... cause in a moment of madness happiness can surely turn to sadness.

The scene is set at the traffic lights down in Tooting Bec. Blazing out my set pushing this Honda V-Tech. Get the picture? IA 1999 boy racer. We're in the season summer, where everyone's a poser. Whatever you prefer the Benz or Beamer. You drive. It's all good for the eyes. Y'get me. Summer girls wearing less showing breasts and thighs. My adrenaline's sky high. Then alongside pulls up a GTI with

6

an even louder hi-fi, like a war cry:

Invite.

Green light.

Bye-bye.

Speeding in my 2.2 si, I guess it's best I slow a little before somebody cripple. I triple the speed limit . I put the needle in the red and leave you. I drive like a never-learner, burning rubber I roast, trying to shake off this Golf in my rear-view mirror, sticking to my bumper like glue. Whoops, just missed — oncoming traffic — wing mirror's clipped. Hectic, shit, gotta get a grip, sweat on my gear stick (this Golf must be chipped or perhaps a VR6). Licking his lips (he's hungry) behind me, then alongside me, real close in front he goes and boasts, flashing hazard lights. Like knights we joust this out in the road to the end, fourth gear corner bends, bumper to lens. Boy racing sends me mad, insane, in and out lanes, fifty mile an hour chicanes, all from this rush of blood stain in my vein, road rage on my brain. Temper came to take me over, like a body snatcher, devil on my shoulder, using me as a host — he's using ME as a host!!

'See, I bet he wants his V-Tech to get wrapped round a post.'

I'm so close to the Golf that I can't see up ahead. He swung to the right while I went left instead. Still burning up from this heat in my head. Untamed, I blame the rules of street cred. It's a shame. Cause I'm too deep in to turn back. I'm trapped like a fool. Got me all out reckless. I've lost my cool. I failed to see the sign that said 'approaching school'.

It's like I knew something so cruel was going to happen. Then, from nowhere, a class of kids crossing like a herd on the edge of my nerve. Had to swerve up and on the curve. Missed one then hit one, a second then third.

You heard this lesson: To all boy racer — it's over. Two kids dead and one in a coma. All in a moment of madness. Happiness, happiness turns to sadness. All in a moment of madness.

Am I seeing things? I'm turning loony loopy, eyes droopy.

"Wake up!"

Someone calling me for what? Just stop. It's looking bad, I must be going mad. I had many marbles before, now they're rolling down your floor. Watch it, don't slip, bus' your hip, your head get hit — end up losing it like me, sick in my head, I love the sight of dark red, open wound bled, constant flow like blood blade, sharp ones here tailor made just for you. You know what — fuck this. I'm going to resist the Jekyll, that crafty cunning devil, trying to unbalance the level of my mind. Sublime.

I'm surprised at the time it took to rhyme. My books are signed — line after line I climb heights up the vine, my textures nine, open the blinds and see the light shine. Bout time, don't you think? Now you can blink. It's not a dream, cast away your team for being so mean. Blink. Snap out of it. Drink. More words soon slurred. Vision blurred. Help me! May the lord have mercy. May he have mercy...

Am I turning off key?

Temporarily.

I smoke. It's hazed. I'm thinking about the days I spent blazed and how my mum raised three children. I'm amazed. In this life there's rife days ahead. I value wisdom instead of bread. I read my palms and psalms before bed, spread the word I said. These hungry souls are fed. I see some are led astray. Then they're promised a better way. Would they not stay if they knew the payback? In fact this teaches those that lack knowledge of fact. Feeble followers flap wings like bats, blind to the fact that fiction is packed with truth and witnessed from early youth. But what's the use if we don't prepare proof? Off the rooftops shouting out "Stop!" We got the lot locked, stocked and boxed for delivery. I watched the snake's slick slivery approach, trying to poach people's vote. From now on, just quote everyhting I wrote/spoke in my life rhyme. This is sublime. Is that a crime? What's the time? Mind to those who wanna climb to the top line.

Watch what? Not mine, the sunshine nine, know my sign. Celes-teen/ Celes-tine, extreme rhyme gleam… You know what I mean.

There's man raising their arms, blazing firearms, inflicting heavy harm. Yow, wha' ah gwan? People spraying for fun, uhm, no one knows it's just the way it goes in the ghettoes.. it used to be double-00s and ratchets, now it's revolvers and automatics. Youts rolling up on big bikes outing lights of targets with some hits and some mis-hits, the metalwork spits quick when held by culprits in the crime bits of

Brixton, sticks in your vision like a head-on collision. Now watch Little John going on like James Bond — 'a licence to kill anyone' is his pun.

"You better run, son, run. Before he come — buss it, buss it, buss yuh gun quick," is all you hear from dem man. Stick it, stick it stick you for your shit, nuh worry what they're doing because they still ah shoot guns. Guns full ah lead — negative they don't bizness. No quiz fizz bottle tops popped in a lift, high risk ki's shift for many man ah jack quick. The younger got hunger 'cause they're coming up quick. Big fish is the main dish, also the strangest, for no shit sticks. You have to wonder who the grass is. Gun buck raases, no parcel passes. Worn sawn-off shotguns in post office. They spray like wild novice. They don't care none. Nuff blood run. Running up their reputation, dem man kill for fun. (Their piece weighs a ton). Aware of what they're doing but they still ah shoot guns.

We see big guns, small guns, big guns, small guns, they keep releasing lead in them.

Down Coldharbour Lane we got rock shots, gun shots, that don't stop pop brains from long range, short range in a range. It's nothin' strange to see shots spray frames and people sayin' Brixton's changed. Think again. It may have changed but REALLY it's still the same old Bricky, but with a lot more money — you get me? And that's the attitude of many murdering many more. Hit the floor from four fours to sixteen in the magazine, seen in the newspapers looking mean on the most wanted team in London, Lambeth,

Brixton's dreams.

I see Tech 9s to jack fat white lines, organised crime, slime informers always get the bullet in the spine. "Gotta get mine," that's the talk — I hear it all the time. All the rules are crude and it's all in the mind of many. Think you're lucky with the bucky or the penny to pounds like bloodhounds terrorising towns, spraying up the place with rounds of lead, army green teams with big guns that beam red. They blaze rudebowys, bad man an' feds for days, many many more man dead, they keep the trade alive with the guns by their side. By their side...

"Wha' ah gwan?"

He drove the 3-series coupe colour-coded convertible, yout, 2.5 i brute, shoot live for fruit, the sour apples groups, bitter battles youts, since the early recruits days of constant shop loots. He lived the life he led from the roots upwards. Now he's fat goods, gettin' paid with ink-stained wood — paper money could seriously damage your health for good. Wealth would wonder ways from childhood stun the days of parenthood.

In the day neighbourhood, he watched and watched good. and understood more than the average would. He should by now be good-bye die — over with and don't sigh or cry — but he's alive and living life. And that his enemies despise. All eyes on his prize. Size him up for size. He seems streetwise, spinning the truth out the lies. He's seen the two guys with guns by their sides. He had his one

11

by his flies. His belt buckle tied tight, ready for a fight, today light tonight, he's a target from when he's in sight. Flashing bright, limelight, limelight...

Ear wot, the mission is clear unlocked, the fight's stopped, the crowds flocked to the scene of gun shots where his life flopped. Dropped dead. The bullet pierced his head through and out. Blood bled al the way down to his leg. Look his bredrins fled, thinking about their own heads. And their bredrin's bread. Before the move they both said, "Forget Fred, instead, take the wedge from the cut."

They stuck three man from way up North, never knew bout the fourth til he returned with force. The course of action is their reaction split into fractions.

"For what?"

Distractions. Dis-dis-distratcions.

Now Fred's dead and his bredrins done fled with the bread — took off at high speed they sped, through the streets ahead. Under the seats one gun full of lead is covered in a bed spread. They planned to dump it in a shed. "I wanna keep it instead," one said. With the lust for bigger bread. And to see man dead. Like their friend Fred, no tears were shed. He made the headlines front page spread, the type that everyone reads. Fascinated they said, "It's time to make bread galore, with the Securicor hit — strategic money quick for a long distance trip to lay low for a bit. Maybe live life legit — who knows — consider it. But by now they both fit the description of two suspects under investigation. Done bird before in Brixton prison for robbery and firearms possession... they haven't learned their lesson. Planning out their new mission,met with perfect precision, now the time has risen for them to bring on the action. It's like money and the gun is an obsession, a lifelong companion and common attraction, split to fractions...

"For what?"

Distractions... dis-distractions.

One gun, two man and one plan to hold money in the hand. Stick the Securicor van, grabbed the money and ran. Quick. Then flew to Egypt to lay low for a bit. Jet lagged they needed kip. They swore, after this job, that would be it. No more banks to stick, they planned to live life legit off the big packet. Check it.

Tomorrow they know where they wanna go, because they've got money to blow. In downtown Cairo in a cramped casino, placing black jack bets. Their greed couldn't control. Drinking alcohol from the bar they staggered slow, shoutin': "No one even knows about this life we chose. At robbin' banks we're pros on tour — we just done Securicor, nuff banks and Group 4 the love of it."

Oh shit!

They looked behind quick and saw their photo-fit on Sky satellite dish dun broadcast this. Still pissed, but now they wished they never opened their lips. It's one of the many tips of the trade. Too late they delayed. They got caught up in the raid by the police parade. The undercover surveyed the building for illegal earnings and now it's bye-bye sterlings and welcome to jail wings .

"For what/?"

Distractions — dis-distractions.

Yeah, it might sound rife, but in all scenarios of life visualise and size up the options from these daily distractions. Dis-distractions

"Hello there, gonna tell you a little story. That's right, a day in a death of being a gangster. You hear me?"

"Tell 'em, Brave."

"I'll tell em, I'll tell em… 'Ere have a biscuit, I'll tell you another day in a death of being a gangster…

"Anyway, right, so he's staring down my barrel and he dares me to do it, I'm thinking he's as dumb as my bullets. Course I pulled it. Brains on the carpet. Quite artistic. Shame you missed it.

" 'Ere have a biscuit, I'll tell you another… Charlie's mate, that real big geezer…"

"Eddie?"

"That's the one — bare knuckle guy that don't like guns. Now 'im and Charlie never work with yardies — goes way back over dodgy nifties. Eddie and his girl had a row last week, now he's down in the pub getting drunk on whisky, touchy feely with this girl at the bar — a black bird, nice arse. She wasn't 'aving any of it tho', she soaked him wet with the drink in her glass. Laughs around the room soon increased Eddie's anger. She flew like a Lockheed Blackbird when she felt his back-hander. Now she's back in half an hour with her boyfriend yardie gangster. And he's bigger than a gorilla.

"Not too clever this Eddie fella. He says 'Leroy or Delroy or whatever your name is, boy, I'm a fucking East End hardnut don't you take me for no toy. Oh yeah, I know your sort, lots of gold with hair like Ruud Gullit. Well you're all talk — you've got the guns, but where's the fucking bullets?'

"Now Eddie shouldn't have said that, in fact he should have run the marathon."

"That's right."

"Because after that the doors blew in, and in came half of Brixton. Now you can guess the rest of the story. But what's the moral to it…? Well, you shouldn't hit women — including your own. And never ask 'where's the bullets?'

"The day in a death of being a gangster. Do they know what we mean?"

"I don't think they know what we mean."

" 'Ere have a biscuit, I'll tell you another…"

It's a cold night. Raining. The blood staining. He just got shot for shotting rock now he's fading fast, trying to gasp his last bit of air. He stared, eyes teared. All his life he feared this would happen — times are tense and don't slacken — family's grief stricken, sickened, by the whole situation.

"Why, why?"

Now who of you can answer their question? And what can you learn from their lesson?

To make an impression in life is rife with tensions, we all want succession in this social spectrum. Keep them eyes on your vision. That's the right decision to avoid collision on the streets or in prison. People plan progression, using kindness and aggression. What's the answer to the question? In possession with intent to supply. The answer 'why'?

Tell me and don't lie, it's a blessing in disguise to stay alive and arrive on point forever. Anoint my head in wisdom. I said it's the vision, sliced cut sharp like circumcision with precision — precision...

You see, this life of pain this life of strain... it seems the same...

Some wanna be on top in the spotlight where it's hot. Others say I never get and I don't ask for a lot. But real contentment, is not getting what you want. It's enjoying what you've got. So stop watch man, stop the money plot plan. Now what of your history? No not world wars and slavery. More importantly, the origin of humanity. Today we live according to gender and order with negative teachings spreading from border to border. In their minds there's nothing but soap powder. Brainwashed they got lost again in this life of pain...

Who turned up the violence on my street? On the concrete leaks rivers of red running speech for the dead. Lead led the way from my machine gun spray. Now families pray a thousand a day — let one be heard take the pain away. Another B.L.A.C.K. man gone today and tomorrow, the sorrow will follow in grey. It's dull, it's dark and it stays that way. Man ah gun dung man an' have nothing to say. When the metal spray's spitting your way, you gonna run or stay? Because I tell you, nowadays, you've got to be careful what you see and say. See, streets are watching, roads are raging, tempers flaring, coming to boiling, point the finger…

To something or another in my area… in my area.

Hoxton Babylon
JEMIMA GIBBONS

I'm not going to tell you who he was — I mean, I can't, and if he ever finds out it's me who's written this, I'm never going to get out — but he was seriously seriously famous. He was spending time in London after filming for his upteenth movie. I met him in the queue for the toilets at a club. He was in drag, you see, and he'd been looking in the mirror, fiddling with the fastening of his dress, and he'd got the little hairs on the back of this neck caught in the zip of this green neoprene Galliano thing... and he was swearing and gasping and writhing in agony. The two girls either side of him were oblivious to his pain; one was wearing a fancy headdress full of sequins and feathers and she kept trying to get it just right on her ringletted Kellis-style hair; every time she pressed the headdress back from her forehead another wayward curl sprang loose, she was trying to flatten them down with tap water. On the other side a woman in her early fifties sporting a sassy Baby Doll dress was fiddling with a contact lens. She was peering

18

into the mirror, her nose almost touching the glass, and tutting as she rubbed her reddening eyes. Basically, this poor guy was struggling and no one was doing a thing to help so I stepped forward and offered a hand.

"Here, let me sort that out for you."

"Sure," he said — a sexy Californian drawl.

I tried to edge open the zip as gently as possible. And that's when I noticed it — the famous tattoo on his upper arm, which had been dedicated to a previous girlfriend, another big Hollywood star. There and then I clicked who he was, but I didn't say anything, I just kept biting my lip and trying to tug open the zip.

Eventually – finally — it came unstuck. He let out a great sigh and slumped his shoulders in relief.

"Thanks, I was dying there," — he gave me a big, beautiful grin.

It was best to play it cool so I tried to act like I wasn't impressed, or anything; as if I'd known it was him all along. "That's OK," I said. "Having a zip up the back can be a nightmare, just don't attempt to do it up on your own next time, get someone to give you a hand – alright?"

I was joking but he picked me up on it: "Right then, so… where will you be?"

"Ha, ha."

"No, really, I came here on my own tonight and, to be honest," he leant towards me and lowered his voice, "I'm finding people kind of distant. Where are you? In the main room?"

"Yeah… um, over by the stage, next to the speaker.

19

Come over."

I gave his arm what I hoped was an appropriately casual-but-friendly squeeze and turned to edge my way out of the packed toilets. Back in the crowded, sweaty, main room, Atomic was on the decks and his deep trancey set was building up. The space was heaving; people kept crushing up against me, laughing before pulling away. A blonde dreadlocked guy grabbed me and span me round, his teeth glowing green in the UV strobes. Two girls in full urban warrior gear swung across my vision. They were tall and impressive, striding through the crowd, modern Amazons in their Buffalo platforms and bicycle boots, their pvc mini skirts only just grazing the top of their camouflage tights, their post-punk bondage t-shirts alight with UV stitching. One wore an anti-pollution cycling mask, as if we truly were on the verge of Armageddon. Beside them a doll-faced woman, her expansive pink afro wig offset by miniscule hotpants, danced an energetic solo routine. Glitter sprinkled off her hair as she shook and rocked her head to the multiplying beats. Still swirling round, I saw the Devil Himself, red-horned, pointy-toed, shaking his arse like John Travolta, I blinked and saw a couple of angels dancing beside him, they pursed their cupid-bow lips and shook their peroxide curls in mock disdain.

There was a lull in the pounding bassline and the over-heating crowd boiled down to a gentle simmer. The room filled with a swirl of strobing electronic beats, distorted drums. My dreadlocked dance partner squeezed my hands and let me go.

"K-tcha, k-tcha, k-tcha..." The urban warriors stood swaying gracefully, their eyes tight shut. "K-tcha, k-tcha, k-tcha..." The doll-faced woman hummed as she checked her wig. "k-tcha, k-tcha, k-tcha..." The Devil smiled as each angel planted a cupid kiss on his shiny-sweaty cheekbones. "K-tcha, k-tcha, k-tcha..."

The drums were building up, almost there. "K-tcha, k-tcha, k- k- k- k- k- k- k- k- k- k- k- k- k- k- k- k----TCHAAAA." The bass kicked in. The crowd went mad. Cheers went up. The urban warriors whipped out plastic pistols and water rained across the crowd.

The dreadlocked guy was grinning like his face was jammed. So was the doll-faced girl. In fact, everyone was smiling like Cheshire cats.

It took me some time to get back to my friends. They were right by the speaker, just as I'd left them. Chrissie and Amber were dancing with some guys in fitted t-shirts. You could tell by their attitude that they were probably from Scandinavia or somewhere. They were looking far too keen, and you could tell they were on the pull. London men are quite self-conscious about chatting up girls directly, because they know the girls know exactly what their blag is, they don't tend to be nearly so obvious. These guys looked like they'd just got off the boat. Chrissie was yelling and whooping as she danced, her sleek mahogany hair swinging across her face, her silver glittered platform hells sparking out incessantly from under her long pink sequinned skirt, the tight-honed white-blonde guy to her right was desperately holding on to her hand as she swung around. He looked like somebody about to fall off a whirly-gig.

Amber looked on in amusement, then the white-blonde buy's mate leant over to her and said something. Her bobbed brown curls jiggled on her cheeks as she shook her head. She smiled politely and carried on dancing. Her determined movements built a no-go zone around her; the curves of her copper-coloured dress reflected the light this way and that, sending out a force-field of lazer beams.

Momentarily, she glanced up at the stage to where Atomic was playing. Atomic was Amber's boyfriend, though of course the Scandinavian wasn't about to know that and I doubted she had any intention of telling him. Why spoil the entertainment?

Up on the stage, Atomic was doing his best not to be distracted by our Italian mate, Marco. Marco was yelling in the DJ's ear, gesticulating wildly as he talked, and every so often he paused just long enough to readjust his porkpie hat or take a long drag of his rolled-up cigarette. Ever the perfectionist, Atomic was concentrating hard on the music, he nodded to himself, but he was counting the beats, ignoring Marco's diatribe.

Smiling at the familiar scene, I pushed my way up to the stage where Ben, my boyfriend was sitting. I grabbed his knee and he squeezed my hand tightly, grinning back. Next to him sat our friends Spike and Elvis, our friends from Belfast. Their heads bopped like noddy dogs as they lost themselves in the music.

Ben leant forward and pulled me up on the stage between him and Spike, then gestured to me and shouted in my ear, "look — check him out!"

There was a scaffolding rig along the side wall and a man was clambering up it.

Following him, we tilted our heads up towards the coloured drapes stretched across the roof space. As we watched, he reached the top of the rig and grabbed a cord swinging from the ceiling. Instantly, the drapes parted. A dense sea of silver paper circles swirled over the dancefloor.

"Whooahhhhh!" A roar went up from the crowd. A thunder of base beats richocheted through the air and faces, hair, hands, turned upwards in bobbing unison, catching light and silver snow.

Sandwiched in between Ben and Spike, I grabbed both their hands and sighed.

"Hmmm... buzzing... lovely. Don't you wish life could just be like this forever?"

"Yeah," Spike nodded. Ben reached over and gave me a kiss. We sat there for some time, looking dreamily into the crowd and enjoying the chemical feeling that things were right with the world.

Minutes later the lights came on, provoking a massive groan from the crowd. The nights were never long enough. Atomic put another piece of vinyl on the decks and glanced over at the haggard bouncer to the side of the stage. The heavy shook his head. Uh-oh, looked like it was time to move on.

"Guess what?" I turned to Ben excitedly, now the music had stopped and it was finally possible to talk. "Guess who I met in the loos?"

"Ermmmm…" Ben closed his eyes and screwed up his face in mock concentration, then opened his eyes again. "No, you're right, I'll never guess. Tell me."

I leant over and whispered in his ear.

"What… really?" Ben grinned and raised his eyebrows. "What the hell's he doing here?"

"No idea," I said. "Having a laugh from the look of things… he's dressed up to the nines like Morticia out of The Addams Family."

"How d'you know who he was, then?" butted in Spike, who'd been listening attentively over Ben's shoulder.

"I just know, it's like, he's got this tattoo, right, and he's had it altered, and he's American and… I just know, alright? He looks like him, you know, he's got these high cheekbones, big brown eyes, pouting lips…"

"Alright, alright, calm down," Ben was losing interest. Fair enough, I don't suppose I'd be overjoyed if he'd bumped into Catherine Zeta Jones in the urinals.

"What's this, then?" Elvis leant over.

"Alice has met some Hollywood Megastar in the toilets," Ben had just a hint of sarcasm in his voice.

"Is that right?" said Elvis, grinning. "Who then? Pamela Anderson? Did she ask after me?"

"No she didn't and no it wasn't her," said Spike, impatiently. "A male megastar…" and he whispered the name in Elvis' ear. "Apparently," he added.

24

"Not that twat," said Elvis. Spike nodded. "He's a tosser," said Elvis. "I saw him in one film and he played a right soppy weirdo. Nah Alice, not my cup of tea, you stick with me," he grinned.

"You still hogging that spliff, Elvis? Pass it here," Ben reached across Spike to grab Elvis' arm.

"Feck off, you only just passed it to me!" said Elvis, taking a long provocative drag.

"Where the hell can we get some booze?" said Spike, ever the diplomat. The three of them leant forward in a conspirational huddle.

I looked on in amusement. Spike and Elvis were cousins, and they both dressed and drank to impeccable excess. Elvis was a singular person, and a caner par excellence, the only person I knew who consumed uppers to make himself sleep.

Spike worked for the Home Office and wore Saville Row suits. A few years ago he'd got Elvis a job in the Department of Education; needless to say, it hadn't lasted. Elvis had gone to do Cultural Studies at North London Uni, which was where he'd met Ben.

I sat there for a while, swinging my feet and mulling over the night's events while we waited for Atomic and Marco to de-rig. Well, so what if they weren't impressed. At least I had something to raise a giggle in the office on Monday.

After a few minutes, Chrissie came over and clambered up beside me. Laughing, she gave me a hug. "Hi sweetie!"

I loved Chrissie. She was my best friend, and she was always in a good mood.

"Hi honey. How's it going?"

"Yeah, great," Chrissie said; she glanced at the tallest of the Scandinavian boys, who smiled pleasantly back at her. The crowd was thinning out, but he and his friends were holding back, a bit awkwardly, looking slightly out of place.

"What d'ya think of Sven?"

"Hmm… depends. Does he have a flat we can go back to?"

"Dunno. Think he's checking into the YMCA. Bit too straight-laced for me."

Chrissie dismissed her latest conquest with a flick of her hair, "Techno tourists…!" She looked back at me. "How's your night been anyway, you look like you've been having a wicked one!"

"You know how the weirdest things happen…?" I told her about my encounter in the ladies toilets.

"No way?!" Chrissie threw back her head and shrieked with laughter. "Fucking brilliant. What's he doing later?" She chuckled for a second, then corrected herself. "Nah, I don't fancy him anyway, not my type you know? Far too puny, give me Denzel Washington any day. Oh shit, hang on a sec."

Marco was beckoning. He'd finished packing the sound system away and wanted to leave. He lived with Chrissie, but, although they had a relationship of sorts, it was very much 'off-on'. Chrissie bounced up on the stage. It looked like tonight was 'on'.

"We're outta here." She blew me a kiss. "Catch you later."

"Definitely. See you soon… have fun." I watched as she shimmied over to Marco and led him away. I always felt the flashy but squat Italian looked not quite right, somehow insignificant alongside my dazzling friend, he looked like he was about to be gobbled up by a pink praying mantis.

I never thought for a moment I'd see Celebrity Drag Queen again but seconds later his sweaty, shiny face appeared in front of me. The designer neoprene was soaked through, his longish hair was stuck to his cheeks. He looked slightly green and incredibly rough. He stared wide-eyed at me and opened his mouth as if to say something but instead he fell sharply forward and landed with his face in my lap.

"Well, I give up. Spike says we can't go back to his again. He's had a council letter, and Elvis looks like he's about ready for bed. Maybe we should…?" Ben came back over, then stopped in his tracks, seeing I had company. He looked on, disdainfully, as I tried to ease my new friend's head off my dress and get him to stand up. Instead Celebrity Drag Queen fell sideways onto Ben, who pushed him away, somewhat roughly. The star stood swaying for a moment, the whites of his eyes shining in the bright light, before slumping slowly to the floor.

"Another one of your waifs and strays, babe?""

Ben was right, I did have a tendency to pick up

complete strangers and invite them home. My friends were always ribbing me about it. Ben usually just let me get on with it, reasoning that someone who was my best new mate on Saturday night would usually be forgotten by Wednesday morning. And this one was certainly in desperate need of some pity.

"Oh Ben, look at him. We can't just leave him here. How can you tell what'll happen? Most likely the bouncers will pick him up and before you know it they'll have sold the story and he'll be at the mercy of the tabloids."

Besides, this particular collapsed caner wasn't a complete stranger. I mean, we already knew his bad habits – we'd read about them in the tabloids: hard drugs, divorce, trashing hotel rooms... In fact, I was deadly curious. Was he really like that? What was he doing over here? And why was no-one with him? I felt this was something that fate had literally dropped in my lap, and I wasn't going to miss out on an opportunity. Most of all, and let's not beat around the bush here, surely, if you took a Hollywood filmstar under your wing, there were rewards to be had?

Ben shrugged, still undecided.

"Come on Ben, he's all on his own... and... well, if we're nice to him... you never know..."

"Yeah, invited over to Paris, L.A, Malibu, guest list here, VIP there... brilliant." Ben started out with irony, then his facial expression changed as he realised how this possible payback didn't sound too bad.

"OK, Alice — let's go for it – you're on!" he smiled. "I'll

28

go call a taxi."

"Hello there, how you feeling?"

"Where the fuck am I?"

Charming.

"Er, you're in our flat. London — Old Street. This is where we live, me and my boyfriend. We, um, we brought you home; you passed out in the club."

My new celebrity mate sat up on the sofa and cast his bleary eyes around the room. It was a bit of a disco den, filled with twinkling fairy lights, mirror balls, sequinned Rajastani wall hangings and silver-threaded cushion covers.

Against one wall, stood the record decks. Assorted vinyl was spread out across the floor. Little toys were all around: a plastic water pistol, a UV globe and, on the mantelpiece, my favourite, a delicately-made snowstorm with the London skyline brightly etched across a dark blue sky. In one corner a fluorescent lava lamp bubbled away, still glowing from the night before.

"Bleughh…" said Celebrity Boy, covering his eyes.

"Oh, sorry," I reached for the switch. "Better?" The afternoon sunlight sent spirals of dust mites up through the air.

"Yeah, uh…" he glanced at the gilt framed mirror on the wall and shook his head as if to dislodge some unwelcome body in his ear. "It's… wow. It's trippy, man, you can't tell what's reflection and what's reality."

"Yeah," I said, looking round the light-drenched room.

"I kind of like it that way."

"Do you?" he said, suddenly sitting up straight and looking me directly in the eye. All nausea had suddenly apparently vanished. "Is that right, Alice?

"How did you know my name?" I asked him.

"You told me, last night – you told me?"

"Did I?" I definitely hadn't. He hadn't been conscious for long enough.

"Yeah man, you did."

"Oh… right." Maybe he had seen it written somewhere in the flat? Well, what the hell, he was bound to know it sooner or later.

"Here, drink this," I passed him the vodka and cranberry juice I'd prepared specially. "This'll sort your head out. Hair of the dog, and lots of vitamin C."

He swung his feet off the sofa and sat upright for a while, nursing the magenta drink.

"Man, what happened to me?"

"I met you in the club," I repeated patiently. "Last night, in the loos; you were out of it, you looked like you needed looking after."

"Thank you Alice… thank you, sincerely… um," he smiled at me, sweetly. "I know this may sound corny, but… you, you do know who I am, don't you?"

"Yes, yes… I do."

"Well, I appreciate what you've done, you know? Picking me up, taking care of me… I must have been in a real state. You could have called the tabloids, found a photographer, anything, I mean, that's really cool of you just to bring me home."

"That's okay." I smiled at him. "No problem. I wouldn't leave anybody in that sort of state."

"No, no… I guess not." Celebrity Boy looked like he was keen to change the subject. He nodded his head approvingly as he looked around the room. "Awesome pad you've got here. Yeah, neat pad, cool social life… nice boyfriend," he grinned.

I didn't really think he'd been in a state to notice Ben the previous night, and he certainly hadn't had the chance this morning. Ben was crashed out next door, snoring gently. But then I noticed that Celebrity Boy had fixed his eyes on a photo on the mantelpiece – me and Ben, arms wrapped round each other, together on a night out, looking confidently at the camera, happy & smiling.

"Oh, yeah, that's Ben. Thanks… we've been together a while now."

"And your friends? How long have you known them?" He leant forward, alertly.

"Well, I met Chrissie… well, about ten years ago. Out and about really. The first time we met, we clicked — pretty much. It was summer, Chrissie wanted to go to her mum's in the country and I had a car, so we ended up spending the weekend together. Chrissie lives with Marco now, but they're not really a couple as such — more of an open relationship – 'single together forever' we call it…"

I hesitated, aware that I was probably going on a bit. "Sorry, all this probably sounds incredibly mundane to you."

"No, not at all… I'm fascinated," he nodded, encouragingly. "And… the others?"

"Let's see… Amber, she's a friend from school. She met Atomic at a squat rave last May and they've been madly in love ever since. Spike and Elvis are from Belfast and, before you ask, we don't know why Elvis is called Elvis, just that his mother must've had a sense of humour."

"Sounds perfect — another undercover superstar." My new friend smiled engagingly. "Elvis! Poor white trash turned good turned… baaaaad!" Although the Southern accent was barely noticeable in his usual voice, he brought it back now, full-blown, for emphasis.

"Er… yes." I said, not quite sure what he meant, apart from the fact that Elvis (the King) had clearly had too many fried peanut butter sandwiches in later life. My friend Elvis (from Donegal) did not have an issue with food, in fact, getting him to eat anything solid, likewise drink water, was usually the problem. Elvis, despite his name, had no genuine fame to boast of. Only local notoriety.

"So," said Celebrity Boy, warming to his subject. "Are you guys 'cool'? Are you 'happening'? Do you hang out together most weekends? Clubs, raves, parties?"

"Well… yes," I said carefully, not sure if I liked the tone of his voice. "I don't think it's so much of a posing scene round here. I just like people to be genuine and do their thing, not to be anyone. Nice, open people are 'cool' to me, if that's what you find important."

"Oh, yeah, yeah," he waved his hand dismissively.

"We're all just so 'loved up', we don't care."

"Whatever."

"So Alice, do you... work?"

"Yeah, actually, I've got a job at a TV production company. I'm only a runner but, the great thing is, it's shifts, so at least I can organise my life. The money's ok and then, well..." I looked around the room, "I've got time for what's important. Though seriously," I added. "I wouldn't mind working a bit harder if I had to. I'm hoping for big things. There's a job going as a researcher, I'm going to apply. They seem happy with me so far. Everyone's really nice there.

There's just this one girl, Sophie, she's a right bitch. She seems to have it in for me."

He sighed, and shifted forward to the edge of the sofa. "Well, you're lucky Alice, you know that? You've only got one person making life hard for you. I've got a shit-load. I spend my life surrounded by insincere people, they're roaches: PRs, agents, groupies... journalists. It all gets too much, you know? The press attention, the celebrity fucking circus... Jesus! I can't kiss a girl without it making the National Enquirer. I can't even take a crap without a long lens camera up my butt."

I winced at the verocity of his outburst, but tried to look sympathetic, although the pile of OK! magazines stuffed by the telly made me feel insincere.

"It gets me down, you know? Life is too gnarly. Lately, I've been really confused. I've been living this kinda life so long, I don't know what it all means any more. I don't know who's my friend and who's my enemy. All I know is that everyone wants something. Every time I fall in love the media fucks it up.

I can't see my family any more, I can't relate to them. People just think I'm white trash from the wrong side of the tracks. I've fought for everything I've got and I don't even know what I've got any more. I'm pretty Goddam sick of it.

"That's why you caught me out on my own last night; I'd had enough. I wanted to be a normal guy having a normal night. You know? The drag thing... it's a great disguise. Nobody notices, nobody bats an eyelid. No, really Alice, I envy you. Honest I do. I wish I could have your life, just hanging out with friends you can trust. I'd love it."

I didn't know what to say. I mean, I was really flattered. It's a kind of weird thing to describe but you've got to try and understand what it was like. I mean, here was this guy I'd always admired, always respected. I'd always followed his stories in the papers or whatever. All the time thinking he was super-cool and super-sexy and now, here he was, in my living room, hung-over and bleary-eyed, confessing with all his heart that what he really wanted was to be like me.

To be honest, you know, I actually felt like it was a wee bit of an anticlimax.

Mega-stars just don't come and pour their heart out on your sofa, do they? They only way they enter your flat is via the media. They're there for us to be in awe of, or to take the piss out of, but, whatever, they are on a public pedestal. I mean, mega-stars just don't want to be normal. What's the point?

It's like that BBC2 series where Mick Jagger and Keith Jones run the corner shop. It ain't ever gonna happen, in theory. But, here he was, Mr L.A.Loverman, in my flat, giving me this whole sob story, letting himself go, confessing everything, blurring the lines, my illusions were being shattered one by one. I almost began to feel sorry for him.

And, boy, did I fancy him! I just wanted to lean right over and snog him on those beautiful, perfect lips. All his talk about how great I was, was kind of doing the trick. As far as I was concerned, flattery could get a guy everywhere, certainly if he shared a parallel existence as my favourite screensaver. But you know, fantasy only, I guess. I mean, Ben was asleep next door and we've been together a long time and there was no way, I thought, that I would be unfaithful, still, it was nice to dream.

"Well, you know…" I said, slowly, trying to come across as casual as possible.

"You're welcome to hang out here for a bit, if you'd like… really. You know? If things are that bad, why don't you stick around here for a few days? Relax, have a bit of fun."

While I was talking about my friends, he'd been looking slightly crestfallen, but this comment wrought just about the biggest grin I'd seen from him so far.

"Really? You know, Alice, that would be totally, totally

awesome."

Excellent. I couldn't wait to tell the crew: Hollywood comes to Hoxton – and stays!

"C'mon," I said to Celebrity Boy, "We're going down the pub."

The Pharmacy was in a restored Victorian drinking house – early Dickensian squalor meets post-millennial decadence. The mahogany bar curved in a serpentine curl around the right hand side of the high-ceilinged room. Dulled crystal chandeliers hung from the ceiling and brightly coloured lanterns marked every corner. To the left, and towards the back, youthfully-spotty but otherwise wizened-looking DJs could be found spinning anything from drum'n'bass to ska.

Even this afternoon it would be packed with a jiggling, buzzing Saturday crowd, biding their time between one party and the next.

It was two in the afternoon by the time I'd managed to raise Ben, sort out Celebrity Boy with some suitably incognito attire and get my own act together.

"C'mon guys, c'mon!" It was usually people waiting for me but today I was unusually stressed. I really needed a big night out. The week at work had been kind of strained and I wanted a full-on weekend to take my mind off it.

Besides, I really wanted Celebrity Boy to have a laugh and see some more of London. He'd been the perfect houseguest and I felt I was neglecting my role as host. Because I'd been so tied up at work, we hadn't really had the chance to go out at all. He'd been really good about it, in fact he'd been fantastic. I wondered what he did at home alone all day but he seemed quite happy tinkering about the flat. I'd have thought someone like Celebrity Boy would have wanted people waiting on him hand and foot but he seemed quite able to look after himself. He spent the day watching cable TV and ordering up food over the internet. When we came home one night, there was a massive Chinese banquet laid on the kitchen table; another night it was Moroccan... and there were always fresh-cut flowers, every day.

The only slightly irritating thing was his desire for privacy – he spent an in-ordinate amount of time in the bathroom. I noticed my most expensive face creams and hair products were going down twice as quickly as usual. On the Wednesday, when I was late for work, I tried to barge my way into the living room to get some office papers I'd left there. The door slammed shut, as if by a wind, and however hard I turned the handle, I couldn't prise it open again.

He also had a tendency to use my things, my jumpers were always going missing – he was so skinny he'd fit into anything, and little petty things like nailfiles would disappear. I was furious when, in a foul mood and desperate to get to sleep, I found my hairbrush under the sofa bed. Still, I guess vanity is an inevitable side-effect of being a megastar, in fact, it's more of a prerequisite. I forgave him his sessions in front of the mirror. I was ready to forgive him anything.

37

Celebrity Boy was good fun to have around, in fact, he was enchanting. The evenings were something new and I'd race home from work, no need for outside entertainment. He had a myriad of stories to tell about his life on the celebrity circuit, who was really sleeping with who, who was a junkie, who had a coke habit, who'd been to rehab and, on a deeper level, he was incredibly well-read. He knew an awful lot about Eastern religions — Taoism and Buddhism – he'd travelled widely in India and Tibet. He was well-versed in existentialism –

I know we all talk about it but he really knew his stuff — he'd even been to tea with Simone de Beauviour in Paris! For that week, things seemed perfect… almost.

"He talks complete bollocks Alice — and you know it."

Ben and I were standing by the stairs in the Pharmacy, waiting for Celebrity Boy to get the drinks.

"That's not fair, Ben, he's great."

"You only say that because he wants to get in your knickers."

"Look, whether I fancy him is neither here nor there, you were perfectly fine about us bringing him back from the club. You agreed it'd be a laugh. Just think how great it'll be when he returns the favour and we get invited over to L.A.

You wouldn't say no to that would you?"

"He's a wanker, Alice. All he cares about is himself. I don't know what he's doing here, but he's having a laugh. He's taking the piss, he must earn millions, he could be off staying at the Ritz if he wanted to, what's he doing hanging out with us? Free bed and board that's what. He's taking the piss."

"I know he earns millions, but that's the point, he's chosen to stay with us, he'd rather be in a real London flat with real Londoners going to parties, seeing a bit of the underbelly, rather than living in that false, ego-filled celebrity world. Didn't you hear what he said, he's had enough of it."

"If he wants to see Hoxton, why isn't he hanging out with Guy Ritchie? All that talk has gone to your head, babe, you'r e getting as bad as him. He doesn't think you're special, he doesn't give a toss."

"So what's he doing here?"

"I don't know, if I could get to the bottom of it, I'd tell you. But a star like him, hanging out with us, it's not natural. Never mind all that Cool Britannia bollocks, even cheesy, thick American rednecks can see through that, and he's not thick, that's the problem. He's got a plan, he's up to something."

"Look," I could see Celebrity Boy politely making his way towards us with the drinks.

"You're deluded darlin', trouble is you think you're as cool as him. Well, Hoxton's not Hollywood, it's about time you realised that."

"Stella for you, mate," Celebrity Boy grinned and pressed a gleaming pint in Ben's hand. "Vodka Red Bull for you," he smiled.

"Oh, er, thanks," said Ben.

"Yeah, thanks," I said, as I took my drink. "Ben and I

were just talking about what a laugh it is having you around, and how generous you've been to us."

"Yeah, so generous, in fact," said Ben, "that we really don't think we can accept you treating us for much longer and we wondered when you were leaving?"

"Ben, for f…" I gritted my teeth and glared at him.

"Heh," said Celebrity Boy, "well, not long now, in fact I just got a call from my agent. Seems she wants me back in L.A. by the end of the week."

"Oh," I didn't know why, but I felt gutted.

"It's OK," he put a reassuring arm on my shoulder, "you guys are definitely coming to see me in Cali," he whispered in my ear, "you'd like to experience my world for a little, wouldn't you? You'll find it a little claustrophobic, maybe, a little plastic, very superficial, but Alice my love, you're gonna experience it."

His breath on my ear was sending a sensual shiver down my back. Out of the corner of my eye I could see Ben glaring at me.

"Yeah, sure," I said, pulling away slightly, flushing a little, "we'd love to come, wouldn't we Ben?"

"L.A.'s not really my scene," said Ben, looking Celebrity Boy straight in the eye, "too much bullshit."

"Well, it's an expensive city," said Celebrity Boy, "maybe it's just a bit too out of your league."

"Hey, look," I said, frantically searching for a distraction, "can we sit down in here? It's hot and I'm knackered."

I felt I was in the park between two Doberman dogs

who'd only just met and were trying to sort out who had the largest bollocks.

We got our drinks and edged our way through the crowd to the back of the room.

"Oh Shit." The scruffy but oh so comfortable leather sofa and armchairs against the back wall were fully occupied. A blonde girl and her black dreadlocked boyfriend were deep in conversation in one corner; next to them another bloke, possibly his mate, was nodding frantically in time to the music, his head encased in wrapround Oakley shades. Beside him, two guys looking somewhat the worse for wear were struggling to roll a joint, one kept trying to arrange and glue the Rizla papers in the right order while his friend appeared to be picking up what remained of the previous effort from the sticky-surfaced floor; in the remaining armchair, a pretty but bored looking girl stared out into space, rocking gently.

"Here, do you need a hand?" I looked questioningly at the boy holding the sticky mash of Rizlas. His expression changed from one of intense concentration to one of sneering aggression. "No," he said, defensively. Then, as if suddenly alerted to the precariousness of his exposed position, he glanced nervously around the bar and grabbed at his friend, "Hey, let's go upstairs." His friend grunted, stood up and they were gone.

Well, I was only trying to be friendly. But thank God for paranoia.

Celebrity Boy and I squeezed ourselves greedily into the newly vacated portion of sofa. I beckoned to Ben but he made it clear he was happy to stand.

"So, do you come here often?" Celebrity Boy laughed out loud at the cheesiness of his question.

"Yeah, er, we do actually. It's a good place to fill in the gap between parties.

Everyone's been out the night before, and everyone's going out tonight. No-one wants to stop – see?"

In front of the DJ a group of five boys and two girls were dancing frantically.

The girls were glammed up to the nines, glitter spangled on their nails, shoulders and eyelids; their sequinned dresses reflected tiny beams of light.

The boys were similarly dressed, "smart but casual," boot-cut Diesel jeans and fitted shirts in textured materials – velvet, spun cotton and sharp, navy blue denim. The friends were completely immersed in each other, ever wider grins begetting ever wilder dance moves.

"Well, they haven't been home yet," I said. "So, what do you think of this place?"

"Yeah… yeah," Celeb Boy looked round approvingly. "I like it, it's ok."

"Why is it," I asked, "that when people get famous, they decide to open a bar?

You know,'Michael Caine's Maxim', 'U2's Kitchen', 'Johnny Depp's Viper Rooms'… I mean, I get the idea of it, that you have loads of money and you want to open the sort of place where you'd like to hang out, but isn't it a self-defeating operation? I mean, the minute a celeb opens a bar, it's automatically going to be packed with all the sort of sad groupie types that surely that person is desperate to get away from…"

"Well yeah," Celebrity Boy nodded thoughtfully. "It can be a problem. You have to keep hold of your integrity. But it's inevitable; fame begets hangers-on, that's what I hate about it. I mean, Naomi, Elle et al, they sold out with their Fashion Café, and Arnie and Bruce with Planet Hollywood… I mean, those ideas just stank, so obviously just money spinners… but you can do it right if you have the right management, and – obviously – some sort of pretty strict door policy regarding uncool people, er…" he broke off suddenly.

The pretty-but-vacant girl next to Celebrity Boy's elbow had woken up out of her part slumber and was eyeing him with intense curiosity.

I'd dressed him carefully that afternoon; a Cowboy hat (originally my Dad's, but all the rage, thanks to Meg, Mel & co) and Rayban sunglasses masked most of his face. There was no way anyone could have recognised him… or was there? There was an uncomfortable pause and I shifted nervously in my seat.

"Naomi… Elle…" the girl said, slowly, sarcastically. She leant closely towards him and peered into his face, her breath left little patches of mist on his darkened lenses. "You know, you don't half look like… whatisname… erm… what is his name?"

Celebrity Boy just returned her stare: cold, saying nothing.

"…Aw what's his NAME?" the pretty girl bawled at no-one in particular. Then she twisted sharply back towards my new friend. Her pink leather jacket made annoying squeaking noises as she turned. "Go on," she said, "take em off."

"Excuse me." Celebrity Boy leaned back in mock concern.

"Yer shades, take em OFF!"

"Oh, leave him alone," I said. "He's wasted. His eyes hurt."

The girl looked at me suspiciously. "Bugger his eyes, I want to know if he is who I think he is."

"Well, whoever you think he is, he's not... OK?"

The girl sat back and surveyed the three of us, as if assessing if this were some sad practical joke, of which she were the victim, or a potentially more interesting situation. At that moment, the spotty DJ's set kicked in with a massive cascade of familiar drum rolls.

"Aw, I LOVE this track," pink leather girl leapt up to her feet and spun off towards the decks, bopping like there was no tomorrow.

"Hmmm," said Celebrity Boy. "That was close. Maybe we should cut the Hollywood chat for now, Alice?" He glanced at me momentarily, then smiled, "More Vodka Red Bull, love?" he asked, in perfect mockney.

Perhaps it's a party thing, but my friends and me always prefer to act as if sex is not an issue when we're out, despite us all being aware that pulling, especially if it's someone gorgeous, is an added bonus. And the prospects of unrivalled, unbounded no-strings-attached lovemaking are much, much, infinitely better if you're a clubber than if you're someone confined to the dinner party circuit. I was used to taking it easy with men, to hanging out, doing that best mates thing, sharing a laugh, that's how I'd met Ben. What I loved was the possibility of sex hanging on the horizon, the anticipation of passion being half the fun, the nice thing about the whole party scene was how the blokes understood that, they played along. Everyone was pretty cool.

I felt seriously, that here and now, I didn't want anything to happen, I was simply enjoying the thrill of the chase. I was enjoying hanging out with Celebrity Boy, and I was enjoying flirting with him, but I was surprised at how threatened I was beginning to feel every time another girl came close.

Pink leather girl had come and gone, but a string of other curious women had come up to take her place. Even in a grubby old cowboy hat and in all his unwashed glory, Celebrity Boy had a certain enigmatic appeal, a certain je ne sais quoi. He radiated sex appeal like it was going out of fashion.

It wasn't long before Chrissie arrived. Usually I was more than happy to have her around a guy I was friendly with, I trusted her, and we never went for the same sort of men. But for some reason, even though I had no good explanation for it, tonight her confident presence made me anxious.

"Oh so-rree," Chrissie said sweetly to the girl currently

occupying the chair at Celebrity Boy's right elbow. "That was my place, I just popped up to get a drink, mind if I have my seat back?"

"Er, no," said the girl, getting up, "I didn't realise. Sorry."

Chrissie's butter-wouldn't-melt approach always got her what she wanted. She plumped herself down in the newly vacated armchair and reached in her handbag for a sobrani.

"Hi guys, how's it going?"

"Good, what are you up to? You coming to Alexia's this evening?"

Chrissie shook her head as she scrabbled in her bag for a light. "Nah, I was going to pop home first; I need to get changed for the club I think. I never really saw eye to eye with that bitch anyway. Oh I know, I know, you should never speak ill of the married but, you know, since she's been with that tightwad Tim…" Chrissie rolled her eyes. "Probably best if I catch up with you later."

"Need a light?" Celebrity Boy leant forward and flashed his silver zippo in front of Chrissie's lips.

"Ooh, yes, thanks," Chrissie took a deep drag of her cigarette. "Sorry, we haven't properly been introduced. What's your name?" She smiled charmingly at him.

Celebrity Boy flashed an equally becoming grin back.

"Chrissie! This is… the guy I mentioned," I said. "He's… you know, I told you… we met in the loos at that club, but it's probably best if you call him 'Cowboy' for now."

"Oh right." Chrissie purred. " 'Cowboy!' or, how about 'Bigboy'?"

"Yep – that's OK too." Celebrity Boy grinned from ear to ear. "In fact, I prefer that."

Oh Jesus. A match made in Heaven. But Chrissie's normal game was just to play around. I tried to keep my disturbing feelings of envy under control. I was stupid to be getting upset about this – besides, the minute a man showed interest in Chrissie she always got bored; challenges were more up her street.

I looked around for Ben. With Celebrity Boy clearly eyeing up Chrissie, I urgently needed reassurance. Acting cool was all very well, but you had to have someone to take notice. Unsurprisingly, Ben had vanished, clearly not in the mood to play court.

"Well, I'm off to phone Alexia," I said. "I can't remember what time the party starts, and I think if Spike and Elvis are going to turn up, we might be too many people for her."

I grabbed my mobile and went upstairs to the Ladies to dial the number. Phone conversation was pointless in the noisy confines of The Pharmacy bar.

When I came back, Chrissie and Celebrity Boy had vanished, in their place sat Ben, accompanied by a dapper-looking Spike and Elvis.

"Oh hi," I smiled. "You managed to get home then. Listen, I've just called Alexia, she says it's fine if we all turn up... but where've those other two gone?" I looked at Ben questioningly, raising an eyebrow.

"Oh, no, no," he shook his head. "It's not what you think. Your celebrity mate was starving. Chrissie offered to take him up the road for some decent fish and chips." He gently grabbed my hand and squeezed it. "You look worried. Come and sit down babe."

He pulled me down on his lap and wrapped his arms round my waist. I was happy to be distracted. I supposed anything was possible. Celebrity Boy was not Chrissie's type, but then, nor were fish and chips.

"Mmm... that's better," I said, then spied Chrissie's pink sequinned bag pressed into the side of the sofa. "Guess they'll be back soon then. Let's hang on a mo... who's for another drink?"

The cocktail party was in a converted warehouse just off Columbia Road.

"Darling," exclaimed Mustapha, when we arrived. "Who is your friend?"

"Oh, we met him at the club last weekend, he's staying with us for a few days.

He likes to be called Cowboy." As always, the obvious was the first thing to spring to mind. Mustapha looked Celebrity Boy up and down with palpable pleasure. "You're divine sweetie, you're IN."

Despite the fact that this was a house party, Mustapha's days on the door at Heaven were obviously far from behind him. We squeezed passed his lavish fake breasts and entered the main room. Apart from Mustapha, everyone else was disarmingly straight. These were friends from years ago, but we'd all gone different ways. Alexia and Tim were both actors, and it was their party. Alcohol was plentiful and everything they drank was on the rocks, as was their relationship. They didn't make for the cheeriest of company. Luckily Alexia had told me to bring who I wanted, otherwise I don't think I would have bothered turning up.

Alexia came shimmying over in a smart floor-length Whistles dress. "Hi Alice, come on in. Moscow Mule or Tequila Slammer?"

"Er, Moscow Mule thanks. Here, we brought a bottle." I thrust the dark brown vessel into her hand. It was the least I could do with four people in tow. "You know Ben, Spike, Elvis... and this is, uh, Cowboy."

"Cowboy," repeated Alexia, looking at Celebrity Boy with pity. "OK, well make yourselves at home." She bustled off briskly.

"Nice pad," said Spike. It was a beautiful conversion. Pale Maplewood floorboards and bright white walls. At the far end of the room a pair of large French windows opened out onto a lush green garden. To the right of the doors a fretwork banister signalled the route downstairs. Opposite, stood a white grand piano which, apart from a clutch of strategically placed cream corduroy bean bags, was the only furniture. On the wall hung a single Damien Hirst spot painting.

It was all very Alexia and Tim, all very Wallpaper*. We walked over to the spiral staircase and clambered downstairs. The basement – walls, floor, aura — was an exact replica of the main room, but with a smart line of granite-coloured kitchen units against the back wall. At the opposite end, a giant aquarium full of tropical fish only partially succeeded in masking the bathroom. In front of us, a few bored looking people were dancing half-heartedly to the Pulp Fiction CD.

"Right, well we're not staying here long," said Ben.

"Ah it's alright," said Elvis, eyeing up a sweet looking girl dancing demurely by herself in the corner.

"Don't worry Alice, it's just fine and dandy," said Spike, mixing up a hearty Moscow Mule from the bottles aligned on one of the kitchen units. "We'll stay for a bit. Go on, tabloid king, get soma that down yer neck."

He held the glass out to Celebrity Boy.

"Thanks mate."

I was glad to hear the mockney accent still holding strong.

"So, superstar, how do you like my mate Chrissie?" I said to him, as casually as possible, as soon as the others were out of earshot.

"Yeah, she's nice. You know, Chrissie and I have a lot of things in common. We were having a great chat this evening. "

"Oh really?" I looked away from him, unable to hide my disappointment. I should be used to it really. Men were always obsessing about my best friend. They always felt they had a 'special bond' with her. Here we went again.

"I mean, of course she's attractive – she's your friend," he smiled winningly at me. "Hey, chica, you're not jealous are you?"

"Of course not." There was no point in feeding his meta-ego further.

"Hey, hey... what's up?" He could sense that I wasn't happy.

"Nothing... it's just..."

He leant over and brushed his hand along my cheek. "Baby," he whispered. "Don't be silly... it's you I want. You're the one I'm after."

I closed my eyes momentarily as a delicious tingle surged in my stomach. I couldn't believe what I was hearing, this was fantasy becoming reality. Although I was dying to kiss him, be kissed by him, there was something about this whole situation that was too unreal, not quite right. One minute I'd been insanely jealous, now I was falling under this wind-up merchant's spell. It was all happening a bit too fast. Besides, Ben was across the room and... I decided I needed some air.

"Look, I'm going upstairs," I said, "If you lot are going to drink the place dry I should at least try to be sociable."

I left Celebrity Boy in the basement and stomped up the spiral staircase and out into the garden. Well-dressed guests were milling round languidly; a bow-tied bloke near the French window nodded and held his hand out to me in greeting.

"Hello... Alice?"

"Oh, hi Tim... how are you? Want to show me round?"

It was probably for the best really, I should keep my hosts happy and at least do the obligatory social rounds.

The over made-up living room beckoned, along with its manicured guests.

A couple of hours later and I was getting seriously bored. There were only so many fund managers I could speak to in a year, let alone an evening. Suddenly there was the sound of loud swishing downstairs and I could hear Alexia's kitten heels banging angrily up the spiral staircase. Furious red blotches had appeared on her cheeks. She marched up to me.

"It's no good Alice, your friends have got to go."

"Oh… right…" I said. My God, what had Celebrity Boy done now? But it wasn't him.

It was Spike and Elvis. They followed Alexia up the stairs, looking sheepish.

"What?" I looked at Spike.

"Oh… you know, let's go." He marched past me and grabbed his coat from the hooks by the front door. "Let's go."

"OK, OK." I followed him and got my coat.

"I'm sorry Alice, but I'm just not 'into' that sort of thing." Alexia cut me a scornful glare.

"Right," I said. Further negotiation, even explanation, was obviously futile.

"Bye then… Thanks anyway… Bye Mustapha." The Moroccan queen was still standing in the doorway, looking out hopefully into the street: "Off so soon, sweetie?"

"Well, yeah, looks that way. Sorry Mustapha, might see you later."

"Probably will honey," he cast a withering glance inside, then smiled back at me, "probably will."

"What's up, Spike? What happened?" He was leaning against the wall, lighting a cigarette.

"Oh Alice..." he took a deep drag of his Benson & Hedges. "Me and Elvis, we were just having a wee snort, you know, just a wee line, in the bathroom. Thought it was fine, private. Well of course, we stepped back out, didn't we? And people were looking at us kind of funny. Of course, we forgot about that damn fish tank. They'd seen everything. And Alexia just freaked."

Well, you could just never tell, could you? Some people were live and let live.

Some took it as a personal slight if you did drugs in their house, which I suppose was fair enough; others took offence if you didn't offer them any, also fair enough. I wasn't quite sure which category Alexia fell into, but whatever, we were out of there. She was obviously mortally wounded. Oh well, saved the small talk I guess. I'd been running out.

"I'm sorry Alice but... oops." Elvis stepped out onto the street and collapsed in a fit of giggles on top of Spike.

Ben came out of the doorway and looked sorrowfully at the pair of them. "Just can't take these two anywhere, can you?" he shrugged his shoulders. "Anyway, that's cocktail parties over for the evening, where to now then?"

"Dunno... it's still a bit early. What's the time?"

"Gone midnight."

"Hmm, how about going back to Chrissie and Marco's

for a bit? They're only up the road. Amber and Atomic can meet us there, then we can all pile on to Wonderland."

Wonderland – excellent, I'd momentarily forgotten. Wonderland was an underground party that had been going for years. It happened every few months, each time in a different venue. This one was due to be the biggest yet. Two thousand people in a big converted warehouse across the river from the Dome. The best regular DJs were booked to play, and a few special guests. They were going to have acrobats, side shows, dodgems, a tented chill out... everything.

"Great," I said. "Let's pick up the others. Erm..." I turned around to go, but something was wrong. "Hang on a sec... where's Cowboy features?"

"Um, dunno..." Spike looked puzzled. "Thought he was with you, Ben?"

"Christ – he's not MY responsibility," Ben blurted out, then reneged slightly.

"Look, he must be downstairs. I think he said he had to go to the 'bathroom', you know, in that annoying American drawl he has."

"Right, so you've lost him, have you?" I said.

"No, I know exactly where he is. He's in the house. Oh, let's leave him. They'll love him."

"No," I said firmly. "He came with us. He's leaving with us. I'll go and get him."

"Hollywood groupie," I heard Ben shout as I walked back inside.

"Sorry Alexia," I panted. "It's our cowboy friend... we left him downstairs, alright if I go and get him?"

"Darling," said Alexia, glancing at Tim and raising a scornful eyebrow, "please release us."

I smiled thinly at her before dashing to the back of the room and clambering down the spiral staircase.

"Hey, Celebrity Boy," I yelled, then came to a halt on the bottom step.

The previously-packed basement was in darkness. The rows of candles lining the walls and kitchen units had been blown out. Half-finished drinks and the sorry remains of previously stunning hors d'evres littered the surfaces. A single inert body lay slumped on a slatted chair, an empty glass leaning precariously from his fingers. Apart from that, no-one... nothing.

A shadow moved across my vision and it was then that I saw him. At the far end of the room a gloomy green light filtered through the aquarium. Behind it was a figure who I could just about make out to be Celebrity Boy. He had taken off his hat, sunglasses and shirt. He was standing with his back to me, stock still, staring at himself in the bathroom mirror.

Curious, I moved closer. What on Earth...? I drew right up to the aquarium and pressed my nose against the cold clammy glass. A single golden-flecked piranha swam silently across my vision. Could Celebrity Boy see me? I wasn't sure. The kitchen was dark and the fish tank was humming with tropical life. Besides, he seemed completely immersed in what he was doing.

I saw that his lips were moving slowly and precisely, as if muttering some affirmation; I could hear his mumbling through the bathroom door, it sounded like some sort of ancient, ritualistic chant. His eyes were cast downwards, fixed on his chest. I breathed in sharply. Some sort of symbol was etched there.

I was close enough now to see exactly what it was. It was a large, star-shaped branding, and in the centre of the star was a weird hieroglyph-like squiggle, something I didn't recognise. It looked a bit like an upside down 'V' – an 'A' with its centre taken out.

Now I know the rich and famous lose it a little but this was something that made my heart skip a beat. I pulled back from the glass. Conflicting thoughts tumbled through my head. What was he doing? Why was he doing it? I knew I wasn't meant to see this. I wished I hadn't seen it. I was scared. There was something about his demeanour, something cold and detached, that sent shivers running down my spine. I wasn't sure whether to confront him – or run. I hesitated, my mind racing.

"I see you, Alice." Celebrity Boy looked up. He spoke in a cold, clear voice that I could just discern through the door. He was still looking in the mirror, and his eyes were fixed straight on mine.

"Oh… hi," I spluttered. "Hi…" I wanted to look away, but it was difficult not to hold his gaze. "Um, Sorry… it's just I… I wondered where you were."

"Well, I'm here." He turned round to face me. Without taking his eyes away from mine he reached down. I watched through the murky light of the aquarium and caught my breath as I saw him calmly pick up his shirt, gently shake it out and pull the sleeves up over his arms. Slowly, he buttoned the buttons one by one.

Then he turned to pick up the cowboy hat and sunglasses.

I heard the click of the bathroom lock and he emerged. He walked towards me, a silhouette against the aquarium light, his face swallowed in shadow. I took a step back, involuntarily.

"Alice… Have you been spying on me?"

"No… no, of course not. I just this second came downstairs. I didn't see anything." I lied, searching for words that might be appropriate.

"Really? Because I wouldn't want you to have seen anything that might upset you.

Anything you might not understand, or find disturbing."

He took another step towards me and his face came into the light shining from the stairwell. He smiled, a thin, cold smile I hadn't seen before, and raised a well-defined eyebrow at me. "I wouldn't want you to ask… unnecessary questions."

"No, no… of course… I wouldn't." He had me on the defensive now.

"Good, because, if you had, then our friendship might be affected." He reached forward and felt for my hand. "And… we've become great friends, haven't we, Alice?"

"Yeah… um yeah, we have."

I mumbled awkwardly, I felt I should pull away my hand. But something stopped me. His touch was warm, familiar, comforting. He pulled me gently towards him.

"You know Alice," he whispered gently. "When you're in a trance, it's kind of like being anethetised. Nothing really matters you know, and that's a very pleasant way to be. It's a different world. Nothing hurts, nothing feels. At first it may, but then, the pain fades away, just fades away. Man, it's goddam fantastic."

As he spoke, his lips brushed softly against my ear, almost kissing me. A shiver ran down my spine, but I tried to ignore it. "Look, I really don't know what you're talking about." I mean, I didn't.

"Chill out, Alice, relax, it's only me, chica, it's me." He pulled away and looked into my eyes. His face was gentle, soft. I wondered what I had been so freaked out about.

"But what...?" I caught my breath as suddenly, his mouth found mine and he was kissing me, a deep, delicious, searching kiss. He tasted divine... addictive. My head sank back, my eyes closed. I was floating...

"Alice. For Christ's Sake..." I could hear Ben shouting upstairs.

"Oh my God – stop." I pulled away. Celebrity Boy sprang back, coolly running his fingers through his hair.

Seconds later, loud footsteps came clanging on the spiral staircase and Ben appeared. "Alice! The cabs are here, are you coming... or what?" He glared at us, face darkened. "There's two, so... we'll take one and you can cosy up with Cowboy here." He turned round swiftly, shoulders hunched, and stomped back up the stairs.

A knowing smile flickered across Celebrity Boy's face. "I think we're on our way," he said, quietly. "Aren't we, Alice?"

Ben's arrival had thrust me back to reality. What the hell was I doing? Damn. Up there was my real-life relationship and I was making a mess of it. Right here in front of me was my fantasy, my idol, someone I had always admired. But he wasn't promising me anything. He was stirring me up and spinning me out. Besides, there was something wrong here. Things didn't add up. Too many secrets…

"Ben… wait." Before Celebrity Boy could say or do anything else, I took the opportunity to get right out of there. I ran up the stairs, past Alexia's chi chi friends and out into the street. I stood on the pavement, taking deep gulps of the fresh winter air.

I looked around, anxiously. Only one car, a clapped out Volvo, remained in the deserted street. The generously-proportioned, red-faced driver threw his first edition News of the World onto the back seat, and tapped his watch. "Gonna charge you waiting time." He scowled.

"That's fine man – not a problem." Celebrity Boy had run out behind me. He stepped to the kerb and graciously pulled open the cab door.

"My lady — your carriage awaits," he stretched his arm expansively towards the cab then, spying the dog-eared newspaper, swiftly bent over and swept it to the floor.

"No need for that, Alice," he said, winking slyly.

Going out clubbing is like embarking on a rollercoaster adventure from which you may well not return for the next 48 hours. Raving, ideally, is a celebration of life being lived to it's fullest, ripest capacity, as any one of those smiling, gurning, chewing people will tell you. It's like living your own Star Trek, Fantasia or trip Through the Looking Glass. If someone is nasty to you, it's like a splinter in your crystal vision and you have to rub it out. If someone is nice, the vision just gets bigger and better, it throbs, it glows. Emotions become part of the landscape. You grow, you fade, with every little happening.

With a nice crowd of friends around you, you feel like life can be good forever.

You get stronger with every memory, you form bonds, you become allies against the rest of the world. It's like The Famous Five, Snufkin and Moomintroll, The Merry Pranksters… or Withnail and I. To me, we seemed like that, my own little gang. Impervious, unchanging. Forever together. I could always count on my friends to see me through the bad times – or so I thought.

"You feeling alright?" Amber yelled. "Want to sit down?" I nodded. We'd been dancing for at least five hours. We were up on one of the podiums to the left of the DJ's booth. All around us soft coloured psychedelic lights caressed the shining, beaming faces. The music was brilliant — deep, uplifting, funky house.

Below us, Dan-Dan the tom-tom man had begun to beat his drums, bop-da-bop, da bop da bop da bop. A blast of horns burst through the dense air and the vocals rang out:

"You've got to love me... or leave me." The crowd whooped and waved energetically. "Stop playing with my mind."

"Hey, Alice. You lookalike you seen a ghost." Marco's grinning face bobbed out of the crowd. He laughed and reached out towards me."Yeah-bop," he sang, softly.

"Yeah-bop," he grabbed my hands and squeezed them reassuringly, aware that I seemed concerned.

"Where's the chill-out?" I shouted frantically at him.

"Down there... outta back," Marco jabbed a finger behind him. "You ok? You want I come with you?"

"No, no, it's OK, Amber's here. You stay with Chrissie — we'll see you later."

I assumed Chrissie was around there somewhere but, to be honest, I'd hardly seen her all night. Somehow, things seemed a bit frosty between us. She was probably off with Celebrity Boy, for all I knew. He'd been swaggering around since we'd got here, clearly off his tits, flashing cash around and buying drinks for all and sundry.

"C'mon, honey." Amber caught my hand and led me carefully down from the podium.

We squeezed along the wall, avoiding the worst of the crowd, and out through the aircraft-hangar like back door, into the crisp October night.

"Hey girls – what's up?" It was Ben, on his way back inside. I hadn't seem him for ages. We certainly hadn't managed to talk about the incident earlier. He looked relaxed, as cool as ever, a half-smoked spliff dangled between his fingers.

Maybe now was a good time to talk. "Darling, I…"

Ben looked away, his lips twisted. He inhaled long and hard at the joint before turning back to glare at me: "Listen Alice, I really don't know what games you're playing. But, I tell you, if that vain tosser ever steps foot in our flat again, I'm kicking his arse right back to Poser Central."

"Ben! What the hell's got into you?"

"You think I don't know what's going on?"

"Listen, darling… there's nothing happening. What's wrong with you?"

Until he'd spelt it out that he'd actually seen us kissing, I wasn't about to admit anything. For all I knew he could be annoyed at Celebrity Boy for a myriad of reasons. I decided to play it safe.

"Alice. I don't care what you think is or isn't taking place… his attitude fucking stinks."

I tried to look concerned, but inwardly I heaved a sigh of relief. Maybe he hadn't seen us after all.

"He's slimy. He's a letch. He's a weirdo." Ben took another long, lasting drag of weed then flicked the roach angrily on the ground, stamping it dead into the dirt. "What on earth were you doing picking up trash like him? I don't want to see his face in our place again."

"Honey…"

"OK Alice – that's enough." Before I could say any more, Amber grabbed my hand and tugged me away. "Ben – we're going to chill out, maybe you should too."

"Christ. What the fucking hell's up with him?" she asked, as soon as we were out of earshot.

I glanced back towards the gaping doorway, but Ben had disappeared.

"Dunno," I shrugged my shoulders and squeezed my friend's hand tightly. Amber looked at me searchingly, her big brown eyes concerned. I was reassured by her presence. We'd known each other for years and been through a lot together. She was constant, warm and understanding. I knew I could tell her anything. "Amber… I…" the tears started welling in my eyes. I breathed in the night air deeply, trying not to lose my cool.

"Don't worry honey, it's been a long night. Come on, we'll have a chat. Let's try to sit down."

The chill-out tent was across the courtyard, erected on a bank overlooking the Thames. It was a big, white marquee – a civilised affair with tables, chairs and beach umbrellas, all bathed in UV light. It was filled to the brim with Wonderland regulars. Everywhere people were sitting down, perching on tables, bodies stretched out languidly across the floor, talking, laughing, rolling joints, sharing drinks, reaching out hands and confiding in each other, or simply arguing good-naturedly. The air was humming. The atmosphere was relaxed.

The place was positively heaving.

"OK, well I guess we're going to have to colonize," said Amber, looking round.

Colonizing was easy. The trick was for one of you to gain entry to the area by stealth, preferably levering yourself in at the furthest possible corner (always the best position: greatest view — least movement). If there was just one chair available, just one tiny opening, you plonked yourself down in at and began to busy with something – make up, rolling a joint, whatever. That way people assumed you must have been there in a previous incarnation, earlier in the evening, say, or maybe even another night, but this was your regular seat.

Whatever, if you looked blasé enough, they always left you alone. Then your friends come by, see, and they spy you there and they shout and wave hello, and they clamber over and squeeze themselves beside you, and people move aside for them. It works, believe me, try it.

We scrambled over to a newly-vacated bright pink deckchair against the back wall and squeezed greedily into its womb-like expanse.

Amber looked happily round the crowd and whistled a little tune to herself. Then she turned back and gave me a look of gentle concern. "Rescue Remedy?" She removed a tiny bottle from her bag and waved it at me.

"OK... ummm." I dripped a few drops of the calming herbal tonic onto the back of my dried out tongue. "Thanks, that's better."

"Come on, sweetie, I know you. What's up?"

"It's just... Amber... oh, I'm so confused. That fucking Californian, you know, he came onto me and..."

"And...?" Amber smiled, raising an eyebrow meaningfully.

"Yes, yes... I know. I've always fancied the pants off him. He's gorgeous."

"Oh my God. So... fantastic. And... what about Ben?"

"Well, yes... exactly. I don't know. It's so difficult... I don't know what to do."

"He's not stupid. Looks like he knows what's up. He's clearly upset."

"He is, and... well, that's not everything. It's not even that simple." I paused, not exactly sure if I could tell Amber the whole truth. I wanted to explain exactly what I'd seen in the bathroom but somehow, the words were difficult to force out. I was finding it hard to express myself.

"The thing is, I'm completely freaked out. There's something dodgy going on.

It's not like: he's a filmstar, I've got a crush on him, this is my fantasy coming reality and I've the chance to see it through. It's that... there's something else. He frightens me, he's weird."

And, at last, I blurted it out. I told her about the chanting, the branding, the chill of terror I'd felt in the air.

I watched Amber's face carefully, searching for any reaction. She turned away from me and looked out across the crowded floorspace, frowning slightly, as if lost in thought.

Then she looked back at me, reached out, and gently stroked my hair.

"Oh Alice, don't be silly. You know him. He's covered in tattoos. Not that pretty maybe, not my personal cup of tea, but that's his own style, his taste.

He is from the deep south you know, sweetie, not exactly number one stop for glamour. And well, you know.

He's been through a lot in his life. Not suprising he's got some funny rituals going on. Look at all those Hollywood Stars –

Scientology, Buddhism, self-mutilation (well, if you count plastic surgery) — they're all at it."

I shrugged my shoulders. Maybe Amber was right but, I wasn't sure. I knew what I'd seen. Besides, I wasn't about to throw away my previously rock-solid relationship on a flaky star. Despite the fact I was clearly attracted to him, I was annoyed at Celebrity Boy for grabbing me the way he had, and I was angry at myself for succumbing. More than that, I was upset to see Ben so angry. Things had always been so chilled between us. Now, suddenly, one little mistake and we seemed to be falling apart.

"Oh Christ, let's not talk about it any more – look there he is."

The white Stetson was unmistakeable. Grinning, confident as ever, Celebrity Boy was waving as he picked his way across the crowd towards us. Following closely behind him was another familiar-looking figure. She looked just like... I peered closely, narrowing my eyes to adjust my vision.

"Oh my God – I don't bloody believe it."

It was Sophie, the girl from work who made it her mission to be my nemesis.

"Hey, chicas." Celebrity Boy came to a halt in front of our deckchair and stood, surveying us, as he gently wiped some beads of sweat from his brow.

"Whew... feeling hot," he grinned at me. "Alice... I

believe you know Sophie?"

"Hi Al... oh... wow... what happened to you? You look tired." Sophie smiled, a pretty, thin smile and flicked back her over-styled hair. "Cowboy said you were out here. He said you'd been overdoing it a bit. Ooh, poor you."

This really was the pits. My feelings of queasiness had subsided as I'd been sitting cosily with Amber. Now, seeing someone from work and what's more, someone who seemed to have it in for me, brought all my fears back into full relief.

"Yeah, well, I'm fine, thanks." I said.

Amber intervened. "Hello, I'm Amber," she said.

"Oh yes, Cowboy – Sophie... sorry, this is my good friend Amber."

"So, how do you know Alice?" Amber said. I was glad someone was making small talk.

"Alicia works with me," said Sophie (why couldn't she get my name right?) "In fact, we've got a healthy competition going on," she added chirpily. "We're both up for the same job."

I was feeling really unwell. I didn't want to think about the real world right now. Least of all that I was going to have to compete with this cow if I wanted to get anywhere.

"Really?" I just about managed to get the word out. "Who told you that?"

"Oh... James — the MD? He told me, well, actually," she giggled. "He tells me pretty much everything. We have, ahem, what you might call a 'special' relationship... though, of course, I shouldn't really say that – might not help your prospects at all."

"Alice doesn't need to sleep with her boss to get anywhere." Amber immediately stepped in to defend me, her eyes flashing.

"Ooh, someone's rattled," spat back Sophie.

"Girls! Girls!" said Celebrity Boy. "Easy."

I glared at him with intense hatred. He must have known Sophie was going to come out with crap like that. He clearly only brought her over to torment me. First Ben, then Chrissie, now even my work was threatened. What the hell was going on?

"Hey look, there's Spike, wonder if he's got any water?" Amber shook my arm and pointed into the room, keen to distract me.

Spike waved from the other side of the tent and began to step cautiously over the body-littered floor.

"Hello, you gorgeous girlies," he squeezed into the deckchair beside Amber and me, stretching his arms wide to give us both a big bear hug.

"Hi sweetie. How's it going?"

"Pretty good actually," Spike grinned and took a swig of his Red Bull. "Want some? Actually better not, you may not want to suffer the toilets here – they're beyond a joke."

"You know, in Medieval times, people wore little stilts on their shoes in the kitchens, to avoid the dirt." Amber observed.

"Yeah… maybe we should do a line in those here?"

I smiled to myself. It was good to see Spike, he immediately lightened the atmosphere.

"Listen, you guys stay here. I'll go and find Elvis... he'll need to know we're out here." Spike took another swig of his drink and turned as if to go.

"Hang on... where's Ben?"

"He's gone home," Spike tilted his head back to drain the last drop of Red Bull, then wiped his mouth on his sleeve. "Didn't he find you? He said he was going to look for you."

Home? Ben never went home without telling me. I felt a hideous mixture of feelings welling up inside me: anger, revulsion... and fear. I felt terrified, I felt scared. It obviously showed on my face.

"Uh-oh," said Amber. "Need some fresh air, don't you? Come on, let's get you outside," Glaring at Sophie, nodding at Spike and Celebrity Boy, Amber put a confident hand in mine and pulled me up out of the deckchair I gulped and nodded, too scared to open my mouth in case I was sick.

I staggered up and allowed Amber to lead me carefully through the chilled out bodies scattered all over the floor. All I wanted to do was get out of there. I peered through the throbbing lights, trying to make out the exit. I felt the beginnings of an intense headache behind my eyes. We'd just got to the exit, when someone caught me from behind.

"Hey, chica, not leaving without me... are you?"

It was Celebrity Boy. Where did he spring from?

"Look, just get me a taxi Amber. I want to go home."

"Hmmm, maybe you need company?" asked Amber. "Maybe Cowboy here should come with you?"

I thought about it a minute. I was feeling sick, angry, fed up, but then, somehow I didn't like the thought of a roadtrip on my own, however short.

"You come," I said, looking at Amber, pleadingly.

"Honey, I can't. Atomic's on in a minute. I couldn't miss the set. He'd never forgive me." That was true. This was a big night, and, knowing Atomic, he'd want his girlfriend to be there.

"Oh right." I said, letting her hand go.

"Come on, why don't you go with gorgeous here?" She grinned at Celebrity Boy.

"I'm sure he'll look after you." She looked out to the courtyard gates, her eyes searching in the brightening morning light.

"Look – there's a cab waiting. Go on — you jump in... take care of her," she added, winking at Celebrity Boy.

I was feeling very fragile and, certainly, not up for arguing. Besides, I decided. Ben was at home. Celebrity Boy could escort me home, and then Ben would send him packing. That would sort things once and for all. I rubbed my stomach, unease welling up inside me. I just wanted to be home, out of this, in bed.

Brakespeare and Leroy, the bouncers, were standing at the gates. "Off so soon, darlin'?" they always said that, even if it was ten in the morning. "No after party?"

It was one of those beautiful clear-skied mornings you often get in London. The days frequently start off sunny, but cheat you by turning to rain before you're out of bed.

The game to play is to avoid going to sleep in the first place.

The grey stone City was basking in bright watery sunlight as our mini cab sped past St.Paul's, along London Wall and on to Shoreditch.

But even the gorgeous sunshine failed to lift my spirits. My mind was on other things. By the time we got home I was unable to focus on anything but seeing Ben again, sorting this out and having my normal life back.

The Albanian driver glared at me through the rear-view mirror.

"She gonna be sick?"

"No, no, she's not going to be sick. She's OK." Celebrity Boy reached over and put a reassuring arm around my shoulder. I felt too weak to push him away; as always, his touch was gentle, strangely comforting.

"I'm fine," I said, my head pounding. "Just want to be home."

Not a moment too soon, we pulled up outside the mansion block and I leaped out and scrabbled in my bag for the keys, leaving Celebrity Boy to pay the driver.

I pushed open the main door and ran up the stairs, frantically, I turned the key in the lock of our flat. I could hear Celebrity Boy's footsteps coming slowly up the stairs behind me.

"Hey Ben," I called, "Ben – we're home."

Flinging the front door open, I tore off my coat, throwing it to the floor, and ran straight through the flat and into the bedroom. I expected to see Ben lying asleep in bed, but he wasn't there. I searched the whole flat. It was empty. I walked to the kitchen – there was a note on the table. I could hardly bear to look at it, but I picked it up, struggling to read with the tears welling in my eyes. 'Hi Alice, Seems like I'm not needed. Have fun with your new boyfriend.

Ben.'

I couldn't believe it. I sank against the wall, choked with despair. I wanted to cry, properly, but now the tears couldn't seem to come out. That was it. The decision was made for me. Ben had gone.

"Hey, here... what's all this?" Celebrity Boy appeared in the kitchen beside me.

"Chica! What's the matter?"

He tried to put his arm around me, but I pulled away. My mind was racing. Did I want this, or didn't I? What was happening? I felt tired, confused, I didn't know what was right any more.

"I need to... sit down." I said.

"Come on, then, let's get you up."

He reached out his hand and, somewhat reluctantly, I allowed him to lead me to the living room. Despite everything, it still felt comforting to feel him close to me. He led me to the sofa. "You sit down. It's ok. I'll make you a hot drink."

He left me and I could hear him go back into the kitchen, and put the kettle on.

Out in the street, below my living room window. I could hear the city waking up.

People were walking outside on the pavement, I could hear them talking, greeting each other. It was Sunday and they were going to the church across the road.

Their ordinary lives seemed a very long way off. Way in the distance, a police siren sounded.

Celebrity Boy came back into the room, all sweetness and light. He handed me a steaming cup of some kind of herbal tea.

"What's this?"

"Go on chica, it's nice, drink it, it'll calm you down."

Cautiously, I took the cup. It wasn't too hot. Vapours swept across my nose. It smelt sweet, incredible... I took a sip. It tasted delicious. Greedily, I gulped it down.

Celebrity Boy sat down on the sofa next to me and gently stroked my hair.

"You know Alice," he whispered gently. "When you're in a trance, it's kind of like being anaesthetised. Nothing really matters you know, and that's a very pleasant way to be. It's a different world. Nothing hurts, nothing feels. At first it may, but then, the pain fades away, just fades away. Man, it's goddam fantastic."

His words sounded familiar. The drink did make me feel a lot better. My shoulders sank back, I began to relax. My head seemed to clear.

We sat there a moment, in silence, then I realised what I had to do. "Listen," I said, "I don't want to cause a scene or anything. But really I don't think it's working out you staying here. I'm really confused. I need to sort my head out.

Would you mind, very much, maybe checking into a hotel for a while? I need to speak to Ben. I need to sort out what I want. I think that might be better for all of us."

"Oh, baby, baby," Celebrity Boy laughed, then his eyes narrowed."Alice, you just don't get it, do you?"

Again, he'd thrown me into confusion. What was he talking about?

"Honey, I'm not moving anywhere. You're the one who's leaving."

"What... what do you mean?"

"That little er... potion you've just swigged down so eagerly. Know what it is?"

"What are you talking about?"

"Alice, you know how much fun I've had meeting you. You know how I love your life. Well, now, the transformation has begun. I'm going to start living it."

"What the...?"

"I've got you trapped, Alice. I'm controlling you. I've been hanging on to little bits of you, I've been busy collecting, you know."

Oh my God. It began to dawn on me, the hairbrush, the nailfiles, the clothes, all that time in my flat. What had he been concocting all those hours on his own? What had he been spelling out? What was he trying to do to me?

"I don't know what the hell you're talking about. Why don't you just... get out.

That's enough." I couldn't listen to him any more. Pushing him away, I leapt up from the sofa. I was incensed. He was really scaring me. "Get the fuck out!"

"Honey, I'm not going anywhere. I'm having a mighty fine time." He leant back contentedly, and started to whistle, casually inspecting his nails.

His calmness infuriated me. "What the…? Right. Well if you're not leaving. I will. I can call the police you know."

I snatched my mobile and car keys from the living room table and stomped out of the room, grabbing my coat from the hallway floor where I'd left it. Without a backward glance, I ran downstairs and out into the street.

My familiar silver Peugeot was parked across the road, fumbling, my hands clammy, I thrust the car key in the lock, opened the door and jumped in. For a few minutes, I sat there, gasping for breath, trembling.

What was I going to do? I realised I had nowhere to go. Besides, I hadn't slept, and was way over the limit. I wasn't in any state to drive. I felt terrified, alone. I had no idea who I could call for help. The police? Well that was ridiculous. They certainly wouldn't believe any weird stuff. Ben would probably slam the phone down. Amber was probably at the Wonderland after party by now.

There'd be no point calling her, she'd never hear the phone. Chrissie…? Maybe, she was my best friend after all. She would see I was in trouble. Feeling panicky, my heart pounding, I pressed Chrissie's number on my mobile phone.

"Hello sweetie pie." Chrissie's cheerful voice answered almost instantly. "We've just left Wonderland. How are you? Where are you? Listen, guess what, I've got news."

"Chrissie... I... it's..." her happy voice threw me. I wasn't sure where to start.

Chrissie gabbled on, blissfully unaware. "Listen, you know your Cowboy friend... well, you'll never believe. When we went off for a 'bite' last night? I gave him a lift in my car. He got me to pull over, and well, one thing lead to another — Sweetie, he's fantastic. It was the most amazing sex – ever!"

Oh my God. I knew it. But I couldn't believe it. She was my closest friend. She knew I liked him. How could she do that? How the hell could she go behind my back?

But there was no stopping Chrissie, there she was, gabbling on in full flow.

"Alice – he says he's crazy about me. That's just so cool. He says there are some 'loose ends' relationshipwise... some things need sorting out... but... I just know it. He's really serious. It's so fantastic – he says he's going to get me my own flat."

I just couldn't understand it. I couldn't believe my friend would be so naïve.

And I couldn't bear to hear any more. But as Chrissie talked, the phone started buzzing in my ear. It was Amber coming through on call waiting.

At last – saved by the bell — thank God. "Chrissie, I've gotta go." I pressed 'accept call'. "Hi – Amber?"

"Listen, Alice, honey, listen carefully. Where are you?" She sounded petrified.

"It's ok, I'm in my car. Celebrity Boy really started scaring me. I had to get out."

"Right... that's good, that's good." She caught her breath, as if calculating what to say. "Uh... have you seen today's News of the World?"

"No." My mind flashed back, something, there was something... I remembered Celebrity Boy throwing the paper aside as we'd got into the back of the cab. My heart began to pound in my throat.

Slowly, carefully, Amber told me the story that was all over the headlines. A new cult had hit Hollywood. Something had superceeded scientology as the chosen 'religion' of the rich and famous. The name had yet to be announced, but this belief appealed to celebrities because the followers were promised complete freedom from the entrapments of fame. The cult was thought to use a mixture of voodoo, wicca and paganism. After some weeks of initiation, it seemed the celebrities who were known by their friends and partners to be devotees were completely disappearing, without trace. The FBI were taking this very seriously and witchcraft was no longer a laughing matter. Almost immediately, both Sabrina the Teenage Witch and Buffy the Vampire Slayer had been banned from TV screens.

Star suspects of this cult had been named, Celebrity Boy topped the list.

I sat with the mobile pressed to my ear, staring at my face in the driver mirror, transfixed at my reflection. "Oh... Amber... oh, shit."

"Alice — listen, don't move. Stay right there. Atomic and I are coming to get you."

There was a click as she hung up. I pulled my big, fluffy winter coat tight around my shoulders, but it didn't seem to give me any comfort. I sat, stock still, and waited.

I was surprised to find myself waking up some time later. Had I really been asleep? For how long? I had no idea what time or day it was. Outside the car, it was snowing. Big, thick flakes fell softly, covering the car bonnet. My body ached all over. My head was throbbing. Despite my warm coat, I shivered.

I looked across the street and suddenly, I saw Amber. She was hurrying along the road, her head bent down against the cold. Atomic was a few steps in front of her. He went up to the door of my block of flats, and rang the bell.

"Amber! Amber! Over here." I banged on the car window, but Amber didn't seem to hear me. She hurried up to the front of the building. The door of the mansion block swung open, and Celebrity Boy appeared. He leant over to Amber and kissed her, then put his right arm round Atomic's shoulders, waving his left hand to beckoning them in.

"Amber." I tried to open the car door but somehow my fingers seemed numb and I couldn't grab the handle. "I'm here."

Seconds later, a taxi pulled up, and Chrissie, Spike and Elvis spilled out.

Laughing, they piled into the building. Chrissie seemed to have a key.

"What the...? Chrissie!" By now I was screaming like

my chest would burst, still banging on the window, but nobody seemed to hear a thing. My lungs felt like they were bleeding, my head was spinning, I began to sway. The snow fell ever more thickly. Everything became blurred and I could no longer see where I was.

The horrible sickness welled in my stomach again.

"Hey, isn't that pretty?" says Chrissie, taking the snowstorm from the mantelpiece and giving it a shake.

"Yeah, isn't it?" Chrissie's gorgeous new boyfriend (some say he looks just like a famous Hollywood film star) grins and glances happily around the room.

Atomic's on the decks, Amber's nodding unselfconsciously to the beats as she flicks through a magazine. Spike and Elvis are mixing the drinks, another Sunday afternoon and it seems like all's right with the world.

Inside the glass ball a neon-lit cityscape glitters under the snow; in the foreground a girl in a fur coat sits in a silver car. The snowflakes fall so thick and fast that for a moment, just a moment, it almost looks like she's waving.

Small Talk
NICK BARLAY

The night I speak of is the night someone cleans out the safe in the office and leaves a tampon instead of the cash. The tampon is a Boots Super Plus with Applicator. It is clearly used, and the fact of it being used whatever its brand makes it a kind of calling card, a calling card that says: I bled here. It is also a personal insult to Bonsai, who is the owner of the safe, the office the safe is in and the club the office is in. It is a personal insult to him because Bonsai orders us girls never to work when we have our periods. He tells us many times that if he catches a girl working and bleeding at the same time she is most certainly fired. We call him Bonsai on account of him being very small, very manicured and a total pain to keep happy, not because he is Japanese, which he isn't.

I do not care about women's issues, he tells us many times in his high-pitched non-smoker's voice. My clientele do not care about women's issues. My clientele do not pay to see gummy knickers and tampon strings. What they pay to see is a bikini wax, big hair, big shoes, a big Hello Boys up front and twenty minutes sexy small talk. And that is all.

He has a long list of other rules such as no plasters on your toes, no chewing gum in the gob, no five o'clock shadow on the lip, no stretch marks. He is even known to make rules about teeth and check a girl's teeth like she is a horse.

But the rule about periods is without a doubt his favourite. So the fact of a tampon appearing in the safe instead of the whole week's takings leads most people to get religious about certain ideas. But most people get religious about three ideas in particular. One, the thief is definitely a woman. Two, the thief is definitely a woman with a period. Three, the thief is definitely a woman with a period and inside knowledge. And all these three items, the woman, the period and the inside knowledge, obviously come together at the same small hour in the same small place. Namely, at about 3.30am in Bonsai's safe. So if you are the type who goes around suspecting other people, you would suspect one or more and pretty much any of the women. In a nutshell, all of us girls have motive and opportunity shared out between us like equal rights.

But I am getting way way way ahead of myself. As per usual. Press pause, relax, rewind, soft cushion, glass of red, spliff, clear the mind, slow the heart, then press play, roll the credits, set the scene.

The events I speak of happen around the time when the new millennium is not so new. In fact it is getting on for old, and all the promises people make in the name of the new millennium are still at the warehouse waiting to be delivered.

The cheque is in the post, the bus is due but meanwhile a lot of girls are having a hard time. Everyone talks big about making a wedge or stealing a wedge and getting out, and those like me who do not talk big about it think about it all the time. Because when you are debted up and cannot see a way out, nothing but nothing is sadder than a wig, a false name and a fake tan. At times like this a place like this makes everyone rub each other up the wrong way and gets everyone pressing the wrong buttons. In good times the rubbing is a laugh and even if you press the wrong button you still get a can of Pepsi.

But the millennium is growing leg hair like an ape and needs a full body wax and a good going over with a Remington Ladyshave because all the girls are waiting so long for Bonsai's promises to be fulfilled. Instead of fulfilment all we get is Bonsai ordering us about, verballing us down, clipping his nails, filing his nails, inspecting his nails, making up new rules and getting tighter and meaner than ever. He is so tight he buys special energy-saving bulbs then keeps them locked in a money-saving cupboard. He is so mean he installs dummy cameras instead of proper CCTV. It is well known that Bonsai is the sort to be tight and mean even if the key to the land of plenty is firmly in his hand. As it is he has firmly in his hand two much lesser things: the key to a lapdancing club near Centrepoint and the fun-size brains of his favourite dancer.

His favourite dancer is Tara Ya-Ya. She is twice as tall and half as old as Bonsai and has a day job as Bonsai's ever-clinging girlfriend. It is often suggested that Bonsai should find a sex partner more his size, like a Honda Civic. But Bonsai feels he is trading up and Tara Ya-Ya thinks she is too. One of them is certainly wrong but it is very true that being Bonsai's ever-clinging girlfriend gives Tara Ya-Ya more airs than she arrives in the world with. And Tara Ya-Ya arrives in this world with more airs than is average on account of the hyphen in her last name. This is why she is all ya ya and quickly learns to live up to the hyphen by being a snooty ya ya bitch.

Of course neither her long legs nor her mock croc accessories nor her airs encourage Bonsai to cough up any quicker. In other words he is as tight and mean with his ever-clinging girlfriend as anyone else and she always has to beg hard for a biscuit. The thing is though, everyone is still jealous of her because of course Tara Ya-Ya is the only one with begging rights.

Before the pecking order reaches me (I am advised not to mention my working name for legal reasons) there are three other girls. Mostly what we have in common is no trust for each other, although everyone gets a big ego free when they start work. After Tara Ya-Ya, the runner-up for the ego prize goes to Xana.

She is a flashy Italian dominatrix with a pvc wardrobe, a dungeon in Paddington and Engleesh that is not very well. But her Engleesh is never a problem because Mistress

Xana speaks the international language of domination. She invites me one time to watch her work in her dungeon. She says many things I do not understand, including things like: you eslave batard, you edirty devil, like my boats, I say like my boats now. Mistress Xana hates Tara Ya-Ya and to get back at her she is trying for months to make Bonsai her slave. She says Bonsai is already a dirty eslave ina his emind. Maybe. But Bonsai is not a slave in his wallet and since that is mostly where his mind is, it stands to reason that he is not ready to part with a hundred pounds for a half hour session. For that money he is only prepared to be Mistress Xana's slave for fifteen minutes and that, she complains, is not nearly long enough to train him properly.

Then there is Gold, who is an oiled up bodybuilder who tells everyone she is from California and speaks to everyone, especially men, in an American accent.

She is actually from a place more east than California called East Ham. But everyone knows she is famous because she is once on the shortlist for the tv show Gladiators. Physically speaking she is the toughest of all of us but the condition of her triceps is out of synch with the condition of her ideas. She is always confessing to some terrible thing, like being an addict of some sort, a drug addict, a sex addict, a food addict, a chocaholic, an alcoholic, a kleptoholic, a paramaniac obsessive or whatever. You run into her in the changing room between dances and she starts chatting at you in the following way: I think I'm addicted to knives... Or something. But mainly what she is addicted to is confessing what she is addicted to. Some people say she should never be on the shortlist for Gladiators at all but for Jerry Springer instead.

After her is Aleesha, who is what some people are apt to call a bint. But she is not a bint just a ditsy blonde who is naturally gorgeous and healthy and will naturally go through life fit as fuck. In fact one day she will make the most fit as fuck corpse ever. She is also open-minded. She has to be on account of her dad. One day her absentee dad Tony turns up at the club with his mates. They are celebrating Tony's unexpected release after five years in max security. So what does Tony pop his eyeballs at first thing? Only his baby in nothing but a g-string upside down on a pole. So he sees her pole-dancing and what does he do?

Instead of dragging her down and beating the fit-as-fuck out of her, daddy pays for the apple of his eye to lapdance for him. And after that for all his mates.

One by one. He and all his mates are regulars now and they, Tony and Aleesha, become best friends. Of course Tony is no mug and he sees straight off the business opportunities from this Kleenex-sponsored reunion. He starts to supply Aleesha with coke to sell in the club, obviously on a strictly fifty-fifty basis.

Several of us ask Tony from time to time if he and his mates can muller Bonsai and then maybe charge him protection money. But Tony says he must keep a low profile for a while yet before he makes any big moves. The truth is we think Tony fears Bonsai's bouncer/cleaner who is known as Steve the Sikh and is generally humungus.

Steve the Sikh is not an easy man to reason with because he is an emotional person with only four emotions: chuffed, gutted, well chuffed and well gutted. He also has scars all over his head from bottlings and chair-leggings and weekly divings through windows. But of course you should see the other guys.

Most of these other guys are like Tony and also fear Steve the Sikh. They know that Steve the Sikh is once a real Sikh, maybe around the time he is born. They also know that as a Sikh he has the five holy K's on his side. I forget the other four K's but the one to remember is the Kirpan which is a long silver dagger that Steve the Sikh keeps with him at all times for spiritual reasons.

Steve the Sikh and his Kirpan are very loyal to Bonsai because, according to Steve the Sikh and his Kirpan, Bonsai is the only one who really understands them. What Bonsai understands is that Steve the Sikh is as unemployable as a fully grown man can be in this town. And, even if Steve the Sikh dreams of striking out alone in bouncing or cleaning, the truth is he needs the little cash in hand that Bonsai gives him even more than he needs his Kirpan.

All this is above the heads of the many law-abiding hostesses who also come and go, such as Thai, Dutch and Spanish students scrimping and saving their way through college, like Kiki, Mandi and Lola. Of course there are also hard Northern girls like Shaz and Kirsty who prefer other people scrimping and saving and usually go looking for these other people in distant places. So if you hear of a mugging in Mill Hill and Shaz and Kirsty are in Mill Hill or anywhere near Mill Hill you would not need a college degree to list the suspects.

So anyway, there we all are this one busy night, me, Tara Ya-Ya, Mistress Xana, Gold, Aleesha, Tony and his mates, Steve the Sikh and his Kirpan, with the house band playing Purple Rain very loud and the place full of hostesses and men, over-priced champagne and under-the-table cocaine. Now, the needle between the girls and especially the top girls starts with Bonsai's system. The more he likes you the higher up you are and the more he intros you to the Big Wheels, the Big Wheels being the men with the Big Money. A night in the company of a Big Wheel is worth a week of tourists, two weeks of lads on stag nights and over a month of odds and sods trying to get buzzed on a budget.

The only drawback is that nine out of ten Big Wheels are ugly. I do not know why this is so but in the end it does not bother nine out of ten girls because of course the more a man spends the prettier he gets. The Big Wheels could be anyone from telecom executives, investment brokers and Ferrari importers to gangsters, dealers and ex-undercover Vice Squad sleazebags (like Desmond McGeolighan who should definitely be named many times for legal reasons although with a name like that it is difficult to name him at all).

What is at stake is more than what the Big Wheel spends in the club because the club gets most of that anyway. What is at stake is the chat money (twenty pounds for twenty minutes of sexy small talk) and of course the possibility of a buy-out. A Big Wheel often buys a girl out and you can bargain the price (say a hundred pounds) and you can cashpoint that off them the moment you step outside with them. Then they take you to a club that you suggest like Stars because of course you know the bar or the door and always get a taste of the business you bring. Then they buy you drinks all night, an E or two, and all the time they think they will sex you up or at least get a thorough caressing out of it, even though you clarify ASAP one or both of two things: this may be the sex industry but sex is not on the menu; you have a boyfriend who is a judo master. Of course men are men and the more you say you won't give it up the more they want you to give it up and the more they spend trying to make you give it up. The trick is to pace yourself for a long stint on the tiles and to avoid bouncing off walls on account of peaking too early. In a nutshell, Big Wheel equals Big Night.

And this is where the needle is. Because this one heaving night, with the house band finishing Purple Rain and starting on Black Magic Woman, Bonsai tells us his new strategy for the future, his visualising for the whole of the new millennium, which of course takes a fair amount of visualising. As it turns out, his visualising does not require any of us to live for a thousand years because it is mainly about skinning us tonight and every night for as long as we work for him. And what Bonsai wants to skin us for is twenty-five per cent of the buy-out money in return for doing an intro, and even another fifteen per cent of the chat money for doing the same. Of course it does not need me to point out that all this is like asking Americans to give up guns or Steve the Sikh to hand over his Kirpan. But unlike Americans or Steve the Sikh there is little we can do.

Then, to rub salt in the wound, Bonsai gets the ever-clinging Tara Ya-Ya to bend our ears about how to make it in this business, about how to get ahead in lapdancing, about how we should always respect the owner, and especially his millennium visualising, because of course there are plenty of other girls out there, plenty of other wannabes out there in times like these, plenty who would just love to step right in and take over at a moment's notice if not sooner so we better watch our step all of us.

Bonsai thinks all this talking down of the girls is well timed because nobody is going to argue when the place is rammed and there is money to be made. So, with the air of someone who is just revealed to be the world's smartest man, Bonsai goes back up to the VIP gallery overlooking the stage to file his nails and keep an eye on everyone, although of course in a place like this you cannot keep an eye on everyone all the time. Tara Ya-Ya is someone most people do keep an eye on, a green eye, as she swans off to her Big Wheel intro. Tonight her intro is none other than the ex-Vice Squad sleazebag Desmond McGeolighan, a man so close to Bonsai that one or the other surely requires a strawberry Jiffy.

And here we all are, the rest of us, lumping more than liking it and very minded to scheme anything that can be schemed by way of revenge. All the Kikis, Lolas, Lalas,

Lilis and Lulus in the place act the herd and follow orders. Them aside, there is much seething and gnashing of teeth. Tony and his mates are usually ready to sit out disputes but all this is apt to arouse the king kong chest-thumping alpha male in them. Tony's mates (who have confusing names like Nazza, Chazza, Dazza etc) nurse their beers and keep an eye on Tony for a signal. Meanwhile, Mistress Xana entertains them with her plans for Bonsai, such as tying him in her donjon in order to weep ina his bolls. Aleesha wants a more permanent solution which includes her dad getting a contract out on her boss before dawn. These ideas are lost on Gold who wonders out loud several times why she is addicted to abusive men. And who knows what hard skulking Northern girls like Shaz and Kirsty are thinking, especially after slim pickings in Alperton.

Between dances we are all chirping in the changing room among our bras, g-strings, glitter and six-inch gift from god mules, with the aroma of Obsession and Wrigley's Airwaves and the sound of mobiles in the background. The chirping we are doing mainly consists of everyone cussing off the world, the boss and his girlfriend and thinking up ways of leaving big marks on all three. We are all doing lines off the toilet seats and wishing we could make easier money erotic dancing on the internet. Gold says that after her boyfriend gets out of rehab he is setting up a live webcam site, so all of us can make a hundred pounds an hour for getting messy with our favourite vibrators. Aleesha is more concerned that the coke she is selling should go further and asks us whether to cut it with Vit C powder or baby lax.

But the basic problem is that while all the sharks are moaning in the changing room, the prawns are cleaning up in the club. Lolas, Lulus and Lalas are being booked and double booked and bought out like there is soon to be a national shortage of them. Worse, the house band is playing a Madonna medley. They start with Material Girl which everyone old enough to remember hates, and only the really young Lolas, Lulus and Lalas love because it is what their magazines tell them is retro chic. Retro chic or no, all this amounts to a very sorry state in the here and now.

So mostly we are left in two minds about what to do. But luckily we have only one instinct. Which is to say we do the inevitable and go back to work. Although if you ever see a girl pole or lap dancing when she is pissed off you will know it does not make for a pleasant evening. Me myself I am dancing for two blubber buddies in suits, one of whom just keeps on eating his spaghetti dinner in a very disrespectful way. So he is the one whose lap I sit on and I make sure to give his crotch a good grind until bolognese sauce starts to form around his mouth and his eyes start to water because of course he is choking. Before his blubber buddy steps in to referee or he swallows enough spaghetti to save his own life, a commotion begins at one of the other tables.

The commotion becomes a ruction in no time at all and this development comes as no surprise for it is none other than Shaz and Kirsty who are working this table. Whatever the argument, Shaz has a broken champagne glass ready in her hand and there are slaps flying from Kirsty and a certain member of the clientele is very much on the receiving end. From the VIP gallery Bonsai is waving his polished cuticles at Steve the Sikh in what you might call a frantic manner. Steve the Sikh is well chuffed and hardly needs much waving at to get him to wade into the thick of a ruction. In fact, with his five K's and a sixth sense he is already so near the ruction he is the ruction, which is really a skill he shares with the cream of bouncers.

Most people who are not bouncers are inclined to give Steve the Sikh the benefit of the doubt in such a situation, even when there is no doubt. The clientele in question does just that, hands up, backing off and hoping to walk away from this with his suit and face in the same condition his suit and face are normally in. But Shaz and Kirsty are not the kind of girls to give a person a break until that person gives up what he or she can towards their good cause.

The rest hover around and about keeping away from the trouble. Tara Ya-Ya is safe in the gaze of the Vice Squad, Gold is dancing, Aleesha is by the bar, Xana is on another table and me myself I get well clear of all of them into the shadows.

In a ruction it is management policy to side with girls until the situation is taken care of and then fire them or, worse, reduce their hours to zero, which is the terrible condition of being neither hired nor fired. But Shaz and Kirsty are not types to be put off by zero hours and carry on accusing the slapped up clientele of touching where they have no right to touch. One well gutted look from Steve the Sikh and the clientele is leaving his car and house keys, watch and wallet, as security while he goes to the cashpoint to settle his bill, a bill which as per usual is revealing many hidden extras.

Bonsai is moving around the tables reassuring people and ordering the house band to play something less likely to provoke people than Madonna. After this we expect him to call Shaz and Kirsty to his office in order to reduce them. But on this twisty old night, with the house band playing Sex Machine, Bonsai goes to his office only to get severely heart-attacked. In fact he is more severely heart-attacked than ever before in his short life. Of course this is because his safe is totally open and his money is totally stolen to the point of no longer being there. On the other hand what is totally there in place of the stolen money is a used Boots Tampon Super Plus with Applicator.

Most people, if their safe is open and their money is gone, shout THIEF or POLICE. But when the thief and the police are very much in the vicinity it makes more sense to shout other words altogether. What Bonsai shouts is not easy to make out above the din but his eyes are glaring and his well-kept little hands are well clenched into little fists. It is the Vice Squad who first gets to hear the words Bonsai is shouting, him and Tara Ya-Ya together on their table. The reaction of the Vice Squad is to make a chopping movement across his throat, either because he believes in the death penalty or because he is advising Bonsai to shut up shop for the night. Closing before closing time is not something Bonsai can bring himself to do even when he is the victim of crime. But the Vice Squad is very persuasive because of course it is also the Vice Squad's money that is usually in Bonsai's safe. So very soon Steve the Sikh and his Kirpan are enforcing an unnaturally early licence.

Ten minutes later the clientele is dispersed and there is a full lock-in, not in a nice drinks-on-the-house kind of way but in a nasty nobody-leaves-till-someone-confesses kind of way. This is because it is clear to both Bonsai and the Vice Squad that, since stealing from a safe requires inside knowledge, it is best to keep such knowledge inside. The Vice Squad rounds up all us girls in a very small space, which is what the Vice Squad is mainly trained to do. The only one who is not rounded up in a small space is of course the ever-clinging Tara Ya-Ya. Lady Twat, as Shaz and Kirsty are more apt to call her, has a large space all to herself at a table and sits there with her typical ya ya expression on her typical ya ya face.

Also, nobody tries to round up Tony and his mates even though some people might say that Tony and his mates are the criminal fraternity and ought to be rounded up on principle. In return for not being rounded up, the criminal fraternity behaves very well, innocently choosing to sit out the dispute until proven guilty. The Vice Squad then takes charge of the investigation and Steve the Sikh is instructed to take charge of the searching of the changing room.

Mistress Xana, who is not used to being dominated in this way, is the first to protest. Who know fucky money where beetch Tayaya no? Which means the bitch Tara Ya-Ya is the thief because nobody else knows where to find the fucking money.

But the truth is everyone knows where to find Bonsai's fucking money. Not only that, everyone knows Bonsai's safe is dodgy because of course Bonsai is too tight and mean to fix it or replace it. The question is how to get even a dodgy safe to open. And that is the kind of knowledge that truly is inside knowledge.

Steve the Sikh is meanwhile turning handbags and clutchbags and bumbags and shoulderbags inside out looking for signs of illegal activity. It does not take him long to find thirteen cashpoint cards, four credit cards and six Blockbusters video cards all crusty with coke. Then he finds five straws with traces of the same, as well as eight wraps, three razor blades, unidentified pills, tablets and powders. Then he finds two dole cards and a dole cheque that do not match any known names, twenty-four bottles of Obsession clearly for retail, and two binliners stuffed with more glamour-wear than is reasonable for personal use. All of us girls are connected to one thing or another, and the only new discovery is Gold's fix kit because it is not widely known before that Gold is a brownhead or that she uses Rimmel No. 5 to cover her needle marks.

Still, all this only tells Bonsai and the Vice Squad what they already assume.

In fact, the Vice Squad says he would be quite stunned not to find evidence of such wrongful lifestyle in such a wrongful place. But him and Bonsai know that any attempt to use this evidence to threaten one or any of the girls into confession is sure to result in generally bad publicity for those making the threats. Then the Vice Squad hits on what is very likely the first policeman-like idea of his long career: a DNA test on the tampon and a fingerprint analysis of the crime scene. He has an old mate in Robbery who is well used to unusual requests and could oblige on a 'no win no fee' basis. Of course nobody needs to be a big fan of courtroom drama to realise that all this testing must be carried out in accordance with the sort of rules that big fans of rules like Bonsai really hate.

So Bonsai hits on a much simpler idea. He asks Steve the Sikh what evidence he finds in the changing room by way of women's monthly affairs. What he actually says is more like: What I want to know is, is any of them girls on the blob?

Steve the Sikh of course finds too much evidence of girls on the blob. He finds Lillets, Tampax, Illusions, Always, Bodyform, with wings and without, with applicators and without, all of which amounts to flagrant abuse of Bonsai's favourite rule. In Bonsai's mind, which is very neglected when compared to his nails, all this points to one thing and only one thing: conspiracy. Of course you do not need to be a big fan of detective thrillers to see the totally absorbent hole in this conspiracy theory: none of the evidence is a Boots Tampon Super Plus with Applicator. This is because of course most girls would not be seen dead wearing a Boots Tampon Super Plus with Applicator.

Except perhaps the one person yet to be rounded up, searched or robbed of her dignity. Tony's mates are quite vocal on this subject and one of them, Nazza or Chazza or possibly Dazza, points out that Tara Ya-Ya is now due for the same treatment. But the Vice Squad and Bonsai decide that it is Tony and his mates who are now due for the same treatment if they fail to leave the premises immediately. Of course Tony is not the sort to leave his naturally gorgeous fit as fuck baby Aleesha in a bind and refuses to leave without her. So Bonsai glares and clenches the way he glares and clenches when he is angry and tells Aleesha that she is reduced to zero. And then while he is on a roll he tells me I am also reduced. And then he tells the same to Gold and then Shaz and Kirsty and then any of the Lulus and Lalas in sight. And he would say exactly the same to Mistress Xana but luckily for her she is temporarily out of sight.

This is the cue for the house band to pack up their instruments in a well-rehearsed hurry, suck the dregs out of their complimentary beer and leg it to the exit before they too become part of the reduced workforce. The reduced workforce is just as keen by now to leave but Bonsai says everyone stays until he says everyone goes. Until could be a long time off, especially if Bonsai starts to give himself a full manicure.

Steve the Sikh obviously twigs that if a night fails to die of natural causes one must stab it to death because this is the very sudden moment he chooses to astonish everyone present. Stepping forward, he holds up a mock croc shoulder bag and produces from it the sort of magic rabbit that closely resembles a pack of Boots Tampon Super Plus with Applicator. It is well known that mock croc and Tara Ya-Ya go together like two names with a hyphen in the middle and it does not need me to describe the general surprise and delicious malicious cocktail of joy when the snooty ya ya bitch is revealed to be the thief. Everyone waits for Bonsai to speak. When he does, he complains bitterly that his ever-clinging girlfriend has the period, the inside knowledge and the most opportunity of all to steal from him and that no girl ever betrays him like this before and that she will never work again if he can help it which he certainly can.

For her part, Tara Ya-Ya acts the most surprised and least joyful of anyone.

She tries to cling to Bonsai and to protest her innocence by saying she is clearly framed. She says she is never in her life cheap enough to go to Boots to buy cheap necessaries to put inside expensive accessories. Furthermore, she says, there is no sign of Bonsai's money anywhere. This, as anyone with public school on their CV can confirm, is the only proof that counts. She also spells out the words facile est inventis addere or something, which she says anyone with Latin on their CV would take to mean: it is easy to add to things that are already invented. Or to put it another way: it is a stitch up. Whatever it means it cuts no ice with anyone who does not have public school or Latin on their CV, which if truth be told is most of the reduced workforce. In fact, the stuff old Tara Ya-Ya comes out with is the sort of stuff that would Fedex a saint to max security and keep that saint there with no hope of parole. As it is, it convinces everyone, especially Bonsai, that she is just a smart skinny bitch.

And a totally guilty smart skinny bitch at that.

The Vice Squad tells her to accompany him outside to his motor for formal questioning. The generally satisfied rest of us are generally free to leave. So me myself, Tony and his mates, Aleesha, Gold, Lalas and Lulus, Shaz and Kirsty all start to go in our own directions. Mistress Xana is still nowhere to be seen but Steve says he will find her since he is staying to clean up the place.

So with my wig in my bag and the dawn coming up I trot down Tottenham Court Road to take my place on a stool in Stars, my favourite bar. I guess if I am way ahead of myself earlier I am now almost fully caught up. Actually I feel I should celebrate because with Tara Ya-Ya branded a thief, Gold revealed as a brownhead, Aleesha and her dad out of favour and Xana nutty as a bag of dry roasted, I am in with a very good chance of being number one as soon as Bonsai increases everyone's hours from zero.

But of course some people might say there are still one or two loose ends to tie. Maybe there are. Because as I sip my Bloody Mary and chat with the barman I am waiting for Shaz and Kirsty. Because it is quite possible that me myself and Shaz and Kirsty have arrangements to meet here. It is quite possible that me myself and Shaz and Kirsty have arrangements to meet here for certain purposes.

Because although I cannot say for sure it is always quite possible that Tara Ya-Ya is never the thief. Maybe her eye strays that way from time to time but she is not the type to think a thing like this through. For instance she would not know how to get girls like Shaz and Kirsty to start ructions and create diversions. Because although Shaz and Kirsty are types who often start ructions and create diversions, they will only actually organise these things for the right person and for the right price, which is usually a big laugh and two drinks. In this case it is for the same plus twenty per cent of the safe.

Of course if Tara Ya-Ya is not the thief with inside knowledge then it is most likely someone else. And the someone else is quite possibly none other than the ever-loyal Steve the Sikh, a man of not many emotions but capable of visualising the millennium as good as anyone. And what he visualises as good as anyone is nothing if not the good life. And the means of getting a piece of this good life is busting in to a dodgy safe with a Kirpan while a ruction kicks off. And the means of getting clean away with the same piece of good life is to make sure Someone Else gets rumbled instead for the whole thing. It is also quite possible that it takes a certain other party to bring Shaz and Kirsty and Steve the Sikh together as well as to place tampons where tampons need placing. But of course even if me myself I know for certain of such a certain other party me myself I cannot reveal them for legal reasons.

All this may be the loose ends finally tied but unfortunately it is not because of what Shaz and Kirsty say when they arrive. After their two drinks each, they have their one big laugh: it seems Mistress Xana is not missing after all. In fact, says Shaz, while everyone is being reduced, it seems that Mistress Xana is just hiding. And the place she is just hiding, says Kirsty, is Bonsai's office.

And when Bonsai goes in there to wait for the Vice Squad to come back with a confession and the money from Tara Ya-Ya, Xana closes the office door and locks it. Then what she does, says Shaz, is well serious by anyone's standards.

Because, says Kirsty, after locking the door, Mistress Xana throws the key out of the window.

Sure the Vice Squad is planning to return to the scene but, as everyone knows and Shaz and Kirsty remind me, formal questioning in a Vice Squad motor takes at the very least half an hour. And half an hour is easily enough for Mistress Xana to work up a head of steam in the international language of domination and make edirty edevil Bonsai her edirty eslave once and for all.

Shaz and Kirsty find this very very funny but of course it means that in half an hour me myself I will have no chance of being number one at all. Well this too could be the gloomy loose ends really and truly tied up. But the night I speak of carries on and does not end here. In fact it continues not to end because Steve the Sikh, who is supposed to be arriving to divvy up with Shaz and Kirsty and a certain other party, does not arrive at all. In fact he continues not to arrive at all well past the night I speak of and well into what most people call morning.

By this time me myself and Shaz and Kirsty are too bladdered to think straight.

Eventually they stop laughing and stop retailing the story over and over to the barman and get as gloomy as me. This is because it dawns on them like it dawns already on me that Steve the Sikh will in fact never arrive to divvy up. This is because of course he is gone for good. Most likely he is setting up a cleaning business in a place far away from this place and even in a town far away from this town.

And this all means that the night I speak of amounts to just another night of heaps of big talk swept clean by commuter time like so much waste. And it means that most of us, like most of us people, are left in the daylight with what we should most likely stick to all along: a false name, a wig, a fake tan and twenty minutes of sexy small talk.

Snow Never Settles In This City
FRANCESCA BEARD

We should go up to Primrose HIll. Just as the day dips into night and the hem of the sky turns violet and all the lights of the city come up, twinkling in diamond-point, honeycombing office blocks and tower blocks where life goes on in tiny squares and all the roads of London scrawl a love letter to homecoming aeroplanes and underneath and in-between, 7 million people come and go, talking in 300 languages, in bars and streets and trains home where kitchens steam in electricity and children fight for the last corner of tv and outside taxis trawl and the homeless bed down in rivers of silver and gold.

All the mess and pain and sweat and struggle of 2000 years of history translated into a moment, an abstract, a poem to the stars.

And each of us a word, a piece of the mosaic, a simile for something else, meaningless unless in context.

All this is true, as if I never told you.

We were magic until we are named.

Snow never settles in this city. Today, the sky is a ghostly ballroom filled with giant forms that dip and piroutte. They cling to the air in a trembling waltz. But eventually, the surface gets them, flake by flake. I watch them dissolve on the green enamel of Bea's bike.

The woman opposite has an orange imac. She often sits in front of the window, naked. Now, she is talking on the phone and painting her toenails.

'Bea', I say 'That naked woman is always painting her toenails.'

'Yeah', Bea says. 'There's a whole lot going on in that room. We have no milk.'

I trudge through the virtual snow to Tescos. The homeless man is there and I buy him some chocolate milk with the rest of my shopping. One time I got him banana-flavoured milk and he said 'No thanks', quite sarcastically. In the queue, I read the Standard. The economy is faltering, we will have war, and Catherine Zeta Jones has a battle with the pounds. I on the other hand, according to my horoscope, am due a lucky break. Then, when I come out of Tesco's, the snow has stopped and the sun is shining!

Back home, Bea tells me that Jo, my boss has called.

'I told her you were in bed', she says. 'I told her you were sleeping.'

'Did she sound pissed off?' I ask.

'She appologised. It's amazing.'

'Isn't it!'

I work for a human rights charity based in Fulham. I've

worked there for a year and a half now. I only go in a couple of days a week. I found out that you can go for 4 days off before you need a doctor's note, so I just call in sick and you can't fire someone for being sick. Maybe it's because I went to the office party with Bea. They're scared of firing me because I'm a poorly lesbian. It wouldn't be charitable.

"What shall we do today?' asks Bea.

'Let's go to the Serpentine.'

We love the Serpentine even though it's not very serpent-like. I like the drab oblong exterior of it, beamed down in the middle of Kensington Gardens. Bea likes the exhibitions. She appreciates the fact that it's free. She says it has a very European feel to it.

We go to the tube, feed the fat coins into the machine and shiver on the platform. When the train arrives, I glare at the driver and look at my wrist where my watch would be.

At Baker Street, tourists peer into the carriage.

'Is yellow Line? Circle line?' says a man in a tweed hat.

'No Circle line today' the passengers tell him.

His hopeful face crumples as the doors close and the train pulls away.

At Edgware Road, the train stops and the driver gets out and stands on the platform. He chats to another man in a blue driver's jacket. They are laughing and one of them is texting on a mobile phone. No-one else in the carriage pays them any attention.

'Bea!' I fidget against her. 'It's unbelievable.'

'It's Edgware Road', says Bea. She is playing snakes on her phone.

'They don't care. They aren't even embarrassed.'

'It's all an act. One of them might snap at any minute. Look at that man's neck.'

I look at the men. Bea is right. Under their jokey banter is a rushing undercurrent of emotional violence. What can they do? They are mere individuals in a complex system riddled by decades of underfunding.

The man next to me is unwrapping a sandwich. Flecks of foil remain embedded in the cream cheese filling. He chews and winces and writes in his diary. 'We are puppets ruled by hostile angles and have lost our way.' He has made the entry in at March 12th, even though it's Febuary 12th today. Under March 8th he has written 'Saw J again today. Was wearing in disguise. Situation is undercontrol.' Undercontrol was underlined heavily and written again in the margin.

At Royal Oak, we get out and walk up the damp residential streets to Queensway, gathering speed. Striding under the high domed glass of Whiteleys, we push past gaggles of Saudi teens in Diesel and Moschino, past Ann Summers, all pink and red for Valentine's Day, past the Morroccan cafes and the guy handing out leaflets for the Indian restaurant, past Office and Starbucks and the queues at the Barclays cashpoint till we stop outside Lee's.

'Shall we?' I say to Bea and she looks at her phone.

'It's 4 o'clock' she says, so we go in and order prawn cheung fun and turnip paste and won-ton soups which arrive glistening and steamy. We feed each other with the slippery cheung fun clenched and balanced between chopsticks, slurping down laughter as the soy splashes on the crisp linen table-cloth. Without Bea, I'd probably go to work a lot more.

It's five by the time we make it to the Gallery. Inside, there is an exhibition of Japanese manga paintings. The colours and shapes are peachy lush and hella cute. Bea's favourite is the one which has dripping penises coming out of a giant space toadstool and mine is one with a mutoid rabbit and some magic vomit. I look till my eyes feel wide open to my brain.

Bea says 'I wish we'd brought a joint'.

We walk back across the park, just as the sun sets.

'Look at the sky', whispers Bea. 'It makes you believe in God.'

The clouds are gold and silver cherubim, blowing trumpets of fire across the violet light and the trees stretch to catch the flames like saints in extacy. We hold out our arms to the West crying 'I love you'. Tears stream down my face, making the colours even more intense.

When the sun goes down, we run for the gates before they shut.

Back at the flat, everything feels closed and dull. I don't know if I'm hungry. Bea wants to go to bed, but I roll a joint and start watching t.v. She falls asleep as usual on the couch, but I stay up till 4am, smoking and watching the learning zone. When I go to bed, I wake her up and she stumbles after me. I don't set the alarm – if I wake up naturally at 8, I'll go to work.

Upper Street. She slips through your hands like spaniel ears in the lap of a man drinking beer, watching Angela Lansbury, technicolour princess of the Philistines in saffron and rose. On some alternaSunday maybe you went out and now she won't sit down and watch, she won't stop, she's still there where you were without her, still she laughs, looking up at your frown and the puzzled faces of your college friends as she folds slowly to the varnish of some pub in Camden. All this as the kettle boils, steaming up Delilah against the ply-wood walls of Gaza and from the sink she stands her ground and glares at steam and curls into the blink and click.

I'm walking along Edgware Road, underneath the billboards for wonderbras and Big Macs, when I pass a woman in a yashmak, wrapped up in black from head to feet and this time, it really got under my skin, that woman, bagged up like porn, what did she have under there — a bomb?

So I follow her home.

I was thinking — 'who's the man behind this fetish uniform, how dare he advertise his supremacy on my day to day?'

Sometimes PMT really makes me keen to explore cultural difference hands on.

So I follow her home, past the new pub in what used to be the bank, the gym and the job centre and the bus-stop with the angry tramps and she beetles into a tower block and up the stairs to the 4th floor and I climb up after her, trying to be quiet, but I'm breathing heavily as I peek through the window.

The place is a real pit, full of dead pizza and half-drunk cans and from under her yashmak, she takes a bottle of Tequila, 5 packets of Scottish Smoked Salmon, a tube of Nair Hair Remover and a pair of 10 dernier tights.

Then she takes off her sex camoflage and it's a skinny guy with bum-fluff.

"Hey Erol," says a voice from the kitchen.

"Alright baby," says the boy.

A girl comes in to view, wearing a mini-skirt and a boob tube. "What d'you get?" she says, kissing him hello, rubbing the top of his shaved head with the flat of her palm.

"Some Nair and smoked salmon mainly."

"Did you get the vodka?"

"Nah — tequila."

"Fair enough, that'll do."

They kissed some more and, at that point, I decided to leave.

I'm not a voyeur.

It's the saturday before the Carnival, that amber between afternoon and evening, when everythings's a little bit abstract.

The bass of car stereos discombobulates down Ladbroke Grove, and the plane trees like saints in the slant of avenues and Jo asks me, 'What do you want?' and I tell him, 'Something bad for you, American.'

He disappears into the shade of Video Shack with 'Crouching Tiger, Hidden Dragon' 12 quid overdue, while I go on, through this melting part of the city.

Tower blocks tune jazz and geometry and money suns itself in Georgian crescents, and the homeless guy who lives by Tesco's sprawls in a tall glass of gold. He salutes me V for victory as I pass though the sliding doors.

Inside, the air hums with choice. If you are what you eat, I 'm a rubix cube of biochemistry, consumer of international scandal, global cuckoo, diverting food from other people's mouths to my sleek fridge.

But we buy free range eggs and fair trade coffee. It's too easy to feel guilty. I have a responsibility to this economy to spend money on stuff. And it's tough making decisions. What do I want? 'Pick me, pick me,' shine the new Zealand fun-size Fuji and the Danish bacon shines fatly and the South African Merlot winks ruby and the French brie shrugs, 'If you want.'

I'm examining some vegetarian sushi when a fight breaks out in aisle 2.

'Scuse me! Hello! '

A man has queue-jumped. Perhaps an accident. Zig-zagged trolleys, jostling for position, could happen. Still, he can't be allowed, not when there's so much feistiness around. If he were sensible he'd retreat but he stands his stolen ground.

'Get back in your own line' shouts a matron in a sari.

'Get back to your own country.'

Oooh, that was the wrong thing to say.

The Phillipina cashier squeaks in dismay. The security guard with the tribal scars pushes past Japanese art students to her rescue and the Australian chef from the Brazilian cafe, says 'No offence, but you're out of line.'

Three Jamaican women in three different queues are shouting abuse in a pincer-movement of righteous sisterhood and the only other English-looking guy, in a suit, organic chicken in his basket, takes his mobile out and ooh, look at his thumb go, he's not really here at all, he's texting.

The queue-jumper senses it's not his crowd and leaves.

Everyone starts talking.

The chef asks me where I come from.

Malaysia, I tell him.

'You're Muslim,' he says and I reply, 'No, I'm Chinese Malaysian.'

'Mee hao? Wau hern gkau shing?' he intones and I freeze because I don't speak chinese but I don't leave and now my smile fixes in a grim rictus as his fades and now he's thinking that my expression is politely inscrutable rage because stupid foreign devil has just called my ancestors a herd of goatfuckers by mistake when actually he's asked me 'How's it going, mate?'

It's unfair on chef but I'm fed-up confessing I don't understand Cantonese or Mandarin — people look at you like you've cut off your mother's tongue. So he slopes off with his basket of emergency lemons and I'm left stricken in front of the gift section. They sell all-sorts and there's an air plant priced £2.99, an unprepossessing weed, all wisps and suspirance. The tag says it gets its nutrients from air. It's rooted nowhere. So... what's the point of that? If it can't be planted, is it even a plant? No, it's a misfit or wouldn't it be in the flower section with the heritage roses and the jade palace jasmine, instead of sat between the bath salts and I love Mum mugs. And now I'm identifying with this wierdoid freak. If I was a plant, I'd be one of these, sucking colour from anything it can.

In London today, it's all about your roots, your identity, but there's banana bio yoghurts over there who've got more live culture than me, I've got to get out of this place, I'm having a negative epiphany in the dairy section of Tesco's, double disgrace to my race — a crisis of chineseness surrounded by cheese.

Empty basket dumped, I exit onto Portobello market. Straight into a walking Bennetton ad of, people of all colours, class, orientation. Stroll in the middle of the road, turning it pedestrian.

This is where I belong, in this privileged mix, this moment of ordinary democracy, where everyone can be equal, everyone can be free.

(Democracy, from the Greek word, demos, the people, rule by the people, a system that flourished in 5th century BC, with the Athenian system of citizenship, where all men were free to vote and own land. When I say all men, I mean all free men, not women or children or foreigners or slaves. This system went hand in hand with a system of slavery.

Of course our democracy is different. Our democracy doesn't depend on an underclass. The word democracy in our culture is synonymous with freedom, equality and justice for all. And that's how I use it here.)

Sure I know where I come from, my childhood homeland, the palm-fringed skies, the sea-swell lullabies, Malaysia, balanced on the equator, 8 hrs ahead, 20 years behind but you can't rewind time, and I can't go back, except on a tourist visa.

My soft world, I'd be an outsider now, lost in the swirl of Hokkiens Tamils, Sihks, malays, the odd sweating, besuited Europeans. Cheese-eaters, the chinese called them. Dad. Us. I remember cheese frozen solid because the only place that stocked it was Acmee Cold Storage, so frigidly polar, it gave you brain-ache. They also stocked tins of chocolate covered ants, which I took to be a popular snack food in Europe.

Acmee was a ghost shop, everyone was downtown at the markets, no air-con, but cool and dark as caves in the banging heat of midday sun, the stench of durian crowding out the sweet perfume of sugar cane. I'd follow my mum, serene through the throng in her lime green cheong sam, past the bloody backs of oxen, tails hanging down, and daffodil chicks peeping in cages as she haggled in arcane equations of tonal spells and sign language for starfruit and curry paste.

We spoke English at home, not because my dad was the big white chief but because English is what you speak when you're all from different places, and in my family we were all strangers, I mean emotionally it was like the bar in Star Wars, wierd melancholic aliens mumbling into their beakers.

I'm from a long line of miscellaneous other, my people are traditionally unsure of who they are — one grandfather hailed from Cornwall, magical land of kings and legends, now symbolised by the pastie. My greatgrandmother came from Canton, carried by six hand-maids, technically slaves.

She couldn't walk — her feet were bound.

Her daughter married out, married down, to the son of a Thai labourer. My mum was born speaking a quilt of dialects around the time when Malaya became Malaysia.

My mum couldn't marry a Malay man without converting to Islam and perhaps she was doubtful that Mohammed would sip soup with her hungry Ghost Ancestors.

No doubt she found my father strangely familiar, they were both running away from the suck of their own cultures, magnetised by the combined vacuum of their longitudes, united and tied in an ox-bow lake shaped ribbon of love, in a Church of England wedding with the Govenor's blessing, the Church of England, the one religion more pragmatically pick and mix than the Chinese.

I never learnt chinese, we did latin at boarding school. The East India Rubber Plantation Agency, in compensation for a life lived beyond the pale, off the map, paid for the children of their employees to school in England and so off I was packed, 7000 miles, in a scratchy wool skirt to

Wiltshire, which might as well have been Antarctica, they might as well have sent me to live with a colony of penguins I'd have probably ate better. If I sound bitter, it's just that those strawberry and vanilla daughters with their pony gymkanas thought they were the centre of the universe. And what was the rock upon which this belief was founded? Sheer ignorance, stupendous towering thickness. And I thought, well, I can do that. That's what privilege means, right? Unawareness of anything or anyone but yourself.

Meanwhile on the other edge of the world, my alternate sister sits inside a factory running Nike swooshes through machines and I wonder if she wonders what it would be like to be me. Does she see the same stars, feel the same sun, stand under the same satellites, space chunk, understand chaos theory, quantum mechanics, quarks, all the songs that are sung by the scientists that comfort no one in the dark? Does she burn paper money in the cemetery to honour the souls of her ancestors, while mine hunger, ghostly under the frangipani, mosquitos tangled in their hair.

When I go to Jo's folks, for Friday night, they light candles and chant in Hebrew and I feel uncomfortable, an intruder in the temple, even though his mum says I'm part of the family.

'You're like a daughter to me', she smiles and shows me how to stack the dairy plates seperate from the ones they use for meat.

And meanwhile, on the outer edge of the spiral, my

alternate sister, my great grandmother, is carried those long miles on a bridal litter, to marry a stranger, never saw her mother again, feet as small as sea shells, slippers sewed with tears.

If I could hear her, through the distance of language and years, what would she whisper?

'One generation builds the road, the next generation travels down it, but you have abandoned us to shame and dust. You have spat out history and now you are a husk, a piece of chaos. Empty selfish girl, what are you bound by? Nothing. Living in freedom, enclosed in a nutshell, your guilt-barred cage is as wide as the world.'

And how will I answer her? In the age-old whine of the young.

'You don't know me! You don't know my life' and I'll run away, in my size 5 Nikes, because I can, because I'm not bound by anything.

Not bound by anything, except the limits of my imagination.

But where are we in the story? In the middle of the road, and the light fading at the end of yet another no-show London summer and no shopping done. So I call Jo on my mobile and tell him I'm coming home and what does he want? And he says he really fancies fish and chips for a change, so while I'm waiting in line, I give my mum a bell, and tell her that I love her and she says 'What's happened, where are you?' and I tell her I'm fine, I'm home.

W10 Closer To Heaven Than W11
MONICA GRANT

Oh yes, I'm the great pretender...

Remember those days? Oh boy, those were the days, y'know. When last you heard somebody sing as good as that?

Remember me? Ouno mus' remember me. Jamaica Bunny Limbo! Gold teeth, back teeth, front teeth... all kinda teeth. Yuh don't remember that? Bwoy, go home an' ask yuh mudda an' faada dem. Ask dem about Jamaica Bunny... Me was the original — front teeth, back teeth, canine, incisor, molar, cavity an' even wisdom teeth, seen?! Original bad boy of comedy. Yuh nuh even remember dis one: 'Leroy say to his father, 'Faada, is why we have long, powerful legs?' And his father answered, 'Well, son, it's for when we're running through the jungle and a lion comes after us, then we'll be able to use our long legs to run away.' 'But faada, how comes we've got such long arms'. 'Well,' his father continued, 'it's for when we're going through the jungle and a lion comes after us, we can use

117

our strong legs to outrun him, and then we can use our long arms to grab the branch of a tree and pull ourselves up away from danger.' 'Oh?', said Leroy.

'But faada, why do we have such tight, curly hair?' 'Well son, it's for when we're going through the jungle, and a lion comes after us — we can use our powerful legs to outrun it, our long arms to reach up to a branch and pull ourselves up, and our hair won't get caught in the branches.' 'Oh,' says Leroy. 'Then faada, how come we live in Brixton…?'

Yuh nuh know seh I was the original? Who you know can make people laugh like dat? Lenny Henry?" He kisses his teeth in disgust.

On the gramophone — 'Red Sails In The Sunset'

Nothing like the old days… Now that's what I call music… You remember The Platters…? Nat King Cole, Brook Benton and all those guys? That's what I call music… Not like this noise they're playing nowadays. Compared to that, today's music is crap. Oh, you think I'm old fashioned? No, you know music — it's supposed to be melody, it's words you can sing, that you can hum along to… It's supposed to make people feel good. A lot of this music nowadays makes you feel bad, you know. You feel like throwing yourself through a window… That's why most people can't dance nowadays, y'know. They can't dance. I don't go out much nowadays. I was at this club with an old mate, y'know, for a reunion. And we were at the bar and watched the dance floor, it looked like a fight down there. You can't call that dance. Men and women don't even dance together anymore. In my days, you just hold a woman's waist and start to dip — you know dem way? Even women... I mean, women don't even look like women nowadays. It's either they dress up like man, or, they're undressed, y'know.

Frightening.

You don't remember me? Ouno mus' remember me. Jamaica Bunny Limbo! Gold teeth, back 'teeth, front teeth... all kinda -teeth. Yuh don't remember that? Bwoy, go home an' ask yuh mudda 'bout the original Jamaica Bunny. Me was front teeth, back teeth, canine, incisor, molar. I like a woman to look pretty, y'know.

Back in those days, you couldn't use patois on television, you couldn't sound too black. Now it's all the rage. Dem nuh even wan' yuh fe talk proper nowadays... what a t'ing! Yuh haffe chat foolishness to go 'pon television as a black man. Imagine. Back in the old days it was strictly King's English, y'know — Oxford, Cambridge an all dem t'ings. Yeah, I was big... Yeah man!

International star of stage screen and television — Bunny Limbo!!! I even met Nat King Cole once... Yes man, I met Mr Velvet Voice himself. The King, King Cole. Most youths nowadays don't give him no respect. I heard one fool-fool boy start talk about how Nat was a sell-out, about how he was an Uncle Tom an' all dem foolishness. Look, me can tell you about Nat. He was my personal bredrin — ask anybody. Yuh haffe respeck dat man deh. He opened the door fe 'nuff ah we.

Me ah tell yuh. First black man to live in Hollywood.

Buy up his house cash, an the whole neighbourhood bring down pure distress about how they're not racist, but it's just that the price of their houses will drop if a black man moves in.

Nowadays it's pure black people complainin' when white people move into Brixton or Harlesden that the price of their houses are going up. Nuh true? Yuh haffe give respect to Nat still, because he went through tribulation for all of us as black people. I even meet his daughter the other day. Wha' she name? Natalie? I meet her an' I hug her up, an kiss her up, y'know, no big t'ing.

Back in the old days, a man couldn't make a living by comedy alone. You had to be an all round entertainer. I used to play as a calypso act with comedy. They used to call me Jamaica Bunny. I used to drop one and two sweet songs, y'know, an' then make people roll with laughter afterwards. International star of stage screen and television... Ladies and gentlemen, a man of comedy...! I was always the number one. Front teeth, back teeth, PhD in dentistry, man — the original don gorgon.'Hey brother is that a gold tooth? You've got a gold tooth in your mouth with the streets as dread as they are. You better not go to Brixton with that gold tooth! Dem youths will start prospecting in your mouth — dig a mine in your face... Dem youths nowadays not joking youths — especially the girls dem. At the dance the other day, you shoulda seen some of those girls. Mosta dem dressed — no, undressed... half naked... in — wha' dem call it — batty rider?! I blame the parents. Yuh cyaant have your daughters dress up like that. You have 'nuff man, who will take advantage, man. I wouldn't mind a taste meself…

You mus' manners your pickney dem. Spare the rod an' wha? Yuh spoil the child!

Dem mus' have discipline. Young people nowadays are too rude. Yuh see, love is a serious t'ing. A very serious t'ing. That's why old time people used to, y'know, take time! In the old days when you met a woman, you had to court her all two years or three years before you even get a kiss, not even French kiss neither. You just (kiss)…

That was it! And you had to wine and dine her and romance her and sweet her up for all six and seven years before you even get a feel. And if you want to go any further, you'd better go dung to the jewellery store and buy a big ring, otherwise her father might come ah yuh yard with all cutlass an' him ah go try fe circumcise yuh… Today's style is the quick style. I'm not complaining though, y'know. After all, if it wasn't for the quick style, this evening wouldn't have happened.

When you check it you hardly hear about divorce in the old days. You hear about when all new year come in, you have to dash 'way the old and bring in the new. Well there's sump'n positive about new an modern technology, but you can't throw away good things neither.

Some of them old time ways, y'know, dem mek sense. I like a girl to look pretty.

But that's not what they want anymore. I mean, that same night I went out with my friend, I thought since I was there I might as well check out what was happening, check out the action y'know. An' I see this girl. She was dressed in — uhm — how can I describe it? It was a two-piece bathing suit and some boots.

Shiny boots. So I kinda tried to strike conversation and — uhm — I said to her, 'It's a different kind of outfit you've got on, y'know.' And I ask her if she always dress like that when she goes out. She looked at me, serious y'know, and smile, an' tell me that 'Yeah, I like to look rough!'… I left her rough.

That's not really my style, y'know. I mean, the question is, would you like your daughter to look like that? Would you even like your wife to look like that? In my day you see, a girl dressed like this — you don't want a hooker, you leave her alone. But nowadays it's hard to tell the difference. But dem t'ings is dangerous now, because you don't know who you're talking to. I can't afford to make a mistake. Money isn't flowing like it used to…

But seriously, it gets really difficult to meet a woman nowadays, let alone get on with her. Because it's not about charm any more, but how much you've got to give her. In my days, you had charm and the right lyrics, you stood a good chance… you were in business. Not anymore… Nowadays, unless she sees you stepping out of a seven series BMW, you've got a long way to go. I don't drive a convertible, that's why I was really surprised when this girl agreed to have dinner with me. Could you believe it? She bumped into me at the supermarket… with her trolley… Almost knocked me over. She apologised, and we started talking.. Very nice girl. Very shapely, very fit.

He chuckles to himself, talking very comfortably, very boastfully.

It's nice to see I've still got the touch. They never used to call me 'Bunny Slick' for nothing. In my peak I used to have women lining up to get in my hotel room. That's one of the perks of being a top class entertainer. A lot of you youngsters don't remember me. Bunny Limbo. Yeah, you see I was the first black comedian. Nowadays they talking about Lenny Henry and all these people, but me I'm like the original. But you never hear them acknowledge me. I toured the whole of England. I was on television every week. One of the highest paid entertainers in the business. Lenny Henry can't touch me — I'm the daddy.

Anyway, dis nice gyaal me jus' meet, she was decent and well dressed and speaks well. That's the kind of young girl me used to meet in the old days, you know wha' I mean? So I got a date. Who would have thought it? A man my age getting off with such a nice young gal. The old boy can still pull it, y'know. In the old days, I roped in enough pussy. That was part of the perks of being an entertainer. Plus I always had an ability to make women laugh. And from you can make them laugh, you got it. You're made. I was so big and famous. Every night on the television. You really don't remember? You don't remember the old catch phrase? You must do — 'This is Jamaica Bunny Limbo, front teeth, back teeth, gold teeth — thirty two different kinda teeth!'

I suppose you're all too young. They don't show me on TV any more. Because the comedy's changed. These

123

comedians nowadays don't even tell jokes. Everything has changed. When I first arrived in '56, I was only sixteen. And it was rough. It wasn't what I expected. It wasn't what nobody expected as a matter of fact. When they used to talk about England back in Port of Spain, it sounded like the land of milk and honey. When we left Trinidad, my daddy said to me, you're gonna taste milk and honey'! Well... I soon realised that it didn't taste like that at all. After a little while it started to taste like bitter cerasee. Like everybody else, I wanted to make a little raise for myself, and go back home and set up something, y'know, and retire. But this is where I ended up... In a bedsit, in a high rise in West London.

We had it hard to make a way for the youngsters in this country. You think there's racism now, you should have been there then!

Hey, you remember that joke, 'Why do black men wear baggy trousers — cause their knee-grows... get it? Dem's not my sunglasses, man, dem's me nostrils?'

You think Lenny Henry can make people laugh? Bwoy him couldn't make people laugh like me... He is a bwoy — pure and simple. He couldn't tell a saucy woman joke, like me. Lenny Henry cyaan drop dem style deh... Yet still, he never gives me respeck. I was the original, the foundation. But nowadays, is jus' small bwoy out dere.

Mmmnh-mmnh... Well, I'm ready now. I know women usually come late on purpose, but I hope she won't come too late, because I'm hungry too. I cook her one of those curries she won't forget — HOT, with pepper...

The nightmare began in the lobby. Stench of urine, beer and stale sweat seeped from shadows — lights smashed again, lifts vandalised into gloom. Silence did not mean no one was there laughing, waiting patiently to mug you. It isn't safe, but then again nowhere really is safe any more after dark. The 'decent', the prostitutes, drug addicts and the scum, stick together like tyres and tarmac.

Breathing in and breathing out. Two kids, hoods over their heads looking for something, looking suspicious. Fast and gone in seconds. Police would arrive four hours later, dusting for fingerprints.

There was no turning back. No turning back.

Westway Tower, Royal Borough of Kensington and Chelsea, West London storeys, gradually becoming gentrified with 'professional' types moving into the area.

Not long before it becomes unaffordable.

Twenty storeys later. In front of the mirror. Listening to the dial tone. And talking in his drink. A tall brown-skinned man of sixty in a dusted down dinner suit. The great pretender bawls out of an old style gramophone. Behind it is the 'kitchen' — a stove, a sink and a small fridge. Between the settee and the kitchen — a dining table set for two. He admires his reflection, fixing his famous bow tie, patting down his hair and splashing on some after shave. He is obviously pleased with what he sees. A loud, satisfied sigh. He picks up a glass and shuffles a step long since out of fashion. He takes a sip and talks to his reflection.

The doorbell rings.

Bunny comes back to reality. He runs around clearing things up quickly and smarting himself up for a last look in the mirror then kills the light. He lights the candles on the dining table with his Zippo, leaving it on the table.

The lighting is now more seductive.

(Aside to his reflection). "I can't talk to you right now… It's been a lot of fun, but this is business, y'know."

He goes to the flat door and opens. He returns with Rosie, a gorgeous, sexily-dressed young woman of about 25 years old. She walks slowly and determinedly to the side lamp and looks around the room as if inspecting it dispassionately. Bunny takes her nice three quarter length coat, to reveal an expensive evening dress underneath. Far to glamorous for the surroundings. She remains standing with a large bottle of champagne in her hand. She wanders over the window and takes in the spectacular view of crammed city streets with pugnaciously driven Volvos and jeep-loads of pollution spewing out from behind.

From Paddington Green and Kensal Rise and Harlesden NW10, right out to the Wembley triangle in zone 4 and the Harrow playing fields from one direction.

Hammersmith, Fulham, W12 and Londonistan to the west. If you crooked your neck you could just make out Waltham Forest E11, 11 miles away east. There was no southerly aspect. Down below — thieves in Little Venice, Portuguese delis and Thai places on the Harrow Road, loads of police on the junction of Elgin Avenue and Shirland Road — the North side is sealed off, it looks quite serious… always feel so safe in Maida Vale.

"Isn't this the most lovely view you've ever seen?" he asks.

His guest smiles and replies, "Impressive."

"…It means 'wrong hole' — wrong hole, get it?"

Rosie laughs. "That was funny, really funny," she says.

Bunny smiles. It had been a long time since his jokes were that well received and appreciated.

He gets up to get another bottle of champagne from the kitchenette. He pops it open as Rosie eats a last morsel of the dinner.

"That was delicious — really delicious."

"So you didn't think I could cook?"

Rosie smiles coyly.

"Why not? Back home you've got to know how to cook — man or woman, boy or girl.

A lot of younger men nowadays can't cook. I'm from the old school. Back home you learn how to cook, or you starve."

"Well, what can I say? I'm certainly impressed."

"Women like a man who can cook for them, nuh true? Especially nowadays."

"Nowadays couples have to share the tasks."

"Except for pregnancy!"

Rosie smiles. "Of course… except for pregnancy. You know any man willing to share pregnancy, you give me a call. But seriously, it's like some men forget that you one are bringing up the children, going to work and bringing home the money, an' still they expect you to come home and have their dinner ready every evening." She kisses her teeth.

"I know what you're saying. It's slackness really, y'know. It seems like the youth nowadays have forgotten the meaning of those old time marriage vows — to love honour and obey."

Rosie hangs her head in quiet contemplation. "Well I don't know about the 'obedience'..."

Realising that he has slipped up, Bunny tries desperately to salvage control.

"Well, when I say 'obedience'... in those days it wasn't like 'obedience', it was more like 'respect', y'know."

Rosie contemplates. "Maybe that's what women mean then. Women are always talking about how they want 'respect' from their men. Maybe they really mean 'obedience'..."

Bunny is confused.

"No, you're taking it the wrong way, man. All I meant to say was that my mother taught me to love, honour and obey my woman — or respect if you like. It's a two way t'ing. There's a lot to say for those old time ways y'know, but young people nowadays are too quick to talk about old fashioned. Every month they throw out the old and bring in the new. Well, I don't know. You need to keep some of those old time things."

"You're right. I must say that I prefer mature men generally. Men who know how to treat a woman like a lady. Gentlemen. I like a man to have modern views, but also to be a gentleman."

"See't deh! Any woman I check, you can bet she's going to get a hundred percent good loving. She must get it. Seen?! Full time lovin', twenty-four seven. No part-time business, but good old fashioned romance. Oldies but goodies dem call it."

Rosie smiles back teasingly, but changes the subject quickly.

"Were you ever married?"

Bunny waves his hand dismissively obviously not wanting to embark on that subject.

"Come on Bunny. Don't tell me you've got something to hide."

"No, I've got nothing to hide. It's just that I made some mistakes in my life and that was one of them. I don't like talking about my mistakes."

For a moment an uncomfortable silence, as Bunny becomes meditative.

"Do you have any kids?"

"Kids? Yeah I've got a couple of kids. Both boys, y'know. Well, they're not kids anymore. They're big now. My kids have got kids of their own."

"What are they like?"

"Like? Let me see…"

He gets up and pulls a family album from the dressing table. He flicks through the pages until he finds what he's looking for and presents it to Rosie.

"That's Gladstone, we call him Gladdy, taken in his first year at secondary school. He must be eleven or twelve there. And this is William…"

"And this is your wife?"

"Ex-wife. I was divorced fifteen years ago. We don't have any contact any more.

Even the kids don't come to see me. I don't know why."

Bunny obviously wants to change the subject. "You said you were working… what kind of work?

"Guess."

"You look kind of sophisticated… public relations? Hostess? Lawyer? No, no, no. Let me see, it's something glamorous… Modelling?

"I work in journalism. I'm a reporter for The Black Mail."

"Blackmail?! What kind of fool man name a newspaper blackmail?!"

"No, not blackmail," she laughs. "Black Mail."

"Oh, Black Male? Like a black man?!"

"No, wrong again. Black Mail, like Daily Mail."

"Oh Black Mail, yes man. That's a wicked name. I thought you said blackmail."

They enjoy the joke.

"Yeah, I work on the entertainments page on the paper."

"Really? What a coincidence. You should do an article on me."

"Why, what do you do that's entertaining?"

"You will find out soon enough," he teases. "Seriously, I used to be a big artist, y'know." Dreamily. "Yeah, I was big in the old days. My name, up there in lights — six feet high. Appearing here tonight…"

"What did you do?"

"Well, I started out as an all round entertainer. You had to in those days. It was just showbiz — there wasn't no singers here, dancers there, comedians there.

You had to do everything. People paid good money to see you, so you had to entertain them. The more you could do, the more work you got. But when I got really big, it was as a comedian later on — in television and all dem ways.

Stand-up comedy really."

"You never did you? Really? I don't remember you."

"You don't remember me?"

"No, I don't think so."

"Come on, you must have… I was the biggest name out there. Bunny Limbo. The first black superstar in the UK. Oh I suppose you're too young to remember. But your parents, they must have mentioned me. I was the number one."

"Not that I can recall. Bunny Limbo…? That's a funny name. Why did they call you Limbo?

"Oh, that was in the old days when I did my act. They used to call me -'Limbo -

How Low Can You Go'?"

Rosie laughs. "You still do it?"

"What?"

"Go low."

"Nah, I stopped that a while ago."

"Oh, that's a pity…"

"I haven't lost it all together…"

"So what about the jokes? You still do comedy?"

"Well, I do the odd gig, but nothing too big these days, y'know."

"When was all this then? When were you the number one?"

"Up to the mid seventies."

"Seventies? So how old are you?"

"Well, not that old really. It's not your age, it's how old you feel inside...

And I feel young tonight?"

"No seriously, how old are you?"

"Well, let's say I'm in my fifties... Is that a problem for you?"

"No, no... Not at all. I like older men. They're... more mature."

"That's right. I've still got my stamina. I'm as fit as any yout'. And I've learned a few things since I was a yout', things that these youngsters nowadays don't know about. Cho, what do kids know about life, about love and all dem sump'n deh?

"Well don't worry yuhself, I'm not a youngster either."

"I'm pleased to hear that ... So you've never heard my old catchphrase — Bunny Limbo, gold teeth front teeth back teeth — all kinda teeth, and you ain't heard my best joke yet? ...Yes, the old magic is still there. I've always been able to make women laugh. That's one of my talents. My humour always puts women at ease."

"Have another drink."

Rosie fills his glass.

"What about you,which kind of places do you go to

when you want to enjoy yourself."

"Clubs usually," she replies.

"Oh, you mean disco?"

"No discos, that's old time. Nobody goes there any more — apart from kids. No, I go clubbing, raving, I go to raves, y'know."

"Raves? So what kind of music they play down at these raves?"

"All kinds."

"Like wha'?"

"Y'know, dance music."

"Like who?"

"Lots of people. I don't think you'd know any of them."

"A lot of the music nowadays is just noise. There's no melody. Like the old time singers. The greats like King Cole or Sam Cooke, The Platters. You don't know all of these people do you? I prefer like melody and song."

"Actually, I really like Nat King Cole."

"Yeah?"

"Yeah. I like all kinds of music, especially the old time stuff."

"What about calypso, you know anything like calypso."

"Well actually my mother is from Trinidad, so I couldn't help but like it?"

"Wha? Your mother from Trinidad? You been there?"

"Yeah I went there like a few years ago, for the carnival."

"Oh you must have had fun... Carnival?!"

"Yeah, it was really nice."

"Oh so you must have heard a lot of the old style at home."

"Dad used to play a lot of music especially on weekends and Sundays."

"Yeah, well that's what I call real music — I can't stop bigging up that old time music deh."

He makes a reference and starts singing a couple of bars. "You remember this one?"

"Oh, I didn't know you could sing?"

"Well… y'know."

"No really, you sing well. Nice. Sing some more."

"Well, if you insist.

"Yes, I do insist. Come on, I won't take no for an answer."

Bunny sings something even more romantic — a couple of bars.

"Yeah, well, you know, my voice sounds kinda rough because I ain't had much practice recently. I used to sing in the old days, but nowadays it's like nobody wants to hear some real good time music with melody and so on.

Nowadays it's all that crude ragamuffin stuff. You can't even understand what they're saying."

"So you used to sing at concerts and so on? I didn't know."

"That was part of my act, before I became famous as a comedian, I used to sing and tell jokes. Hey, you're not drinking … Come on, let me pour you another glass of champagne. Come on, have some more."

She nods her head reluctantly and he pours her another

glass.

"Well, all this could be a good article for my column… It's not every day you get invited on a date with a real star. So why don't you do the comedy anymore?"

"All that was before. Nowadays I might have a couple of little gigs with the old boys but nothing more. Every now and then there's a revival of the old time comedians and sometimes I get invited along, but you know those things are getting more and more seldom. As time goes by."

"But you're so talented. Why give it up? Oh, have you got any old videos of your show?"

"Well dat is the t'ing now, because you see most of my shows were in the sixties and early seventies, long before video came about. The only way I could get the stuff recorded on video now, is if they showed repeats on the telly, but they never do. For some reason they never show my shows anymore. I did a couple of shows on BBC but they don't show them anymore. I could do with the royalties. So if you know anyone at the BBC tell them to repeat the Bunny Limbo Show."

He downs another glass of champagne and puts a drunken hand on Rosie's knee. She pushes him away.

"Take it easy. Nice and slow. There's time for everything. Don't rush.

"Well drink some more champagne then."

He pours champagne into a glass and pushes it towards her. She pushes the glass back.

"No, you drink some more."

She smiles at him sweetly, encouragingly. Bunny is confident he's going to get his end away tonight with a young thing so drinks happily. He pours more champagne into her glass. Pushes it towards her again.

"No, I really don't think I should drink anymore, I'm driving."

"Oh you're driving? Don't worry, if you've drunk too much you can always stay here."

She kind of smiles, neither rebuffing nor encouraging him too much.

"Perhaps I will…"

"You want to see my photo album? I've got pictures of me from when I was famous and with all the big names in there too."

"Yes, I'd really like that."

Bunny produces his showbiz album from under the sofa and sits down beside her.

"That's me and Bruce Forsyth. There's Jimmy Saville and me. Enoch Powell… This was when I did a live show, a cabaret at the Dominion. And this was when I did the Royal Command Performance in front of the Queen at the Palladium. She came up to me afterwards and told me she thought I was wicked, man… Yeah, at that time I thought maybe I'd get an OBE or a knighthood or something, but they just forgot about me I guess… Let me pour you some rum from the old country… I know, I know, you're driving, I won't give you too much, but this is the best rum that you're going to find anywhere — rum with some nice coconut cream — just the way the ladies love it… Hang on, don't go anywhere, I'll soon back. Don't fly away or disappear. Your host will return in a moment."

"Don't worry, I wouldn't dream of going anywhere."

As soon as he disappears into the bathroom, Rosie very naturally replaces the record playing with another and casually goes to her bag which is hanging on a chair and fumbles briefly, picks up something, goes back, sits down and stops for a second, before slipping a couple of tablets in Bunny's drink. She returns to her seat and sits composed until his return.

"Yeah, that's one problem with being a mature man... your bladder shrinks with age, so you can't hold the drink like you used to. I'm telling you, old age is not for weakhearts."

He changes the record again and puts on some early mento sound and dances around the room.

"That's how we used to dance back in the days."

He starts winding up slowly and coming towards her, picks up his glass naturally.

"Come on, let's dance."

"No, really I couldn't."

"Why not?"

"I'm too shy — you dance much better than I do. You go ahead, I'm enjoying it."

He's confident now as he dances. She's not going anywhere. He thinks he's in for pussy shortly. He sips rum from the glass in his hand.

"Come on ... nuh worry yourself, just relax, let yourself loose and dance."

"I can't dance like that."

"Come on, man. It's easy. You say your parents are from Trinidad, innit? Then you must have the music in your blood, man. Come on man, of course you can dance. You say you go clubs. So what do you do when you're there? You dance, ain't it?"

"Yeah, but I dance to modern music. I've never danced to these old sounds."

"From your feet can dance you can adapt to any tune."

She is reluctant but he takes her by the hand and pulls her towards him. She tries to take a sip from her glass to deter him. But he is forceful, so she relents. They start dancing together, with him leading her along and pulling her close to him. Rosie giggles.

"Yeah, you see, I knew you could do it."

The record finishes abruptly. Rosie collapses on the sofa exhausted. Bunny remains standing but is clearly unsteady on his feet.

"I can't believe it… I can't believe that you actually got me dancing those old styles."

"But you enjoyed it, ain't it?"

Bunny changes the record to Alton Ellis' rock steady 'I'm Just A Guy'.

"Yeah, I know that tune, they still play it… No, I really don't think I can…"

"Come on, a little rum won't hurt you one way or another. This is the real stuff — the genuine article … the same rum that Captain Morgan, Long John Silver and all those other pirates used to drink."

She takes a little persuading but eventually takes a sip.

"Yes, what did I tell you... this kind of rum makes you fall in love."

He thinks he's gonna get some... She's neither confirming nor running away.

"Who is that?" she points to a photo on the wall.

"That's my brother, Robert."

"You look alike."

"Yeah, he's only two years younger than me."

"And who is that?" she points to a framed photo above it.

"My auntie back home — she's dead now. And sitting on her knee..."

"Oh my god...!"

"Oh well, everyone was a baby once, you know."

He grabs his crotch as if dying to take a piss.

"Hang on, don't go anywhere, I'll soon back. Don't fly away or disappear. Your host will return in a moment."

"Don't worry, I wouldn't dream of going anywhere."

Bunny rushes to the toilet. As soon as he goes, she slips a couple more tablets into his drink and switches the music with a really fast ska tune. She returns to her seat and sits composed and awaits his return from the bathroom. Bunny comes back having relived himself of his jacket and loosened his bow tie.

"Bwoy we can really start dance now."

He pulls her by the hands. This time she obliges willingly and they shuffle to the music — quick tempo. They dance for a while, Bunny increasingly unsteady on his feet. He stops and puts his hand to his head, wiping sweat off his brow.

"Do you feel hot in here?" he asks. "Is it me or do you feel hot in here also?"

Rosie seductively, "Yeah, I feel hot in here. Hot but sweet."

Bunny tries to feel good about her statement, but his knees start to wobble. He looks down momentarily and then collapses to the floor with a thud.

When he finally comes to, everything is exactly as it was except that he is tied fast to a chair with rope and his wrists are cuffed behind his back. Rosie is sitting casually on the sofa reading a magazine and smoking a cigarette. Bunny looks unsure of what has happened to him.

"W-w-what's going on?" he stutters.

Rosie coolly takes a drag from her cigarette and blows the smoke in his face.

"You tell me," she says. "You're the comedian."

"Woman, have you lost your mind. Untie me."

He shouldn't have said that. She stubs her cigarette on his forehead. He screams with pain. The smell of burning flesh wafts in the air.

"Now that we're agreed that I give the orders... why don't you make me laugh."

"Two elephants fell of a cliff — boom, boom!"

"No, tell the one about the monkey ."

"Monkey? W-w-what..."

"Come on, you know the one about how you tell the

difference between a monkey and a sambo. Remember that."

"B-b-b-but..."

"How does it go again... put it in water and if it drowns it's not a monkey. Because everyone knows darkies can't swim."

Bunny's eyes are filled with terror, the joke sounding worse today than it had ever done back in his heyday.

"It was just a joke..." he protested.

"That's right," she agreed. "Do you remember a nine year old boy called Peter Ohana-Kena...? Yes, I know you do. Well, I'm Rosemary Ohana-Kena..."

A damp patch appears in the crotch area of Bunny's trousers and spreads across his thighs.

"He was my big brother... I was so proud of him. I miss him so much." Rosie stifles a sob. From her handbag she pulls out a can of lighter fluid and squirts it in Bunny's face. He smells the fumes and screams "No...!"

She continues squirting the fluid over his head.

"...Peter was a nice kid... but those two white boys were just having a laugh... that was their defence. They heard your joke on Saturday night and went to school on Monday to see if it was true. They threw Peter in the river, even though they knew he couldn't swim. They just had to prove whether he was a monkey or not."

"It wasn't my fault..." Bunny screams. "You're crazy... that was a long time ago. I'm an old man, don't do this.. please, I beg, in the name of the father, the son and the holy ghost..."

Rosie empties the whole can of lighter fluid on Bunny. Then pulls out a lighter and says, "Did I ever tell you the one about the old man and the devil? Guess how you spot the difference…"

A Fly In The Alphabet Soup
VIC LAMBRUSCO

"Can you feel anything?"

"It's starting to happen."

Breathe out the lungful you've been holding deep, wobble through a few hazy seconds, then bang! Whatever you used to call "reality" is nowhere, and it ain't coming back for the foreseeable. You're catapulted out of time, out of your body, into an orangey-brown world of flight, panic, horror, wonder, cartoon actuality, nightmare made flesh. Acid — for all its bright shifting colours and distorted sounds — is like aspirin compared to this shit. Even DMT — when the elves want to speak through that strange clicky noise — is just a dose of Diet Coke. You've still got a purchase on the world you left behind. You still can remind yourself you're on something.

But with salvia divinorum, forget it! The world you're cannonballed into is real with a capital R-E-A-L. You don't question it. It's indomitable as the death of innocence; authentic as the onset of anxiety; there behind the

143

forehead, at the seat of your perception.

Cy, who seconds ago was at your side, is remoter to you than candour from a politician. He's gone: engulfed in the same vortex which swept away your position on his sofa, your quotidian moorings, your ability to filter experience through concepts.

And you're flying. Not machine aided aircraft flight, but actual bird flight: the kind infants often fantasise and adults usually forget. You swoop and flap precariously, high above your early childhood home — solidly familiar and yet made strange by a tawny, clay-like shading. From somewhere some how "behind", yet simultaneously "within", you hear a voice. It is your mother's. Gently she intones a nursery rhyme-like phrase, over and over. It has the quality of a profound, reassuring truth. You have a clear sense of its intention: to help you through whatever lies ahead.

As her voice stops your flight becomes instantly, anxiously erratic. You're no longer swooping, but tumbling.

Your senses become a large orb — like an orange or a tennis ball. As you plummet towards the fence its earthy-toned aspect overwhelms you. It's a kaleidoscope in four sections, twisting your consciousness, mind, perception (or whatever else it would be called in the concrete-notion world which no longer exists) completely inside out. Not for a second — if there were still seconds — do you doubt this is actually happening.

You clutch mentally for some respite from the twisting,

plummeting terror.

Somewhere the phrase, "Cy will make it all right" shoots across what you are aware of. You don't know if you say it, think it or shout it. All you can tell is relief will come once your twisting-orb-seat-of-perception turns 360 degrees.

Crash! Just a tiny fraction short of full circle you smash into the fence. The top of Cy's head appears just above it. Somehow you hold him responsible for this terror trip into the terra incognita. You're overwhelmed with the desire to escape — from what and to what you cannot begin to imagine.

The contours of Cy's flat begin to become perceptible. But you're not sitting on the sofa; you're floating gently into his bedroom, his kitchen, the spare room. Your view has become an inquisitive fish-eye lens, probing these once familiar surroundings which have shed their aura of solidity, attained the quality of dreams.

At the window you stop. The sense of dreamy floating is replaced by a sense of being fettered to the floor. As your physical body slips gradually back to you, you feel your feet anchoring you in position, holding you somehow against your will.

You become aware of bright colour, shimmering and yet confusing. A huge dark purple takes over the whole window. It's neither the sitting room window nor the spare room window, but both simultaneously. This causes you an anxiety which mushrooms into a profound quivering terror. You are convinced, as much as you have ever been convinced of anything, that you must not look out of the window!

All you've ever known has been reduced to a single certainty: everything outside — Wandsworth Road, Stockwell, the rest of the country, the world, the universe — has turned into a purple Martian landscape. And the only respite, the only way to prevent being totally engulfed within it, is to avoid looking directly at it...

Seconds — decades! — later you begin to segue into more regular, more integratable consciousness.

The shock of what has just happened to you causes you involuntarily to stand.

"Sit down!" shrieks Cy, whose journey, you will soon find, has been even more harrowing. You find the instruction strange, since moments ago you were flying around the entire flat, but see no reason not to comply.

"Are we going to be like this forever?" you ask, with child credulity.

"No!" he snorts desperately, willing himself towards the comforting knowledge that no, the world hasn't spun apocalyptically off its axis into a pile-up on the celestial M25.

Cos this time he's peaked. Cy, who has taught you just about everything you ever wanted to know (and, today, something you wished you didn't) about drugs; Cy, who — if the government appoint a drugs czar — could quite easily apply to be drugs emperor; Cy, whose magic flask is a real alphabet soup of intoxication:

LSD, 2CB, DMT, MDA, DET, MDMA, STP, PCP and,

latterly, H, has finally gone as far out as he is wont to go. This salvia divinorum, this "sage of divinity", which Mexican shamans use in caves to talk to the ancestors and read the future, has reached the end of his trip.

"Fuck, man!" he concludes, slowly coming round. "That's as far out as I ever wanna go."

"Yeah," you concur, as sagely as your befuddled returning senses will allow.

"And you can fuck off with that salvinorin A!"

"Mmmm," you mumble, in relieved acknowledgement that salvinorin A is the active element of, and many times stronger than, what you've just taken.

Imagine!

You'd rather not!

In the succeeding minutes, which seem like five but prove a measurable thirty, you babble over a Becks about the experience.

"Did I do anything I shouldn't have?"

"Dunno. Did I?"

"It was just like flight, man! Flight in the sky and flight as in escape."

"It's like being in a cartoon, but for real!"

"I'm glad I did it, but no fucking way am I doing that again!"

"Did you have your eyes open or shut?"

"Dunno."

"It's like I woulda done a shit in public just to get away from it. Nothing mattered except escape."

Your mobile rings. Fuck knows what would have

happened if it had gone off thirty five minutes earlier! It's a woman, rebuking you for not ringing when you agreed to.

"Sorry sweetheart," you say, smiling mischievously at Cy. "I just lost all sense of time."

Cy's not much of a pub man, so after another bottle you leave him to his bong and his Saturday night TV.

Normally you cycle, but for some reason today you're walking back to Brixton. In Larkhall Park a surreal scene makes you wonder if the SD hasn't worn off yet. A fat, pugilistic woman with an unattractive tattoo is berating a group of ten year old urchins. The cause of her dismay is a pitbull's carnal zeal for her rather unremarkable mongrel.

"Get 'im off!" she shrieks. "You little cunts!"

The "little cunts" giggle as their rampant hound struggles to consummate its deepest urges. Its height, however, does not measure up to its homoerotic inclinations, and it fails to sate its doggie desire.

"Go on! Fuck 'im!" squeaks a freckly malcontent, his yelpy tone heaping absurdity on an already bizarre scene. But, flail as he might, pitbull can't reach his target.

In Dalyell Road you ponder this afternoon's phone conversation with your Mum.

It's the first time in the twenty years since you left home you've got short with each other. OK, you acknowledged: you haven't got a BMW (like your younger sister), or a detached house and a leather sofa (like your younger brother); you didn't go the parent pleasing marriage-and-offspring route (like both of them).

But at least you're still out there. Still having a go, still chasing some kind of dream. You haven't caved in to the remorseless arithmetic of "thirty-plus" equals "start-to-die". You're proud you've never joined the M-People: the Married, Mortgaged and Mating classes. Whatever the future holds, you're going to stride towards it, grab it by the lapels, pin it face down and give it a robust rear-entry seeing to. To hell with being afraid of life! You did enough of that at school and uni-fucking-versity.

Maybe it was your point, maybe your turn of phrase, which prompted your Mum to cry. Your immediate guilt you smothered in effusive apologies. But now, several hours later, you feel an insistent unease. Though you push it from your conscious mind, it still persists, a dull, nagging ache within your chest.

Where's it all leading? you wonder.

And you don't mean the Prince Albert. But that's where you end up. Best pub in Brixton, bar none! Once – to champion this conviction – you got into vociferous debate with the devotee of a rival boozer. It almost came to fisticuffs, until you realised the "my-Dad-could-beat-yours-in-an-arm-wrestle" risibility of the exchange.

Most times in the Albert you recognize plenty of faces. Saturday night, however, is tourist season. Regulars are resolutely outnumbered by the gilded youth of more affluent but less cool neighbouring districts, who've come to check out the "flava". They spill from taxis which enable cosy access to the "streetcred" zone, but save them the irksome travail of a pedestrian interface with the crackheads, junkies and dealers of Coldharbour Lane.

You hook up with Glyn and Ed for a couple of pints. Normally, you'd be off out to "have it large", but tonight you're a bit subdued. You pass some lighthearted moments mocking a table of "tourists". Their animated chat of the clubbing night ahead has all the guileless enthusiasm of the Secret Seven embarking on an adventure. Lashings of MDMA!

At chucking out time Ed and Glyn announce their intention of going to the Queen.

They're both souped up on cider, and will blend in well with the scary late night drunks who gather there like flies round shit.

Despite Glyn's swingeing appraisal of you as a "part-timer" and a "poof", you manage to extricate yourself from the bacchanalian brethren, and head off home for an early(-ish) night.

Ah, but the best laid plans of mice and miscreants! You're nearly back to your squat. You've fought (and sneered!) your way past the tarted-up pub on the corner: where clueless wannabes beg charmless bouncers for admission to a soulless trendy rats' nest. You're even feeling for your key, when who should emerge from one of Saturday night's more mischievous corners but Johnny.

Johnny, the big smiley likeable rogue! Jamaican born, Brixton-bred: the boxer who didn't quite make it turned dealer you can't quite trust. Even though he stiffed you on that last bag of weed, you can't help feeling warmth for the geezer.

"Wha'gwan, star?" you joke as he embraces you.

"Not bad, rude boy," he quips back; partly in response to your question, , partly in mock approval of your cod patois. "So, you wanna come for a smoke then?"

Thoughts of recompense for that moody weed deal guide you, and you agree.

Goodbye early(-ish) night!

Ten minutes and a million miles from the trendy main drag see the pair of you at a door. This is the Brixton that doesn't get in the style mags: the piss-stenching, graffiti-addled precincts of the Tulse Hill Estate. No streetcred-seeking Clapham dwellers here. No "flava"-hungry Fulham-ites on these mean thoroughfares. Not even passing through in a cab!

Johnny's knocked four times, and you're getting twitchy. You glance down the hall, past all the doors, which, unlike this one, stand wretchedly framed behind security gates. Rubbish spills from a plastic bag: with an appositeness that transcends metaphor. It's a wall-to-wall hot and cold running shithole.

"No-one's in," you assert uneasily.

Johnny knocks again. "Look, man, he's coming!" And, indeed, stirring from within is audible.

"Quick, man!" Johnny snaps. "Gimme that tenner!"

What tenner? you are minded to ask, since no money was mentioned hitherto. But, unnerved by these surroundings, you hand one over anyway.

The door creaks open with ponderous caution. Johnny is given a visual frisk, the chain comes slowly away and you're in.

You've long known the meaning of "down by law", but this is the first time you've lived it. You keep close to Johnny as you pass through the hallway.

"This is my spar," quips Johnny. "He's white, but that's not his fault!"

Unmoved by the attempted joke three faces eye you with suspicious contempt.

Shit! You think, as the penny drops. It's a fucking den! Johnny wasn't talking spliffs when he offered a "smoke" but this! A night on pipefuls of the new social evil, the little white rock that prompts terror in the shires and hysteria in the tabloids: crack cocaine.

Johnny leads you into a dimly lit bedroom and sits you down, then goes off to do whatever business your tenner will run to. You're seated opposite a sparsely clad, light skinned black woman. A white geezer is sprawled awkwardly across a mattress behind her.

"Lucy," says the woman, offering her hand. "That's Richie. Don't mind him; he's got the flu."

You shake. "Hi, Lucy. Hi, Richie."

"Respect, bruv," murmurs Richie, without raising his face from the pillow.

There is an awkward silence. This may not be a suburban dinner party or an accountants' convention, but small talk is still called for.

"So what you up to, Lucy?" you essay.

"Lookin' for a punter."

Shit! You walked straight into that one. Leaning back, to

compose yourself, you draw relief from her heavy scouse accent, which provides an easy small talk recovery conduit.

"So... You from Liverpool then?"

"Yeah, but down 'ere twenty years."

Before another awkward silence can descend Johnny's back in, holding a pipe.

"Ash, man!" he demands, not looking up, as he tests the tightness of the tube, pricks holes in a new layer of foil. Lucy passes him a full ashtray.

Slowly, with the dexterity and solicitude of a craftsman, he sprinkles a layer of ash, then some crumbs of white rock on to the foil.

From the darkness of the hall you hear the grumbled sounds of dissent. The heavy patois is hard to understand, but you get the gist: what the fuck is Johnny doing bringing Babylon round?

Johnny looks up from his handiwork and turns his head.

"I told you, man, he's my spar," he hisses over his shoulder, at the open door behind him. "He's cool!" His gentle yet insistent tone carries enough menace to assuage the hiccough of disquiet.

"Chu!" he demurs, with a petulant kissing of teeth.

Once calm, he returns to the task in hand. With practised co-ordination he moves a lighter flame over the foil. The little rocks pop, then glow, as he inhales deeply. Removing the pipe from his mouth, he closes his eyes and holds his breath hard.

"Whoah, fuck!" he exclaims, breathing out the smoke. "'S good gear, man.

" Ladies first," he smiles to you, handing Lucy the second pipeful. Her inhalation is as skilled as his; her reaction less histrionic. She smiles affectionately, as if at the thought of a distant, but fondly remembered lover.

When your turn comes round, you struggle to hide your apprehension. Though fairly well tutored at narc-school, you've never indulged in the Big Nasty before.

Treat it like a bong, you think, as you breathe out and spark the lighter. This idea calms you as you take a measured draw deep into your lungs. Even as you hold your breath, you can't hold yourself from a simple, tempting thought: I want some more of this.

When you finally exhale, the violent headfuck you were expecting fails to materialize. You feel a pleasant, manageable rush, which exhilarates you. Then a tingly mild euphoria. Then... well, nothing really. Just a vague sense of emptiness and the precise desire for another go.

Cos it's over very quickly, this Kentucky fried hit, this cocaine for the underclass. And, much as you've long despised the powdered bravado of the bullshit-babbling charlie brigade, there's something altogether more wretched, more last-ditch about this. It promises little, delivers less, and leaves need in its wake.

If religion is the opium of the people, you, muse, then crack cocaine is the opium of the desperate. And now you begin to understand those corpses-in-waiting down Atlantic Road. Their eyes are so dead, their expressions so void, for a reason. It's not for a high they loiter around amid the needles and discarded Kitkats on the steps of Brixton BR. It's not for a kick they whore themselves, nick phones, snatch change or pose as street dealers and clip the money. It's because of the need this stuff shoots you full of: the overwhelming compulsion provoked by this pleasant but unspectacular hit for another pleasant but unspectacular hit just like it.

Shit! You decide. I bet it's dead easy to get hooked on this fucking stuff.

Better be careful.

"Cheers," you mumble, seconds later, nearly ripping Johnny's arm off when he offers you another pipeful...

After the fourth, maybe fifth, cycle of smoke-rush-buzz-fade you feel pretty damn jangly. The conversation has slumped to the level of grunted commonplaces, punctuated by sluggish "yeah man"s and "innit"s. The squalid surroundings have now lost their initial threat, and slide with disquieting ease into sync with your fogged and debilitated senses. The term "wasted", so often used about the after effects of many drugs, was never more appropriate than with this. Your money, your time, your effort, your expectations – all wasted; all spunked away; all flushed down the toilet. Briefly you succumb to the promptings of something approaching anger. But they're too vague. And you're too, well........ wasted to lend them expression.

A slam of the front door, a kerfuffle in the hall and you're rudely aroused from your musings. Lucy, who had sloped off a couple of pipes ago, is back in full leery scouse effect.

"Right, you lot," she snaps peremptorily. "Out, now!"

You immediately jump to your feet and edge into the hall, where you clock a young-ish white guy who looks both awed and anxious at having blundered into some A1 urban degeneration.

Lucy, if it were possible, becomes even more insistent. "Look, I don't wanna lose this punter. Come 'ead!"

Johnny slopes out with studied petulance. "Chill, man!" he snorts, with another kiss of the teeth.

Richie struggles in his wake, shivering and disgruntled, wrapped in the quilt.

In the lounge, which is even darker than the bedroom-cum-brothel-cum-crack den, the three of you jockey diplomatically for a seat. You ease yourself carefully between two figures engrossed in Milan versus Roma.

You're not sure why, but their earlier hostility appears to have softened.

Perhaps it's Johnny's influence; maybe it's cos they're reassured you're not "Babylon"; or it might be down to your occasional comments in the boysie lingua franca of football ("They were the fuckin' bollocks when they had Gullit." "That ref wants some new glasses!" "Tell you who else is good, that....... wossname? Edgar Davids!") Whatever it is, you feel something approaching relaxed.

Like the proverbial traveler in hope who arrives to disappointment, you feel strangely flat. The danger which made you baulk has given way to a discomfort that makes you bored. This den thing ain't all it's cracked up to be (boom boom!) and now you've done it you just want fucking out. But – seasoned in the scuzz though you might now be – you still don't know the protocol for withdrawal from such an establishment. Several times you mentally rehearse a nonchalant exit.

Before you have time to rise and bid casual "laters" there is an interruption.

Lucy, whose punter seems invisibly and inaudibly to have evanesced, appears in the doorway. Sidling up to the main man, whose name (it suddenly occurs to you) you have never been told, she hands him some money. He pockets it inscrutably, never once averting his gaze from a nifty right-sided Roman manoeuvre.

Johnny nods Lucy out into the hallway. An argument ensues. His patois-ed petulance again goes past you, but it's clear from her responses the dispute is over money. Suddenly he pokes his head back into the room, looks at you and snorts, "Come on, man!" Bingo! The retreat you craved has come about without any action on your part. So insistent is he to get you out, you don't even manage valedictory pleasantries.

Ten minutes of grumpy trudging down the hill and you're outside the HSBC.

Johnny's importuning you for the loan of a tenner you'll never see again, while you're rather unconvincingly pretending to have forgotten your PIN. The crisp dawn and the comedown lend an uncomfortable spikiness to the exchange.

"Fuck you, then!" Johnny suddenly snaps and stalks tetchily off. You notice, with amused suspicion, he's heading back the way you've just come. But without the price of another rock...

Five hours' erratic sleep, plus two cups of coffee, plus a ride courtesy of one of Brixton tube's most spectacularly cadaverous junkie travelcard touts, and you're at your destination. Charing Cross. The comedown might not be as bad as an "oh-fuck-I-didn't-did-I?" booze hangover, but it still puts you seriously short of harmonious communion with your environment. As you struggle through Trafalgar Square you're filled with sullen impatience: for the tourists clutching maps and guidebooks babbling incomprehensibly; for the wage slave placard bearer advertising a nearby sale; for the rats with wings relentlessly dedicated to covering the whole world, starting with Nelson's Column, in a rancid coat of pigeon shit.

Backstage at the ICA you perk up a bit. There's a rider. The visiting Americans, here to get the UK hip to the slam phenomenon, are all depressingly teetotal, while your fellow performers mostly sip wine demurely from half-filled disposable beakers. Gulping greedily at one of the Stellas you've snatched, you bid manfully – through a two-pronged attack of indifference and alcohol – to block out the inane, pretentious conversation which fills the room. Cos you really don't give a fuck for the funding apparatchik's waffle about "bringing the arts to the people" or "developing new audience strands". The notion of setting up a stage on Brixton tube concourse to achieve such ends occurs mischievously to you. But you keep it to yourself.

Halfway through your second can the show begins. One of the septics has finished reciting worthy verse from the height of what you suspect is a gigantic ivory tower, and is explaining the rules of a slam. Basically, it's a competition decided by a handful of self-appointed audience judges. Four heats of five, then four in the final.

You're on last in the third heat, and in the interim you get the right hump. The performers, without exception, have been from the end of the scale you and Cy contemptuously call "proper" poetry. Precious, guilty verse for metropolitan liberals who could patronise for England; dripping with feigned compassion, clumsily preoccupied with causes dear to, but remote from, the performer's life.

Boring, serious, bollock-less, proper poetry!

By the time your turn comes up, you're seriously steaming. The stray half an E you just located in your combats, and immediately gulped, is well short of coming up. A shudder of booze-fuelled anger jolts you towards the stage. There's no way on this (or any other) planet you're gonna win. You walk on eggshells for no-one! So you elect instead to make an impression.

"Good evening," you snarl, lunging into the mic, tearing the ring grenade-like off another Stella. "My name's Vince and I can do this."

Calmly, and with your best Johnny Rotten sneer, you empty the can over your head.

From the disdainful silence you expected to descend rises a clamour you did not.

"Whoah! 'Oo wants it?! Serve 'em up!"

Fuck! You can't see them under the lights, but you sure as shit recognize the voices. It's only Glyn and Ed, isn't it? And by the sound of it they've come eight or ten strong with some Albert locals. Chelsea versus Leeds at the ICA!

Bringing people to the arts.

Recovering swiftly from the surprise, you launch into your harangue. "I only write about what I see around me. This one's called 'Dismal'. You won't like it."

And away you go...

"Tulse Hill Estate in the drizzly rain

A timid soul too scared to complain

A baby who'll never know its daddy's name

What is it?"

"Dismal!" comes back the retort, as unbidden as it is uninhibited, from the Albert element.

"A bingo hall and a fish'n'chip shop

A seven year old cussing at a bus stop

Fed on plastic, watered on slop

What is it?"

"Dismal!"

After about five verses one of the more regular punters is minded to take remonstrative action.

"Get off!" he shouts, with weedy contempt.

You can't see him, but it's clear he's injudiciously close

160

to Glyn and co. And it's well and truly off...

Before you know it you've been ushered backstage by security. The event has been abandoned and you're the butt of much exasperated invective, mainly from the uncomprehending Americans. What apparently happened was Glyn, high on cider and indignation, waded into your detractor, the "firm" followed, and wallop! Instant Wild West saloon brawl.

Two security blokes detain you in anticipation of plod. Given your onstage belligerence, they seem a bit disappointed when you don't resist.

One of them answers a knock at the door. But it's not the police. It's the world's media. Well, three broadsheets, one tabloid, the World Service and a Dutch camera crew. You've never given a press conference before, and you could think of more conducive circumstances, but what the fuck? You field their questions playfully. They're obviously hoping for more quotable aggression, but your pill's coming up and you feel all fluffy. You want to hug them all, especially the Dutch TV girl.

When the old bill do arrive, they clock the absurd scenario, look at security as if to say, "You must be having a laugh!" and immediately withdraw. Clearly, filling in the paperwork for a case of poetical incitement to affray is not on their Sunday night agenda.

Twenty-five to midnight and you're hopping off the tube a stop early. It's not big, it's not clever – it's far more down to impulse than intention – but you're going back to Cy's.

The wet grass of Larkhall Park squeaks under your apprehensive footsteps.

At least his light is still on when you knock.

You decide to blurt it straight out. "Look, Cy," you stutter at his back as he ushers you in. "I know it's a bit cheeky... you can tell me to fuck off if you like, but... well... I'm raggedy as... I could really do with some..."

"Mother's milk?" he smiles, through eyes pinned as pissholes. "Yeah, sure."

This wasn't supposed to happen! You expected a bit of resistance, a little eliciting of guilt which might enable a bottle out. You'd practised your "yeah-maybe-it's-not-such-a-good-idea" patter more than the actual request. But no! There he is chopping out a fat one on his stereo.

And there you are, seconds later, snorting it up a plastic straw.

"Thanks, man," you say, sitting down, as the bitterness sears your nostril.

Opposite Cy, you still feel shaky. You're awkward with how easily this particular Rubicon has been crossed: asking your mate for a line of heroin. So you keep reassuring yourself it's all OK: this is a one-off; you've never injected and you never will; in future you'll only take it like before, when he offers it; and anyway it's not brown street shit, which neither of you have ever touched, it's pure – smuggled from source via Cy's arse and Bogota customs to its current location. Mother's milk! It'll be all right!

Slowly the sour taste hits your throat. It won't be long

now before the smooth smacky feeling eases through your stomach, your joints, your thoughts. Anyone who calls it a buzz doesn't know it. It's a gentle cushion, a delicious glow. It radiates softly through your being like treacle. It offers nothing by the way of edge, of rush, of hit. In fact, that's precisely what it does offer: nothing. A big beautiful void, dominated by a sweet absence of pain.

Just what you need right now.

But, before you float off, a few mundane questions linger to assail you.

Like:

Shit, it's pissing down. Have I got enough money for a cab?

Or:

I don't fancy moving just yet. How long can I stay without Cy getting the hump?

And (most pressingly):

How the fuck am I gonna face those kids at school tomorrow?

The Gatecrasher
KENNY MACDONALD

"A million people are expected over the two days of this year's Notting Hill

Carnival which starts tomorrow. A West Indian festival of pageantry, music, dancing and food. It is billed by its organisers as the largest street festival in Europe. This year the police have ..."

Pringle flicked off the radio. Living on Ladbroke Grove in a first floor balcony flat on the main parade route of costume floats and steel bands, he knew as much about the Carnival as he needed to. He had a Carnival party every year — the only way to avoid it would be to escape London altogether for the August Bank holiday weekend. Pringle had no intention of doing that — he loved the Carnival.

He had lived on Ladbroke Grove for six years but this year there would be one major difference. His girlfriend of seven years had left him six months previously so he would be solely responsible for the organisation of the event. In fact, Pringle was only vaguely aware that her absence would make any difference. It had never been apparent to him that there was any need for organising further than telling everyone he met in the previous two weeks to come along.

The Saturday beforehand he went out and bought four dozen cans of lager and a lump of cannabis. On Sunday morning he pushed some of the living room furniture back and stuck a couple of chairs on the balcony which two sets of French windows, one from the living room and one from the kitchen, opened on to. That was it, he felt quite contented that everything was ready for the big day tomorrow.

It dawned bright and sunny which meant that this year's Carnival would be jam-packed. By ten o'clock the air was filling with curried goat and fried fish aromas from the food stalls and the 1000 watt sound systems were being constructed on the street corners. At one o'clock there were a couple of dozen guests in the flat and the trickle of Carnival-goers down Ladbroke

Grove had turned into a steady human torrent. Pringle was well settled in the best balcony spot complete with joint and can of lager. As far as he was concerned, all he needed to do was to sit there receiving the guests and their compliments about what a marvellous flat he had, the same as every year.

He knew nothing, because he'd never bothered to notice, of the filtering out at the door of unwanted guests; of the diplomatic separating of confirmed enemies, ex-lovers and feuding friends; the cooling down of the obstreperously drunk; the careful choreography that had to go into a rumbustious party with fifty guests in a flat big enough for an absolute maximum of thirty. Pringle didn't have a clue that as host it was up to him to make the party appear effortlessly successful.

The Carnival was taking off. The crashing steel bands worked against the thumping sound systems towards a cacophonous crescendo for which the word

'NOISE', even capitalised, was puny. Below him, people were dancing and laughing unbritishly. Pringle waved patricianly from his superior vantage point at them through the thick haze of dope smoke he was generating. The gorgeous colours of the fantastical Carnival costumes, some of them twenty feet high and needing the support of two helpers as well as the person wearing them, shimmered in the afternoon sun as the crowds parted to let the floats through. Magic! This was what the Carnival was all about!

Then the first black cloud of the day scudded across Pringle's horizon.

"Pringle, there's someone here at the door looking for Nigel."

"I don't know any Nigel," he frowned, "I'd better come and see."

By now his kitchen, which he had to traverse to get to the front door, was a heaving mass of drunken sweating bodies. He started to push his way through and accidentally knocked over a beer belonging to a girl he'd never seen before.

"You fucking prick, that was my last can and they're charging £2.50 a shot out in the street now."

"Excuse me, I only live here."

"Pardon me. I'm sure," she said in unapologetic tones, turning her back on him to show that that was the end of the exchange as far as she was concerned. A stinging riposte was just taking shape in his mind when his attention was captured by a loud crashing noise from the back of the house where the bedroom was. He elbowed his way through the hordes, most of whom were complete strangers to him. Passing the front door, he expressed something of his changed mood by slamming it shut in the face of the non-existent-Nigel seeker.

In the bedroom he found the bed propped up on its side against the wall, his book shelf toppled on the floor spewing out books and one of the window panes smashed. There seemed to be about five or six people wrestling on the floor together under the ripped-down curtain.

"What the fuck is going on here?" he yelled.

Someone he at least knew, a notorious drunk called Stan, arose from the wreckage, "Hey man no need to get wound up we're just having a bit of fun…"

Before Pringle had a chance to explain to Stan that he couldn't at all see the funny side of having his bedroom smashed up, he was interrupted by the noise of someone hammering at the loo door and screaming, "I know you're both in there, how dare you humiliate me in front of all these people. OPEN THE DOOR AT ONCE!"

He dashed to the bog to try and prevent the mayhem that was surely imminent.

It was an old acquaintance of Pringle's, Carol, and she was thrashing the bathroom door with an empty can as hard as she could. Behind her a long queue of bursting bladders was becoming increasingly irate. Pringle realised what was going on. Carol's boyfriend always ended up in the toilet with another girl at parties and Carol always cottoned on to what was happening, a dreary but inevitable drama. Pringle would have to intervene before he had a toilet-queue riot on his hands.

"Excuse me Carol. Listen you two, you'd better get out of there NOW!" he shouted in his most authoritative voice as he banged on the door with his fist. He was answered by giggling. He turned helplessly to the queue, "I'm sure they'll be out in a minute."

He retreated to the kitchen.

"Stan you canNOT piss in the kitchen sink!"

"Oh yeah, right, sorry man."

Pringle had only just been in time.

Pringle and the flat managed to weather the rest of the afternoon with only one fight, two forcible ejections, one collapsed coffee table and a broken glass or nineteen. It was seven o'clock, the flat and the streets were beginning to empty. Half of the remaining handful of guests were out on the balcony when Pringle spotted a gang of fifty or sixty youths, fourteen to eighteen, black and white, come steaming down Ladbroke Grove at the trot.

The crowd parted fearfully to let the mob run through.

Then they got someone in their sights, mainly because he'd started running from them, and the baying pack was after him, a man about thirty.

A group of about fifteen uniformed police, barely older than the steamers, were standing at the side of the road. The man being chased fell at their feet and two police grabbed hold of the youth at the front of the pack, an eighteen year old white boy. The gang stopped in its tracks, faced the cops and started chanting, "let him go... let him go."

The cops looked at each other anxiously — there was no sergeant amongst them and none of them wanted to take the lead. They let the white kid go and the steamers ran off up the street.

If there were incidents like this happening around the dying embers of the

Carnival, Pringle knew the police would have no hesitation in putting the riot squad on the streets with their combat gear and perspex shields.

That was a guarantee of ugly scenes to come.

Sure enough, five minutes later a squad of about thirty riot police, sinister in one piece navy blue fire-proof suits and visored crash helmets, appeared from a side street, fanned out across the width of Ladbroke Grove and started advancing, beating their shields rhythmically with their truncheons and flashing their powerful hand-held searchlights at the buildings around them. Other squads could be seen materialising up and down the length of the Grove. The people who were left in the street, carnival revellers wearily making their way home, took one look at that lot and ran for it. Some didn't get away fast enough and the police shoved them roughly out of the way with their shields, knocking one man over.

People were shouting from a house across the road, "leave him alone, he hasn't done anything," but the police shone their dazzling lights at them and ordered them inside. The police line was below Pringle's house when he saw out of the corner of his eye that a girl three feet to his right on the balcony had her arm raised with an empty wine bottle in her hand, ready to hurl it at the police.

If he'd had time he would have reflected that if the bottle missed the police and smashed at their feet everyone in the flat, but especially him, would be in very serious trouble. He would probably then have realised that if the bottle actually hit one of the policemen the word 'trouble' would become redundant. It would have to be replaced by 'Armageddon'. Finally he might have calculated how long it would take the police to break down the street door, run up the stairs and smash his flat to bits, beat them all up, arrest them and charge them all with conspiracy to murder police officers while going about their lawful duty.

Before there was time for him to think any of these things he reacted by grabbing the bottle and wrenching it from the girl's hand, catching her round the waist with his other arm and pushing her through the open French window into the living room.

"You bastard, why did you do that, those fucking fascists out there..." She was beside herself, spitting with rage, and went on in that vein for a minute or so. Then she ran out the flat. That put the final kibosh on the party, the rest of the guests mumbled embarrassed farewells and slunk off.

Pringle flopped down on the sofa. The living room was ankle deep in discarded food wrappings, empty bottles, cans and fag-ends. He was knackered. He went through to have a look at the damage in the kitchen and that was when he came across him. He was an insignificant looking little guy, sitting on his own in the kitchen.

"Look pal, the party's over now, time to go home."

"You kidding, the place is crawling with police outside. I'm from Derry, I know what those bastards can do to ye."

"Don't be daft, everything's calm out now, anyway I'm not asking you,"

Pringle's voice rose, "I'm telling you, get out of my flat."

"No way, man, the cops are everywhere."

This was too much for Pringle, he grabbed the guy by his jacket and yanked him to his feet — he was only about five foot four at full stretch.

"You're leaving now."

The bloke slipped backwards on a bottle, Pringle clung on to him and fell with him, landing on top of him.

"You gonna go now pal, you gonna go now, ya bastard, bastard… "

Pringle stuttered the staccato inarticulacy of violence as he jammed the heel of his hand under the man's chin pushing his head back. The guy began to panic, clawing wildly at Pringle and catching him across the cheek with his nails, drawing blood. Infuriated, Pringle struck him on the face with his fist.

Although he was a good six inches smaller than Pringle and must have weighed two stone less the guy's fear gave him the strength to writhe out from under

Pringle and jump to his feet. Pringle got up too and they stood panting heavily, facing each other, wondering how to get out of this nightmare.

"C'mon, man, maybe if I could just stay here the night."

Pringle couldn't believe his ears, he'd jumped on this guy, actually assaulted him and now he was asking to stay the night as if he was an old friend. The wee man reached inside his grubby polyester windcheater. A knife, the little bastard had a knife! Pringle jumped on him with all his strength knocking him backwards so that his head crunched of the corner of the gas cooker. Shit, he was unconscious, that was all Pringle needed.

"Wake up and get out of my house you poisonous little bastard! "

He was still shaking with the adrenaline that the struggle had shot through his veins. He sat down on the floor beside the cooker. Why were the guy's eyes wide open, was that normal in someone who was unconscious? Pringle gently slapped his cheek to bring him round but all that happened was that his mouth sagged open and a plate with three false teeth on it slipped half-way out of his mouth. Pringle recoiled partly in disgust and partly in the realisation of what he was dealing with. He forced himself to put his ear to the man's chest and listen, he held his breath but he could hear nothing.

This guy was dead. The shock of the knowledge started to work on Pringle and he began a conversation with his increasingly unwelcome guest, as if talking to stiffs was a pastime he engaged in most days.

"Why me? Why did you have to come and snuff it, OK be fair, get killed in my house? Shit, I don't even know your name. Let's have a look at that knife you've got stashed in your pocket."

Inside the jacket there was nothing except a bright blue nylon wallet with three fivers in it. The guy had probably been going to offer him money to stay there the night.

"It's too late to say I'm sorry now, so what am I going to do about you, pal?"

The corpse didn't seem to have any bright ideas.

"I mean here you are an actual cadaver, I can't just leave you here. You don't fit in with the kitchen decor."

The pure gibberish of shock and fear.

Pringle fingered the cuts on his cheek where the man had scratched him. They were quite deep and added to his ripped and bloody shirt they put paid to any ideas of phoning the police to claim that a drunken guest at his party had slipped and fallen, killing himself in the process. The best he would be able to do along those lines would be to say that he had been attacked by a drunken gatecrasher and hope to get off with a manslaughter charge. Pringle looked down at the body and things became clear to him.

"Listen pal, I don't have the least intention of spending

even five minutes in any gaol on account of you, you miserable little runt of a gatecrasher."

He looked through the rest of the wallet. There was a piece of paper with the address of a North Kensington doss house which meant that the guy was homeless. There was a dole card — Sean McFitt was his name. Since the card was for an office in Londonderry, he must be a recent arrival in London.

Despite the fight and the gross inconvenience of the demise Pringle felt a pang of pity for him.

"Fifteen quid, nowhere to stay, no friends, what a fucked-up life, why didn't you stay in Ireland?"

Pringle realised he would never find out what had brought McFitt to England and the exquisite melancholy of the thought made him burst into tears. What a shit day he'd had. The Carnival was supposed to be fun and all he'd had was hassle, hassle nothing but bloody hassle and now this inconsiderate little bastard had to choose his kitchen as his last resting place. A banshee police siren wailed in the street and brought him back to his senses.

He looked at his watch. it was nine o'clock, he had a dead body in his kitchen and he was going to have to do something about it. The one thing he'd decided was that he was not going to the police. What did people usually do with unwanted stiffs? Squeamishness ruled out chopping the body up and flushing it bit by bit down the toilet; he didn't happen to have fifty gallons of sulphuric acid in the flat that he could dissolve the body in the bath with either. That meant transporting the body somewhere to dispose of it.

Pringle's degree in History and the ten years that had brought him to the middle echelons of a town hall bureaucracy were not, in truth, the best possible preparation for the streamlined and discreet disposal of a corpse.

But he had as much knowledge about murder and forensic medicine as any average crime thriller consumer has, which is a surprisingly large amount.

He pulled the guy's head forward to see how much blood there was. He was in luck. Although the back of his head was quite obviously misshapen only a couple of dessert spoons full of thickish blood had dripped from a small wound corresponding to the corner of the cooker. Pringle took off the guy's jacket and started cutting it into strips with the kitchen scissors. With one strip he carefully bandaged McFitt's head to stop the blood. He tried to ignore the squashy feeling that the back of his skull had but once he'd finished tying up the material he had to go and vomit in the toilet.

He came back with the bathroom disinfectant and with another part of

McFitt's jacket he mopped up the little blood that was on the floor. He realised that some of it would have soaked between the floor tiles into the wooden boards but he would have to live with that. Finally, holding his breath, he grasped McFitt's false teeth in a piece of the material and twisted them back into his mouth. For the first time, he noticed that

McFitt's trousers were wet and that there was a strong smell of shit in the room. He went back to the toilet for another puke; it was dry boking now.

He looked out of the window and although there were still regular patrols of police in twos and threes there was no one else to be seen. Pringle calculated that it would be safe to make a move at three am, five hours to go. Then he would have to get the body down the two flights of stairs to the ground floor hall of the house, down the short but steep steps to the street and into the car. The car! He'd have to go and get it, it was parked about a half a mile away because the streets had to be cleared for the Carnival.

What else would he need to do? He'd have to disguise the body to get it from the street door into his car. How? Black bin bags, he had plenty of them, he could pull one over the body's head and another over its feet. In fact two bags over each, and then tape the whole lot up with plenty of gaffer tape.

He set to the task straight away. A body is an awkward thing to manhandle, even one whose owner had been fairly small in stature. 'Had been' — another wave of panic flooded over Pringle. This was a real dead person he was planning to dispose of; if he was caught doing this he could be sent to nick for years and years. Maybe he should make a clean breast of it after all, before it was too late. The police would understand that sheer terror had prevented him from reporting the death right away and with a good lawyer he might get off with a short sentence on a self-defence plea.

He got a grip on himself. He wasn't going to gaol, he was going to get rid of this body and no one would be any the wiser. He found the remains of a half bottle of overproof rum where he'd hidden it that afternoon in the oven and took a slug that left him coughing and gasping for breath. McFitt was laid out on the floor, wearing his shiny black shroud. It was midnight, he might as well go and get the car.

He got back and there were still over two hours to kill until three. He set to work tidying up — activity seemed a better idea than contemplation. When he had finished clearing up he went out on the balcony and looked up and down the street; there was no one in sight. He went back into the kitchen and stood over the body. How should he do this, grab the body by the feet and drag it or haul it over his shoulder in a fireman's lift and carry it?

If he had the strength, he hadn't done any physically demanding work since university summer vacations and he wasn't sure what he was capable of.

Heaving at the body it was quickly apparent that he was scarcely going to get it off the ground, far less over his shoulder. He'd have to drag it and pray that the neighbours were sleeping soundly.

He manhandled McFitt along the floor and out of his flat door easily enough but his skull was making an hideous coconut clunk on each step as he dragged the body down the stairs by the feet. He decided to turn him round and pull him along by the shoulders. He got him half way round but then

McFitt seemed to get himself jammed in the narrow stairway. Pringle heaved and tugged. The bags started to tear and come off, he was shaking uncontrollably and the time-set stair light went out. In the darkness

Pringle stumbled over the body to where the switch was and put the light back on. Ten minutes that had seemed like an hour and all he'd managed to do was get the body stuck six feet outside his own flat.

He sat down and took several deep breaths. Recommencing his labour, he methodically worked at the body until he had it round. The top bags were hanging off, he'd just have to replace them at the street door. At least

McFitt was now lying on his back with his head pointing down the stairs so that Pringle could grasp him under the arms (trying to avoid looking into his glazed eyes) and drag him down the stairs without that horrible noise.

Pringle's clothes were soaked with the perspiration of unaccustomed labour and fear. He understood now why Burke and Hare had always worked double-handed.

Eventually he got the body down to the foot of the stairs and the end of the entrance hall. If any of his neighbours came down now, what would he say to them. 'Oh hello, Mrs Jones, just throwing out this old body, lovely day isn't it.' If he could still laugh, maybe he'd have the strength to carry this through.

He went back up the stairs to get some more bags and tape, returned to the body and repackaged it. Right, one last blast outside and into the back of the car. He had a hatchback and with the seat down he should be able to fit the body in easily enough. Car keys. Car keys? Where the fuck were the car keys? He could have sworn they were in his trouser pocket, but they weren't there now. He must've had them earlier when he'd gone to pick up the car.

He'd left them up in the flat. He trudged back up the stairs to get them.

Kitchen table, top of the telly, bookshelf in the living room, toilet cistern, the keys weren't in any of the places he usually put them. He'd sat down on the sofa and in that armchair earlier. He burrowed his fingers down the side of them, tearing the top off one of his fingernails, but no keys.

He got down on his hands and knees and crawled around scanning the floor, no keys. Marvellous, he had a stiff lying at the front door and he couldn't find his car keys.

He swallowed the last inch of the rum from the oven and the jolt cleared his mind — he had left the keys in the car. His heart jumped, what if it had been stolen, he leapt up and looked out the window, there it was safe as houses. He couldn't take much more of this. He ran down the stairs out into the street and yanked the unlocked car door open. There were the keys. In the ignition. He took them out and went back upstairs.

Pringle opened the street door and peered up and down the Grove. A car drove by, then nothing. He got the body down the steps, half falling with it. He dragged it across the short stretch of pavement, still covered with a thick layer of Carnival detritus that wouldn't be cleared up until dawn. Opening the boot, with a last superhuman effort he hulked McFitt into the back of the motor covering him roughly with an old blanket that was there. He shut the boot, climbed into the car and started it up. Only then did he realise that he hadn't the first idea where he was going and exactly how he would carry out his brilliant body-dumping plan.

Where to? The docks, the River, Epping Forest, a building site, a quarry, where did people usually get rid of bodies? Perhaps he should phone up the

Body Disposal Advisory Service, an end to unwanted-body misery.

Ha-fucking-ha, Pringle was getting sick of his own jokes in the way that you get sick of your own smell when you haven't bathed for too long. He was very tired.

Pringle drove aimlessly for half an hour until it came to him. Take the bags off the body, put it behind a wall in the heart of the area where the

Carnival and the subsequent trouble had been. When the body was found the next day the police would assume that McFitt had been a victim of the violence. As a convincing touch Pringle would take the fifteen quid and leave the empty wallet by the body.

It was three years later, another Carnival. Stan and Carol, who had married after one bathroom incident too many for Carol and a successful drying-out for Stan, were being swept past Pringle's flat by the momentum of the parade.

Looking up and seeing the flat locked up and deserted,

Carol shouted in

Stan's ear, above the noise, "Pringle used to love it so much, I wonder why he always goes away now at Carnival time?"

"He told me the last party he had was murder."

Fearless Footsteps
AOIFE MANNIX

The smell of burnt toast curled its way through the kitchen.
He put the paper down in a hurry and rushed in to pop the
bread up. It was charred black, but she stopped him just as
he was about to drop it in the bin in disgust. She started
scraping the ash into the sink with a kitchen knife. He liked
his toast lightly done, practically still bread but warm and
soft. He liked to get the butter on in the first thirty seconds
so that it melted right in. He had a moment's flash of
ripping the knife from her hands and plunging it into her
heart, but told himself he was probably overreacting.

The charred remains broke as he attempted to mash the
butter in. She insisted the butter must be kept in the fridge
even in summer, so it was always as hard as rock. He was
sure she turned up the settings on the toaster on purpose
too.

Her face as he kissed her goodbye was pinched with
reproach. He never knew what crime he was supposed to
have committed.

The rain was a light mist, more a dampness in the air. The clouds put a grey lid on the sky. Turning the key in the ignition, he started to cry for no reason at all. He had done this every single morning for the past month. Even his tears had become routine.

It struck him as stupid to take a car to take a train, but traffic jams gave him panic attacks. His stop was just on the edge of whether there would be any seats left or not. If taking the train before or the train after would have guaranteed a seat, he would have done it. But the rush hour was more like an hour and a half and so he had gotten the same train at the same time for the past eleven years. The 9:05 Express to Paddington. He knew this morning there would be no seats. He could feel it in his bones.

The crowd surged forward into the already fit to burst carriages. It was all so undignified and humiliating. He had a flash of documentary footage of Jews being taken to Auschwitz in cattle trains. He was squashed in behind a man ten years older then him but in a practically identical grey suit, even their ties had a similar small checked pattern. The man was reading the newspaper standing up. Not caring that his elbows were jamming into the ribs and stomachs of fellow passengers. He tried to avoid reading over his shoulder as he knew it made him nervous when people did that to him, but he couldn't resist.

The news was all bad as usual. Recently he'd found himself being jealous of earthquake victims, convicted rapists, war refugees, not because of the publicity or the drama, but because they at least had a concrete reason to be miserable, Instead of his own vague uneasiness and doubt. It wasn't just the unfairness of not getting the promotion, it was the realisation that he genuinely didn't care. She was devastated of course. She didn't want to be married to someone who was passed over. Passed over, it made it sound as if they had just happened not to see him there. Maybe it was because of that phrase that he had started to feel invisible. Not all at once, but as if every day he grew a little more transparent. Certainly on the train in the morning, he noticed that people always stepped on his feet and never apologised.

The man had caught him reading and flapped the paper in irritation as if he were trying to steal something from him. He looked out the window instead. The view from trains always embarrassed him. All the gardens full of junk and the boarded up windows and the grey backs of crumbling office blocks. Out front they were probably clean and smiling, but travelling behind the scenes, they seemed exposed for the sordid frauds they really were.

A woman got on with a child in a buggy and no one made room for her. As if she were breaking some unwritten law about the 9:05 being a train for people on their way to work. She was glared at with resentment. He felt sorry for her until the kid began to cry. At first a low snivel, but soon developing into piercing, panicked wailing. The mother was mortified, but could do nothing.

The train was packed tight. He felt as if all the air were being sucked out of his lungs. He must stay calm. Waves of claustrophobia washed over him. The kid's crying got louder and he had an urge to scream shut up, shut the fuck up.

He held on tighter to the pole, he would make it, they were nearly in Paddington.

The impact sent him flying half way across the carriage. He landed in a tangle of bodies. He lay there staring up at the ceiling. Then realised he could see buildings in the sky. The carriage had come right off the track and flipped over. Everyone around him seemed to be moaning quietly, except for one woman who was screaming in agony. His brain had still not registered there had been a crash. His main feeling was of irritation, first the toast and now this.

He tried to move but his legs were entangled in something. It turned out to be the kid's buggy. He would have given up without a struggle, except the air was filling with noxious fumes and he started to cough. In a panic, he crawled over bodies. His one big fear was not being able to breath. He could feel his lungs burning. He pulled himself up through the door which now opened into the sky.

Gasping for air, he flung himself to the ground.

He could see the front of the train ablaze. There was smoke everywhere. The wail of fire engines engulfed him. He wandered up and down the track in a daze.

Suddenly the whole world had derailed. An ambulance man rushed up and asked him repeatedly if he was OK. He opened his mouth to speak, but no sound came. The man pointed him in the direction of an ambulance and he stumbled towards it mindlessly. On the way, he tripped over something.

Peering down, he saw a man sprawled on the ground. He wore a dark suit, his glasses were smashed, and blood seeped from his head. With a terrible shock, he realised the man was certainly dead. It woke him up. The train had crashed.

People had been killed. Who knew how many? It was a packed rush hour train.

He could have been killed. He could have been burnt to ashes in that terrifying blaze. They'd never even find his body. He could have ceased existing at that very moment. He sat down.

Ambulance people rushed back and forth, but they paid no attention to him. He kept thinking over and over again he could be dead, as far as anybody knew, he could be dead. He would just not turn up for work and some hours later, they would hear the terrible news of the disaster and begin to worry. His wife would turn on the TV and see the carnage. She would know he always got that train.

If he never came home, if he never turned up for work, they would all assume he died in the crash. It was absolutely perfect.

The station had been turned into a temporary hospital. There were stretchers and wounded everywhere. He went into the men's and washed his hands and face.

He was covered in black soot and there was a small cut above his left eye. He stared at his reflection for a very long time. Then he checked his wallet.

Three hundred pounds. His wife always gave out to

him for foolishly carrying so much money around. How wrong she had turned out to be. Where could he get to?

America? He'd need a passport. France? It didn't matter. He was a dead man anyway. He was going to be reborn somewhere else, anywhere else. It was his one chance of escape.

As he left the station, he was laughing happily. The rain had stopped and the city was drenched in sunshine.

So the day had come at last. He couldn't help feeling excited even though time had lost all meaning for him years ago. He had long since stopped looking at calendars. And he wasn't allowed wear a watch. How a watch could be considered a dangerous weapon he didn't know. But there was a clock in the TV room that told him what time his favourite programmes were on so he looked at that. His father had said he would come at midday on Saturday, the 10th of January to collect him. Twenty two years to the day he had first been put in that strange place.

Suddenly he felt frightened. But then calmed himself. It wasn't as if he was being released, just a day trip. A taste of freedom Matty said. They'd never actually let him go, he knew that. His Dad had had to fill in lots of forms to get him this and there'd been all kinds of assessments. The same questions asked again and again. Luckily by now he knew the answers by heart. Only Matty asked him if he actually wanted to go outside, to set foot in the real world. He told him he was worried about all the violence which made Matty hoot with laughter.

'Listen Tough Guy,' he'd said. 'You been watching too many of those stupid cop shows. The world isn't as dangerous as they like to make out.'

Matty was always making fun of the TV saying it was religion for the masses and he'd rather have opium any day. He liked Matty but he wished he wouldn't be so critical the whole time. After all that little box had for over twenty years been his window on the world. Of course he'd had visitors in the beginning, but he'd refused to speak to them, so could hardly blame them for not coming back.

His Dad had never given up on him though. He came every Saturday afternoon regular as clock work. At first they used to sit in silence or his Dad would tell him how the garden was getting on, but then they hit on the idea of playing chess. A game his Dad had taught him when he was only very small. His Dad could have been a world champion, he often thought. All the Saturdays they played together, he'd only ever beaten his Dad once. And he'd felt bad about it and made sure not to do it again. Anyway it had only been because his Dad wasn't concentrating.

He found it hard to focus sometimes himself, though it was better now they gave him less drugs. Matty said it was good to take the drugs. He couldn't understand why people wasted them hiding them under their mattresses. The fact that they didn't work wasn't the point. The main thing was to take the edge off, Matty said. Matty asked him how he'd managed to survive being in this place all these years. He'd told him the first ten years were pretty bad, but after that he got used to it.

Since eight that morning he'd been sat in the visitors room with his coat on and his scarf wrapped around his neck. He was a bit hot and he knew he was way too early, but he wanted to have that feeling of going for a day out for as long as possible. He'd noticed often it was the anticipation of something, rather then the thing itself that gave the greatest pleasure. And it had been so long since he wore a proper coat. Sure they gave them a kind of jacket thing when they got taken out for their exercises, but that was different. This was his Dad's old coat that he'd brought with him last Saturday. A big heavy black one with deep pockets and a collar. His Dad never wore it because it didn't fit anymore. Not that the coat had shrunk, but his Dad had.   He watched his Dad walk in, stopping to say hello to the nurses as he always did. It made him sad to see what a thin old man he'd become. How he walked with a slight stoop and a kind of barely perceptible tremble. If anything happened to his Dad, there'd be no more days out that was for sure. You had to have a guardian and he didn't have anybody else on the outside. These were selfish thoughts he knew. Morbid and unfit for this perfect day.

The sun was even shining, though there was a bit of a breeze his Dad told him.

He'd said to his Dad he didn't mind where they went as long as it was outside.

He wanted to get as much fresh air as possible.   So his Dad had decided upon the zoo. He didn't point out the irony of him spending his day of freedom looking at animals locked up in cages. His Dad was never a great man for irony.

They looked at the monkeys and the zebras and the lions fast asleep. Though to be honest, he was more interested in looking at the people. There were so many kids around. He realised with a shock that he hadn't seen children for years.

He asked his Dad if it would be OK to buy some balloons for a little boy whose Mum was ignoring his desperate pleading. His Dad didn't think this was a good idea though.

They sat together on a bench and ate ice creams. It was a bit cold for ice cream, but he didn't care, it made him feel like he was alive again. The cold creaminess and the flakes of chocolate. He put his face up to the sun and closed his eyes. Smiled at the beautiful feeling of warmth and said to his Dad, 'This has been the best day ever.'

He was already thinking about how he'd make Matty laugh doing impressions of the orang-utans. He was surprised when he opened his eyes to see his Dad was crying. He couldn't ever remember seeing him cry before.

His Dad said 'you know I thought maybe you might attack me, but I never, never thought you'd hurt her.' So there it was. Spoken of after twenty years. 'It's not that I blame you. It's myself I can't forgive.'

Sometimes he thought it would have been easier on both of them if his Dad had never come to visit. God knows many fathers had thrown away the key for a lot less.

Matty had asked him straight out, 'so who did you kill then?' while they were playing poker together.

He'd stuttered 'what makes you think I killed anyone?'

'They don't put you in here for two decades just for thinking you're the Queen of England.'

So he told him, which was the first time he'd told anyone who didn't already know. 'I strangled my mother with a telephone cord.'

That was the only occasion he'd seen Matty at a loss for words. Eventually he'd said, 'Jesus Christ, Tough Guy, I'm really sorry.'

Which was what he was saying to his Dad just now. His Dad took out a handkerchief and blew his nose.

'You were ill, we knew you were ill, your mother always said you couldn't help it. And if I hadn't lost my temper and left the house like that. Leaving you alone…'

He wanted his Dad to stop now. He couldn't think about that afternoon. He had wrapped it up in a thick cloth and dropped it to the bottom of his soul.

'I still miss her you know' he said to his Dad.

His Dad did a strange thing then. He took his hand in his and squeezed it hard. It was the first time he had touched him since it had happened. It felt even better then the ice cream.

Nowadays she just cleaned houses. She claimed her back was killing her and she couldn't cope with more industrial work. But it wasn't just the low ache that crept up her spine from all the reaching under desks for those small metal bins. It was more that offices depressed her. No one ever talked to you. Even if they were staying late, if you attempted a bit of a chat, they looked at you as if you'd bitten them. Really the art of conversation had died among the young. Probably all that loud music. They didn't feel comfortable unless they were shouting. These were crumblie thoughts, she knew Dave would say, if she ever were foolish enough to voice them out loud. But at least with Mrs Richardson you got a cup of tea and a biscuit and she worried about her sons too. Didn't matter how big your house were, kids were always trouble.

Mrs Richardson's youngest, same age as her Dave, wanted to be an actor. This didn't strike her as the end of the world, but Mrs Richardson seemed convinced he would starve to death in a gutter. At least he wanted to do something. Dave thought ambition a dirty word. All he seemed to care about was his stupid moped. She knew it wasn't a moped, it was a Vespa, but she always got mixed up on purpose. The sight of it sent a chill right through her. He swore he always wore a helmet and never rode it drunk. It wasn't that she didn't believe him, but she had a bad feeling about it. "Don't be such a crumblie", he'd tell her as he slammed the door cheerfully behind him. She'd stand for a moment in the kitchen listening to him whistling and the childlike cough of the engine starting. Then shake her head knowing that he was right, she was getting old. She'd peer out the window watching him take off up the road.

She never used to be nervous, it wasn't in her nature. Dave was like her that way, utterly fearless. She remembered one time, when he was only three, she was reading her magazine when he shouted "Hey Mammy, look at me." She glanced up to see he had climbed to the very top of the jungle gym. It was a huge wooden one with four different levels and a kind of extra tower that went even higher. Before she could utter a sound, he had jumped. For a moment that went on forever, her heart froze. Then he hit the sand, sprang up, and ran towards her laughing. She held him tight and told him never to do that again, but she could see he had no idea what she was talking about.

Still, as her sister Anne liked to say, at least he's not a heroin addict. Anne only asked about Dave as an excuse to start in on endless tales of her own daughter who was studying medicine at Trinity. At least he's not a stuck-up little bitch with a face like the bollocks off a cat that's just been neutered. It was Dave who described his cousin like that, she didn't agree of course, but she couldn't help smiling. The main thing, she told Mrs Richardson that morning, is that they're happy. And Dave wasn't one of those sullen young lads all collapsed in on themselves and shuffling round like a shadow. He loved making jokes and teasing her. Sometimes she pretended to be offended, but deep down, she was pretty unshockable. And the gay thing didn't bother her really, just what other people would think.

When the phone rang, she answered it 'Richardson

residence' as Mrs Richardson had instructed, and was surprised to her Dave's voice. He was supposed to be at work. He had a job delivering paintings to galleries. "Tell Anne I work in the arts if it makes you feel better," he'd said. But she wasn't going to lie to her own sister. She said he was a removal man. Anne was always asking if he had a girlfriend, obviously already having her suspicions, there was no need to give her more ammunition by mentioning the arts.

"Why aren't you at work?" she asked accusingly.

"I've been arrested for mass murder and indecent assault of a minor. This is the only call I'm allowed make before they take me off for the lethal injection."

"Better make it quick then. Some of us are trying to earn a living. Mrs Richardson doesn't like me getting personal calls."

"The van broke down so I've come home early. I thought I'd make us lasagne for tea if you're gonna be home."

"You know I don't like Italian food. Broke down? Did you crash it or something?"

"No, no Robbie just chipped it off a post box"

"Who's Robbie?"

"New driver, he's as thick as cement. Forgot to put the handbrake on and the bloody thing starts moving just as me and Sean are stepping out the back."

"You didn't hurt yourself?"

"Course not. God don't start fussing."

The lasagne was delicious, even if it was Italian. Don't

know where he learnt to cook like that. She hated cooking herself and his Dad couldn't boil an egg. His Dad wasn't able to do anything full stop.   She knew she should be glad they'd started seeing each other again, that it was ungenerous of her. But a mean little voice inside couldn't help sneering, oh yeah get in touch when he's old enough to go to the pub with you, no interest in anyone you can't share a pint with. She knew it was unfair because Dave was the one who'd looked him up. Maybe she was a bit jealous.

She caught him swilling two aspirins in the kitchen. "Hung over again?"

"It's worn off by now, Ma. Only crumblies like yourself have hangovers last till evening. Just got a bit of a headache."

And he sloped off to watch telly. She read the paper and fed the cat. He was fast asleep when she went to join him. Snoring like a chimney. Watching some rubbish about gorillas in the Amazon. She was about to flick over when she got caught up in the story about one of the baby monkeys whose mother had been killed by hunters. The other monkeys wouldn't share their food with the new orphan. "Bastards," she muttered to herself.

Dave was still sleeping when the programme finished. He really was handsome, she couldn't help thinking, looking at his fine featured face with the dark hair just beginning to grow back. It had used to be down to his shoulders and she'd hated that. But she didn't like when he shaved it to the bone either. Made him look like he was in the army. He told her they'd never let his kind be a soldier. Just as well she thought. She gave him a little shake to wake him and he mumbled "Leave me alone, Ma." Fine, if he wanted to sleep on the sofa, let him. She went off up to bed, making sure to turn all the lights off and unplug the telly.

The next morning she woke late and it was raining. She'd have to hurry to get to Mrs Richardson's on time. She went into Dave's room to shout at him to get up, but of course he was still on the sofa. The moment she stepped into the sitting room, she knew there was something wrong. Like there was a stillness that hadn't been there before. She shook him saying, "Time to get up, Dave." And even though she knew he wasn't breathing, she went on shaking him and whispering "time to get up." Then she rang the hospital.

Afterwards she couldn't believe she hadn't tried to do mouth to mouth, but the doctor assured her he'd died at around 4 am. A brain haemorrhage. Nothing she could have done. Sean explained to her that when the van had moved, Dave lost his footing and fell out the back. Hit his head. They'd thought nothing of it cos he was still laughing. He hadn't even mentioned it to her, that was what got to her most. If he had, she'd only have fussed. Probably made him see a doctor. Apparently that wouldn't have made a difference either.

Mrs Richardson said she could have as long as she liked off. But she didn't want to just sit around the flat. She kept thinking she heard Dave whistling outside in the yard. She spent a long time staring out the window at the moped. Hours in fact. She couldn't shake off the feeling that somehow it was to blame. She'd be better off getting back to work she knew.

Mrs Richardson's youngest was still eating breakfast she arrived so late. Everything seemed to take her three times as long these days as if she were moving in slow motion.

He went bright red when she came in and stammered, "I'm very sorry about your son."

She looked at him, but said nothing.

"Must have been… the shock and all…" His words spluttered and gave up.

She continued to stare at him. In a panic, he picked up a letter from the table. "I just got in to drama school. Just got the acceptance. Mum doesn't want me to go but… I'm sorry, I really am sorry." He stared down at the letter in embarrassment. He'd always been an awkward kid, she found it rather sweet.

She smiled at him. " My son had a Vespa. It was his pride and joy. It's only getting rusty out in our yard."

He looked up at her in surprise. He clearly thought she'd gone off her rocker with grief.

"I just thought you might like it. Only if you promise to wear the helmet, mind."

Of course she'd never be able to forgive herself if anything happened to Mrs Richardson's son, but she had a good feeling about it. And she didn't want to just throw the bike away as if it were a piece of junk, as if she hadn't felt some strange kind of pride every time she watched Dave speeding off up the road.

It wasn't as if he was mad. He knew he was imagining it. When he was at home in his room listening to music, he knew it was all in his head. He loved 'The Cure'. He played all their old albums for hours. Wasn't so keen on their later stuff. Years ago he used to go for the whole look. The white make-up and the lipstick. He had a black leather coat that reached almost to his ankles. His Dad said it made him look like a faggot. But it was the music he was into, the fact that it pissed his Dad off was only an added bonus. Not that he went around like that now. Though he still wore a small silver skull on a chain around his neck. Sarah had given it to him for his eighteenth birthday. They'd both been as high as kites when she put it round his neck whispering "Happy birthday, lover boy."

He'd kissed her then and it was just as if he could taste all the colours of the rainbow. He wondered where she was now, who she was kissing. He'd heard she'd become a hairdresser, moved south of the river. But he'd lost touch with all that old crowd. The living dead his Dad used to call them. Always shouting out 'where's the funeral' as they headed for the door. Miserable old bastard.

He used to go out nearly every night of the week then. There was a club called 'The Spider' that he spent more time in than his own bed. The walls were painted with webs and there were giant plastic spider legs hung over the bar. That was before he got scared of insects. Before he got scared of going outside. Not that he was afraid of leaving his own house. That would be ridiculous. When he was putting his jacket on, double checking he had his wallet and his keys, re-reading the shopping list, everything felt normal. He liked to make a list partly because it meant he couldn't forget anything and have to do more trips then absolutely necessary. And partly because writing things down gave him a feeling of achievement, like he was getting it all under control. That was the key after all. To remain calm, cool, collected. But it never lasted long.

As soon as he turned the corner out of his street to the main road, he would start to sweat. A kind of clammy dampness would ooze from all the pores of his body. It had nothing to do with being too hot, after he'd be freezing cold and his teeth would start to chatter. He'd repeat to himself like a mantra, there is nobody following you, and he would nearly believe it until he heard the footsteps. Mostly they were sharp and purposeful and belonged to men in suits. He never dared to actually look at their faces, but he could tell. Sometimes they were softer and bounced like a cat on the prowl. He'd always despised trainers himself. Once they were a pair of high heels clacking painfully just behind him. If he moved quickly enough, he could escape them. Another trick he'd learned was stopping suddenly and staring in a shop window. Caught off guard, the footsteps could continue on by. But there was more then one of them after him and they would replace each other. The slap of leather on cement getting closer all the time.

Of course when he did get home shaking and shivering, he knew he was just being silly. He would peer out the curtains and there was nobody there. They didn't know where he lived. The doctor had suggested it was all the acid he'd taken when he was young. But he hadn't taken any more then anybody else. And they were all fine, had got married, had kids. No one was after them. His Dad was always saying to him how all the rest of his waster friends had finally grown up and got a real job, what was he still doing sitting around on his arse all day? But he wasn't lazy. He used to spend hours and hours practising his bass. That wasn't the reason he got thrown out of the band. It was because the singer Robert was an ego maniac who'd always been after Sarah. He couldn't understand what she saw in him. To be dumped was one thing, but for that lanky streak of piss quite another.

The afternoon they told him they'd found another bass player, it was raining hard. He'd hurried home through the streets pulling his coat around him. A slow burning anger working his way up through his guts. If his Dad dared to say one word to him tonight, he'd punch him in the face. He was imagining how his knuckles would feel making contact with his Dad's lower jaw as he put his key in the door. He could hear the TV burbling away asking questions. His Dad was obsessed with those stupid quiz shows even though he never actually knew any of the answers.

The first thing he noticed that was a bit unusual was

that his Dad's shoes were sat on a piece of newspaper in the middle of the hall. They were brown loafers, Italian leather, and he had apparently just finished polishing them. The tin of polish was still open beside them. God he thought, maybe the old man's finally got a date. He couldn't remember the last time his Dad had left the house even to go for a drink.

The second strange thing struck him the moment he walked into the TV room. His Dad was still sat in his regular armchair. An empty bottle of whisky beside him. His Dad didn't drink whiskey as far as he knew.

Then there was the dark stain behind his Dad's head and the shotgun on the ground. He seemed to take these details in slowly, in precisely that order. But he came to rest on his Dad's feet which were bare. The large unclipped toes vulnerable. He'd polished his shoes, but taken his socks off.

At the funeral he heard his Dad's brothers discussing in hushed tones how his Dad could have got hold a shotgun. But it was the shoes that puzzled him. Just where had his Dad been thinking of going?

You collect me from Stanstead, an airport more like a space station with its huge whiteness and strange lack of people.

I feel the coldness of it seep into me.

We've nothing to say to each other on the train on the way back, which isn't the best start to a new life together.

The bedsit is tiny, but you've hung the walls with welcome streamers. It's not true that you don't try, but neither of us tries hard enough.

In the evenings we play cards desperately as I try to push the heat from my head, the panic crush of rush hour underground. I spend hours lost in Tescos, dwarfed by the aisles of soap powder, frozen pizzas. Sweating with shopping bags on Tottenham High Road, I see two men hop out of their cars and start cunting each other. One of them whips a screwdriver from his glove compartment while the small child in the back screams and screams. He strikes him over the head, there is blood and I vow to go home.

Every day on the winding escalators that make me dizzy, the push and shove of elbows, the rudeness, the greyness. I promise to go home but never do, I just come back earlier and you stay out later.

I can never find those fancy Soho bars down tiny little streets always arriving late, work weary and sore, my whole body aching among the shouts of suits. I watch myself from far away, shrinking thin and sick. A cough that clings on through the winter with the boiler broken and you not coming home at all. My skin a frozen puddle, the rain against the panes of my eyes, I never knew I had such foul weather in me.

The clock plays its card tricks and I continue to lose at solitaire. You are full of concerts, crackers, champagne, and girls with blond hair and big teeth. Loud, laughing, so different to me you keep saying, as I struggle to breathe. The doctor says acute bronchitis, I just feel acute. Drowning in slow motion, I start to frighten myself with the walls closing over my head and you don't seem to notice I have turned invisible. Until one evening by chance, I fall into love like a capital city, and move out into the big wide streets as if they suddenly knew my name.

The party's already blurring at the edges when I get there, the sangria makes me thirsty.

The girl from Denver at the kitchen table telling me she got a French cruise from Venice.

We discuss the mystery of how come food tastes so much better on the continent, even the sandwiches you buy on corners in the rain. She says she likes the Italians because they've been there a long time and that makes them easier in themselves. She says Americans are too raw, too much to prove, too little history, kind of like me I think. I tell her I could fall in love in New York, but don't know if I could stay there long. Like everyone you meet these days, she's trying to get a visa. There ought to be a way to swap just for a while, there's nothing like deportation to help you appreciate a foreign country.

I feel guilty for my dissatisfaction, maybe I'm just jealous the way the Yanks lap up the English, maybe I'm just looking for a way to get your attention. I get sucked in by the word mongrel, but soon realise I'm being bated. He's making some fancy trap out of Tory MPs, Martin McGuinness, collapsing racism and terrorism. One of these nights he's going to push my buttons too far. I know he's said I should go back to my own country, where ever that's supposed to be, but I also know what you'll say about burning trouble at both ends, so I cut and dive away in the middle of his sentence.

She wants desperately to go dancing and it seems safer then talking. Everyone's shouting, being left behind, losing the address, the taxi driver a bewildered saint. We finish the beer under the bouncer's coat outside the club. He's big, but he's smiling, later he becomes a referee in our game of pool.

She tells us about smuggling gold in her shoes, wearing the tightest, sexiest outfit, because she says she's not pretty, but she's got a body. Each footstep worth its weight. Seven years if she got caught — but how else was she going to get home, not a penny to her passport.

I consider whether I have the metal for this, decide I'm just running scared with an empty suitcase, hoping to catch the last flight out.

Guns of Acton
MICHAEL BAKER

He had a very bad feeling about this. Regaining consciousness in the boot of a vehicle was not a good sign. Neither was the fact that his wrists and ankles were bound tightly with something cold and metallic, probably wire. He tried to stretch his legs but couldn't, his movements restricted. He knew the 9mm semi-automatic Glock in his waistband was missing before he even attempted to reach for it. He opened his eyes and a sense of resignation swept over him. He realised that this night could be his last as he lay face down in total darkness on a piece of carpet that reeked of petrol. The vehicle bounced over another pothole and explosions of intense pain behind his eyelids threatened to burst his skull.

He'd faced this possibility many times in the past. As the perpetrator of many ambushes and drug rip-offs himself, he knew just how easy it was to become a victim. In his line of work, he knew it was almost inevitable. He had known many in JA, New York and here in London whose lives had ended prematurely in the same way. Here he was, a comparative veteran at the ripe old age of twenty-five. Maybe his luck had finally run dry. Tonight, in the early hours, he and Rica had left the club, stepping into the cool night air. Next thing, he had woken up here, his head throbbing, trussed up like the Christmas turkey.

The bouncing became more regular, as if the vehicle were passing over a rutted lane, then came to an abrupt halt. The boot swung open and rough hands gripped his shoulders, hauling him out. Sliding in the mud, he was shoved to the front of the vehicle, blinking in the harsh glare of the headlights. He lost his footing, falling head first into a mound of fresh earth. On his knees now, but unafraid and defiant, he spat contempt at the figure looming over him. Whenever Forrester had threatened him in the past he laughed in the fat man's face, never believing him for one second actually capable of carrying his threats out. The cold muzzle of the Beretta pressed into the back of his neck. He heard a deafening roar then fell into darkness that engulfed him and claimed him for eternity. Warmed by the dying flames that licked the burning vehicle, the two men ignored the wind and rain chilling the autumn night air, watching as the blaze reflected on the brickwork of the Victorian pub. Rushmore Ellis pulled his baseball cap down tight on his head, turning up the collar of his jacket against the curtain of drizzle as litter fluttered around him in the wind. A mini-cab nosed around the corner from a deserted side street then accelerated away into the night.

"Couldn't happen to a nicer guy..." chuckled Johnny Too Bad, watching the fire crew hose down the oily, smoke-blackened hulk in Harry Randall's normal parking space. The rear personalised number plate hung disconsolately by one bolt. Harry Randall's Jag. His pride and joy. The tang of fuel hung heavy in the air, the tarmac scorched, blistered into craters in a wide circle around the vehicle. Burnt out and blackened, rivers of ash and oil-streaked water dribbled across the tarmac, swelled by the continuing rain. The small audience of bystanders from the pub trickled away, losing interest.

Rush and Johnny Too Bad were both well aware that Randall was not a man to be crossed. He came from a feared and well-established family of West London gangsters and shared many family traits, most notable among them an easily provoked violent temper and a strong resemblance to the late comedy actor Roy Kinnear. No one remarked on this similarity when he was in earshot. Not known for his sense of humour, there were rumours how those foolish enough to cross Harry Randall often ended up nailed to the floorboards of condemned buildings. Whoever had done this would soon wish they hadn't.

"You know what they call that? Karma," said Rush. "Poetic justice. It'd be a bonus if the motherfucker had been inside when it went up, though."

Johnny grinned. "What go around, come around, man." The big man shrugged his broad shoulders and turned away from the scene. "So, what were you tellin' me?" he asked, changing the subject. "They sacked you, just like that?"

"Yeah, man." Rush kissed his teeth in disgust. "Redundancy. Same thing, though. Can you fuckin' believe it, man?"

"That's the way it goes these days, star. Last in, first out."

"Yeah, but the way they did that shit, you know? I thought they had to give you notice or something." He shook his head. "I didn't get no warning, no nothing. The bastard just called me into the office and..." He drew an imaginary line with his finger across his throat, "...that was it."

"Scum," sympathised Johnny.

"I don't know what the fuck I'm gonna tell Aprilia. We got debts up to our ears, man. Catalogues, bills, all kinds of shit... she already thinks I'm leeching off her." He gazed into the distance. "Looks like I'm gonna have a major domestic when I get in."

Johnny shrugged. "Not out tonight, then?"

"You're jokin' me, man." He laughed bitterly. "I'll be looking for work all weekend if Aprilia's got anything to do with it. Anyway, mi pocket bruck right now. Billy Bruck Shut. Why, you got plans?"

Johnny grinned at him. "Tonight, big tings ah gwaan ah Trends. Watch mi nuh; all fruits ripe tonight!"

"Hear wha'," said Rush. "Mind yuh tell all ah the gyaal dem, mi deh soon!" Rush couldn't help but feel slightly envious of his friend — he still had his job and wasn't tied down. The big dread always had all the angles covered. They started walking towards the tube station when a bellow of rage stopped them dead in their tracks.

"You fucking black bastard!" Sixteen stone of furious Harry Randall lunged out of the darkness at them, swinging punches and screaming abuse. Randall caught Rush on the side of the head with one wild punch, sending him staggering backwards. Harry almost lost his own footing in the process, sprays of wet gravel crunching under his shiny Italian loafers as the two men brawled in the road. Johnny tried to force his large frame between them, but not before Rush retaliated, burying a sly uppercut in Harry's gut. Harry doubled up, florid cheeks bulging with air and Rush followed up the punch with a devastating kick in the balls. Johnny pulled his friend away, preventing him following up his victory. Harry, groaning in agony, gripped his crotch, knuckles turning as white as his face and sank to his knees, groaning, "You fucking little shit. My beautiful motor..."

"What? Me?" Rush crouched so his face was close to Randall's. "What the fuck're you on, man? I never touched your car!"

"It was you, Jooksie, you little bastard!" Harry said. He clutched his balls as he tried to catch his breath, his complexion redder than ever. "You were seen — bang to rights!"

"Jooksie? Who's Jooksie?" Rush was about to kick Randall again but stopped as Johnny placed a broad hand on his shoulder. "Easy. Cool nuh, man. He's done." Rush stopped, looked down at Randall for a moment then turned and walked away. Johnny Too Bad followed.

"This ain't over!" Randall shouted at their backs. "I've got a fucking long memory!"

Rush's head was spinning as he walked to the tube station. He halted, illuminated by the dim yellow streetlight, ignoring the drizzle. The left side of his head throbbed; the fat man had at least managed to get one good punch in. He massaged his left temple. "You see that? You see that? That fuckin' arsehole had a pop at me!" He bounced up and down a couple of times on the balls of his feet. "Still went down like a sack of shit, though." Rush attended the same Thai-boxing classes as Johnny Too Bad and was respected and feared for his one-punch KO.

"Yeah, and it looks like we're both probably gonna be looking over our shoulders from now on." Johnny scowled.

"Hey, hold on, don't be giving me bad looks," Rush snapped. "It wasn't me started it."

"True," admitted Johnny. "There's plenty people want to fuck up that guy, still."

They walked on in silence for a while, each lost in their own thoughts. They stopped at the mouth of the alley that ran beside North Acton station.

"More time, Rush. Take it easy, yeah?" said Johnny Too Bad.

"You too. Keep in touch, star." He held out a clenched fist, which Johnny bumped with his own. "Later."

He turned into the alley as Johnny Too Bad disappeared down Victoria Road, heading for his flat in Harlesden.

Rush looked at his watch as he hurried in the station; it was nearly ten and he was late. Aprilia was going to be really pissed off. A tall figure walked fast towards him from the opposite end of the alley, silhouetted against the pale streetlight. On drawing level, the silhouette materialised into a tall white guy carrying a large black sports bag, who stopped and leaned towards Rush, as if to ask the time. He radiated strung-out anxiety and wiped the palms of his hands on his jacket, glancing around nervously. "All right, Jooksie? Long time no see."

That name again. "Sorry? You talkin' to me?" asked Rush.

A shadow passed over the guy's face. "Don't take the piss," he said, thrusting the bag into Rush's arms. "Five ki's as agreed. Readies at the usual pick-up, yeah?" He walked away without looking back and turned the corner at the end of the alley, disappearing from view.

"Hold it!" Rush shouted, still clutching the bag, his voice echoing. "What the fuck is this?"

Bewildered, he put the bag down on the muddy pavement and unzipped it. Inside were parcels of cling film-wrapped parcels of white powder, neatly stacked on top of each other. He lifted one out, weighing its compact softness in his hand. He replaced the package carefully, zipped the sports bag shut and hoisted it over his shoulder, wondering what he should do with it.

The only other person on the platform was an old white

man, hunched into a raincoat as worn as his face, pacing back and forth to keep warm. Watching him made Rush feel the autumn chill even more, huddling further into his bulky puffa jacket. He sat on a bench in the waiting room, which was little more than a wooden hut with a radiator. He warily eyed the sports bag next to him. It sat there like a big black question mark, as if daring him to look inside.

He unzipped the bag once more and stared at its contents. His experience of the drugs trade was limited to buying the odd bag of weed and he really couldn't see himself trying to offload all this gear. This really was the big league. Also, the owner of the five kilos was probably out looking for his lost merchandise right that minute.

A westbound Central Line train rattled to a halt. The doors hissed open, brushing his thoughts away. He left the bag in the waiting room, stood up and walked to the train doors. The stakes were high; amateurs in the drugs trade didn't last long, usually ending up getting a bullet or doing a long stretch in prison. On the other hand, this could be the break he'd been waiting for so long. A chance to take some control over his life by making some loot. He thought about some of the good things money could buy — Versace suits, Prada shoes and top of the range motors, state of the art apartments. But most important to Rush was the respect and influence that money commanded. This could be the turning point where his luck changed in life. He sprinted into the waiting room, grabbed the bag and dashed back to the train, squeezing between the doors just as they closed and the train juddered off into the night.

Although the carriage was empty, he stood, holding on to a strap. The reflection in the carriage window returned his paranoid stare. He flinched whenever the doors opened, all reflexes and raw nerves. He'd felt quite calm until the enormity of what he was doing suddenly came crashing in on him. He was travelling around town with five kilos of charlie in a bag like it was nothing, and it wasn't as if he was an experienced criminal of any kind, let alone a coke-slinging gangster. He almost expected half the Met to come bursting into the carriage at any moment, choking him with pepper spray, rigid handcuffs clicking shut on his wrists. How many years could you rack up for the amount he was carrying, he wondered, staring out into the darkness? Six or seven years? Eight or nine? Maybe more, even. He desperately needed to work out his next move, quick time.

At Ealing Broadway, a stream of late rush-hour stragglers made their weary way home into the evening traffic, while a few early Friday-night drinkers and clubbers hung around the station waiting for friends to show up. Rush felt exposed and vulnerable as he walked out through the swing doors, down the steps and onto the street, the sports bag slung over his shoulder. Outside, neon signs glowed invitingly in the gloom but the taxi rank was empty. The nearest taxi office was up on the high street, and he suddenly felt even more vulnerable. Ironically, he had been intending to buy a second-hand motor when he got next month's pay, but forget that — now he'd buy a brand new Merc!

Someone barrelled into him and he almost spun into the road. "Hey, watch where…" he started, but didn't get to finish the sentence as a stream of saliva splattered his face and a furious female shriek drowned out any other sound. Dirty fingernails tore at his face and his baseball cap flew into the street as the woman launched herself at him.

"You fucking piece of shit, Jooksie!" she screamed, almost perforating his eardrums as the reek of stale alcohol fumes threatened to overwhelm him. Shocked and angry, he caught hold of her bruised, stick-thin wrists, shaking his attacker like a pit bull shaking a rag doll. She was light as a small child, but with the worn, tear-stained face of a much older woman, hair bleached canary yellow, lank and greasy. She sobbed and cursed, wiping saliva from his face.

Shit. He was seriously out of his depth here. All this drama was drawing attention to him. Although bewildered, he was well aware of disapproving glances from several passers-by as he shoved the hysterical woman away from him with disgust. He had to get off the street, fast. A black cab was parked opposite, its yellow FARE lamp on. He spotted the police patrol car prowling along beside him, two suspicious white faces peering through the windscreen and rain at the agitated, young mixed-race guy with the large black sports bag.

Maybe the smart thing to do would have been to head straight for the local nick with the bag, but it was too late now. He really didn't think the Old Bill would swallow the truth somehow; that he'd been given the gear in an alley at North Acton by a geezer he'd never seen before and now he was on his way to the police station to hand it in. Say goodnight and take five years. The police car pulled out of the stream of traffic and slowed to a halt at the curb. Just as the front passenger door opened, a black BMW screeched to a halt in front, in a tidal wave of oil-streaked drizzle. A tinted window hummed and slid down. A large middle-aged white man leant out. "Jooksie! Stop fannying about and get in!"

He didn't have to be told twice. The rear passenger door opened and he climbed in. A ragga bass line reverberated from the vehicle at ear-splitting volume. "One of yours, Jooksie?" shouted the driver over the stereo, as he revved the engine. "You must be fuckin' barmy walkin' round like that. Just can't leave them junkie birds alone, can you?" He laughed wildly as the BM took off, leaving the police car standing as they lurched forward and cut into the traffic on the Uxbridge Road.

The back of the driver's cropped greying head seemed to merge directly into his broad shoulders. His face was craggy, chasms around his eyes crinkling with amusement as he swerved dangerously into a left, then a right turn, following traffic, registering its disapproval with a chorus of horn blasts. He grinned at his passengers, churning gum between two rows of even white teeth. In the front passenger seat sat a tall, dignified black man with his hair in cane rows, a diamond stud in his left ear. They accelerated through a red light, tyres squealing in protest.

"Easy, T."

They narrowly missed a white van in front, the driver

glaring at them in his rear-view.

"Who's fuckin' driving, eh? You or me, Beres?"

"Shit, if I'd known you was gonna kill us, I'd have driven, man," muttered Beres.

"Get out and fucking walk then," said Tony, raising his voice over the stereo.

"Fuck you — and your mother" said Beres, unperturbed. He turned to Rush in the back seat. "So, Jooksie… Wha'you a seh? Good to see you again, man. We all thought you was brown bread or banged up," he said, his transatlantic twang hopping between South London, Brooklyn and JA.

"Nah, just keeping a low profile," replied Rush, watching office blocks and shops pass in a blur. "Out of the country, you know."

"Yeah, nothin' like a break to concentrate and freshen the mind," agreed Beres, wincing as the BMW overtook a line of traffic, narrowly missing a Post Office van with the same idea. "You think Blunt Tony's driving's improved any, Jooks?" asked Beres, putting a cigarette in his mouth and lighting it with the dashboard cigar-lighter.

"Nah," said Rush, shaking his head, which was spinning, as much with confusion as from Blunt Tony's driving. The resemblance between him and Jooksie was obviously stronger than he'd thought. How come he hadn't been sussed immediately? It was a good thing they hadn't rumbled him, judging by the hard resolve on the faces of both men. He'd seen that look before, on the faces of guys he knew that had spent a lot of time in prison. He knew these were dangerous people.

He peered through the rain-lashed rear windscreen into the darkness. Neither Beres nor Blunt Tony seemed unduly worried about the police car behind them, although the sirens and blue flashing lights seemed to be drawing closer, illuminating the interior of the black BMW for a second before plunging it into darkness again. As the traffic thinned out, the chase resumed along the Western Avenue, weaving in and out of the Friday evening traffic.

"Five-O right behind us, T," warned Beres.

"Not for long, pal." Blunt Tony savagely spun the steering wheel through sausage-like fingers, pushing the accelerator to its limit, sending the vehicle careering down the central reservation. The BM hurtled into the darkness for a short while longer, before he threw the vehicle into a sharp u-turn, and then skidded into a left and a right turn. They aquaplaned into a deserted side street, spun sideways and came to a halt as he slammed the brakes on. The flashing blue light was no longer visible, nor could they hear the siren in the distance.

Blunt Tony leant over towards Rush, a chunky gold bracelet dangling from his left wrist. A smile stretched his mouth, no humour present at all. He turned the volume on the stereo down. "So, whatcha got for us, Jooks?" The eyes were cold and hard, expressionless. Blunt Tony was clearly the real thing. Tonight Rush had to be the real thing, too, if he wanted to get out of this mess intact.

He reluctantly handed over the bag. Blunt Tony unzipped it and peered at its contents. He held one of the packages up to the light, examining it closely. He carefully opened it and dipped the tip of his index finger into the powder, dabbing it onto his tongue, tasting it. A broad smile spread slowly across his face. "Fuck me," he said quietly. "Looks like Forrester's really come up trumps." He turned to Rush. "You done all right, Jooksie. Mind you," he said smiling, "it only just makes up for knocking out that moody shit last time." He shook his head, still smiling.

"Well, you do what you gotta," said Rush. He knew he was way out of his depth but, strangely, he was beginning to enjoy the charade. He'd always thought he would have been quite a talented actor.

In another life, maybe.

Blunt Tony replaced the package and zipped the bag, slinging it over his massive shoulder. "You're priceless, you are," he said. He opened the door and climbed out. Despite his width, he moved with the speed and grace of a cat. Meanwhile, Beres rummaged around in the glove compartment. Slipping a handgun inside his jacket, he unfolded his lean frame from inside the BMW. "Abso-fucking-lutely priceless," said Blunt Tony, shaking his head.

They walked to the end of a urine-stinking, litter strewn alley, then down a flight of cement steps to a doorway lit by a single spotlight and a sign in blue neon, spelling out "Dante's". Two doormen stood in the splash of light, talking. One, a short stocky white man wearing a dark suit, hair slicked back into a ponytail, leant against the wall smoking a cigarette. The other was Asian and larger than his colleague. Both seemed bored, waiting for the Friday night rush to begin. They nodded at Blunt Tony and stood aside as he entered, carrying the bag. Beres and Rush followed.

The interior of the club was dimly lit, the peeling wallpaper and ceiling nicotine brown. Situated in a basement, there were no windows; the only light artificial and their shoes stuck to the lager-sodden carpet as they crossed the bar. A tall, black girl with bleached cropped hair looked up from behind the bar, distracted from the magazine she had been thumbing through. The light glinted off a single gold tooth as Beres shot her a grin. "Yuh ahright, Rica?" he chirped.

"Yeah, great," she replied dryly. She frowned, staring straight at Rush, who averted his gaze, looking down at the sticky carpet. Her gaze followed as they walked away, shoving through a small circle of young men and women in expensive designer wear, whose conversation fell silent until they passed. A rumbling bass line from the dance floor filled the gap. A few tables were occupied by large, smartly-dressed men wearing too much gold jewellery accompanied by young women in designer dresses, some deep in serious conversation while others relaxed, drinking and laughing.

One solitary drinker glanced up as they passed, his shaven skull catching the light. A mobile phone clamped to his ear in one heavily tattooed hand, a pint of lager in the other, blurred blue-green elbows on the table. He said, "All right, Jooksie. How's business?" Without waiting for an answer, he continued his phone conversation.

They entered a doorway at the rear of the bar. A full-size snooker table dominated. One man, face screwed up in concentration, bent over the table, carefully taking aim with his cue. A big man, tall but fat from a diet of kebabs and curries, he wore a heavy moustache and a tie at half-mast with the top shirt button unfastened, shirtsleeves rolled up, exposing hairy forearms. Another man lounged in a swivel chair behind a large mahogany desk at the rear of the room, watching the other take his shot. Both looked to be around middle age.

"Have some of that!" The big man took a single ferocious shot, slamming the black ball into a far corner pocket. He ignored the "NO SMOKING OVER THE SNOOKER TABLE" sign hung overhead, tendrils of pungent smoke drifted from the cigar clamped between his teeth. "What a fucking shot, eh?" he said, grinning. The man at the desk shot the snooker player a disapproving glance through steel rimmed glasses. "Watch the table, Gary," he ordered. He fitted perfectly the stereotype of an accountant with neatly parted salt-and-pepper hair, steel rimmed glasses and a neat pile of ledgers and folders stacked on his desk. There were also a couple of fat, neatly chopped lines of white powder on its polished surface, waiting to be hoovered up.

Chastised, Gary crushed his cigar out in an ashtray. The man behind the desk rose, beaming at his visitors. "What sort of time do you call this?" he said, exchanging exuberant backslaps and handshakes with Beres and Blunt

Tony with the air of authority of someone who was used to giving the orders and being obeyed without question. A man who made decisions that mattered. Rush's nagging sense of familiarity suddenly blossomed into full-blown recognition. Jimmy Rawlins was the lynchpin of West London's most influential underworld organisation. He was a legend in the area, feared and respected. Rush couldn't help wondering what such a high roller was doing back in South Acton.

Rawlins turned to him. "Firstly, I'd just like to say how good it is to see Jooks back on the firm again." It was impossible to tell if the remark was sarcastic or not. "Secondly, we got a score today, all thanks to the help and goodwill of plod, including DS Forrester here." They all guffawed loudly at this, except Forrester, staring wide-eyed at Rush, who was close enough to see the frosting of white powder in Forrester's moustache. Forrester's snooker cue clattered onto the terracotta-tiled floor as he dropped it.

"You feeling all right, Gary?" asked Rawlins. Forrester's complexion was suddenly several shades paler.

"Yeah, fine. No problem," he managed.

"Anyway," Rawlins continued. "I've got a little bonus for everyone, tonight." He stood behind the desk and handed out three bricks of red fifty-pound notes. Rush couldn't believe his eyes. There had to be at least a few grand there. Not wanting to appear too eager, he glanced at the wedge, weighing it in his hand, before sliding it into his jacket. "And that's just the beginning of a long, lucrative friendship," said Rawlins, glancing at the gold Rolex on his wrist. "Now, maybe you lot can go and sort yourselves out with some drinks while we conclude our business here tonight."

Rush turned to walk out. "Hold up, Jooksie. Not you." His tone was cold. The others left the room. Rawlins turned his stony glare on Rush, who felt his heart beating in his throat. Now he really was in the deep end of shit creek. "What the fuck did you think you were doing?" snarled Rawlins, clearly very angry. "You fucking doughnut! You were meant to arrange the pick-up with me or Tony, not call Forrester yourself!" Rush had no idea what he was talking about. "What if you'd been followed?"

"I didn't see no-one..." The words seemed to come from elsewhere.

Rawlins turned to Forrester. "You hear that, Gary? 'I didn't see no-one...' " he mimicked. "So he put our bollocks on the block! You are a fucking arsehole, Jooksie. You used to be a good earner, but now you're really testing me." His voice dropped to a whisper. "I just hope for your sake it was a cock-up, 'cos if I ever find out that you're trying to screw me..." he paused for effect. "...I'll cut your fucking bollocks off."

Rush tried to remain cool and composed. "You got nothing to worry about with me. I'm staunch. You know that, Jimmy."

"Do I?" Rawlins glanced at Forrester, who was looking even paler, like he had seen a ghost, then turned to Rush

again. "Go on. Fuck off. And close the door behind you."
Rush quietly left the room, holding his breath until he was
back in the main bar area.

He felt as though he was sleepwalking. The whole
situation had a sense of unreality about it. As if to add to
the hazy aura, shadowy figures waved their hands in the
air on the dance floor, swaying in slow-mo to thundering
German techno-trance. The floor was packed tight with
strobe-lit twenty-somethings; a mixture of shirts-off
ecstasy casualties in combat fatigues and trainers, young
women in PVC and luminous lycra sportswear, and a few
older local faces in their Stone Island and Henri Lloyd gear,
fuelling the bacchanalian rapture on the dance floor with
E's and whiz.

Rush watched Blunt Tony and Beres noisily carousing
at a corner table. A tiny top-heavy redhead in an equally
tiny black dress laughed and squealed as Blunt Tony
squeezed her breasts. Beres poured champagne from a
magnum bottle of Moet into several glasses on the table.
He raised his voice over a juddering bass line. "Yo,
Homes," he called to Rush as he passed a glass over to
Blunt Tony. "Rica's looking for you, G."

"Yeah. I know." He spotted the statuesque young black
woman with the bleached crop cutting a swathe through
the crowd of clubbers like a heat-seeking missile. The exit
was located on the opposite side of a flailing, sweating
dance floor and it was unlikely he would be able to slip
away quietly without anyone noticing. Not wanting to
push his luck, he made his way over to the bar. At least

there, even if he had been rumbled, the conversation would be out of earshot of the others. Other drinkers, two young women in short skirts and low-cut tops and two young guys with shaved heads, shifted aside without a word. He ordered a bottle of lager and waited. Rica strode up to him and gripped his arm, just above the elbow. She hissed into his ear, "I need to talk to you now. Not here. Outside."

"You're very direct," he said, smiling. "Don't you even want a drink first?"

He looked down at the slim, elegant hand squeezing his arm. She drew her hand away slowly, brushing his thigh in the process. She looked at him hard. Her eyes were hazel with specks of silver around the irises. As well as suspicion, there was something else there. Something she did not want to bring attention to. Fear, perhaps. "You're not Jooksie," she said. It wasn't an accusation, just a matter-of-fact statement. "I think you and me need to talk." She shrugged her fine-boned shoulders into her long leather coat and strode off towards the exit without looking back once. Rush left his beer on the bar and followed her.

The damp night air was refreshing after the pressure cooker atmosphere of the club. The doormen had joined Blunt Tony's crew at their table, so Rush and Rica were alone at the foot of the concrete stairs that led to the alley above. Rush retrieved a small bag of weed from his pocket and, cupping his hands to protect them from the rain, stuck together a few Rizlas. He broke open a cigarette Rica gave him and carefully laced the tobacco inside the papers. Once he had completed the spliff he passed it to her. She flicked open a silver Zippo, ignited it, taking a couple of deep draws, the tip glowing and exhaled a cloud of herb smoke. She sighed and looked up at Notes, peering closely at him, as if for the first time. "So," she said pleasantly, "as you're obviously not Jooksie, I think we ought to introduce ourselves." She passed the joint to him, coolly exhaling another column of smoke into the night air. "Rica." She held out her hand, which he shook lightly.

"Rushmore Ellis." He saw no reason not to tell her the truth now his cover was blown anyway. "But most people call me Rush."

"So why pass yourself off as Jooksie? Unless you happen to be police, that is."

"You're having a laugh!" he spluttered. "How did you know?"

She smirked at him. "You might look alike, but that's as far as it goes. You're nothing like him."

He took a toke on the spliff and blinked at her through the weed smoke as she spoke. "Anyway," she said, quietly. "He... retired. Some time ago." Before he could ask her more, she had reached into her mock-croc handbag and handed him a photograph. For a fraction of a second, he thought he saw a trace of sadness on her face, but when he looked again it had vanished.

He gazed in amazement at the picture. Self-assured and solid, a stocky young mixed-race man stood under a tree, leaning against the trunk, framed by an idyllic pastoral landscape. The sky behind him was a brilliant blue and he smiled contentedly. The resemblance between Rush and the man in the photograph was startling; so much so that a casual observer could have been forgiven for thinking the photo was actually of him. Wide-eyed, he handed the photo back to Rica, who tucked the precious memento back in the handbag. As she did so, he caught a glimpse of a shiny, metallic object inside.

"So what was he to you?" As if he needed to ask.

"Everything. He was absolutely everything to me for six years. After that he became nothing to anyone. Even himself. But now he's gone and that's that. All that's history now but..." she leant forward and whispered into his ear, "...unless you want to go the same way, you'd better leave. Now." She patted the bulge in the pocket he had the wedge of banknotes in. "Quit now and you might just stay alive," she warned. "Turn around and just keep on walking."

He wasn't sure if it was a threat, a warning or both. "Why?"

"Rawlins' got an arrangement with the Serious Crime Squad. He gives Forrester a cut in return for delivery of some of the gear they seize from the main suppliers. Most of them are Rawlins's competitors."

"What's that got to do with me?"

"Don't be naive," she snorted, exasperated. "You just passed yourself off as one of Rawlins's right hand guys," she said, as though trying to explain a point to a particularly stupid child. "Rawlins thinks he's just paid

Jooksie for his part in setting up the operation. If he finds out you're not Jooksie he'll kill you. Forrester's a paranoiac coke fiend and thinks Jooksie's come back to take revenge on him…"

"Revenge for what?"

She ignored the question. "…And he'll probably kill you anyway."

"But if I bail out now I'll be OK?" said Rush, unconvinced. "What's to stop them coming to my yard?"

"They won't, trust me."

"What if I don't?"

"You don't have a choice, believe me. You won't live to see morning. I've spoken to Forrester and he's having kittens along with his paranoid delusions. He's convinced you're Jooksie, back from the dead."

"You really gotta be takin' the piss." But Rica was not laughing at all. Rush took a deep pull on the spliff and felt a warm fog enveloping his brain. He found himself examining the neon sign's reflections in the puddles. He thought about the danger he could be in, but it didn't seem real, somehow. He felt bulletproof. And he really needed that cash. Rica stepped up to him, wrapped both arms round his neck and kissed him, mashing her mouth against his, deep and lingering; a goodbye kiss. The door behind them crashed open and Forrester stood in the doorway, cradling an Uzi submachine gun in his arms. "Too late," said Rica, pushing Rush away.

"No more phone calls at 3am, you bastard," shouted Forrester, sweating and dishevelled. "No more standing outside my house at night. You're fucking dead and buried!" He turned to Rica, staring wildly. "You saw me put a bullet in him!" He was desperate, pleading for reassurance. "Tell me you saw it!" He was up close now, his glazed bloodshot gaze meeting Rush's horrified stare. He firmly and deliberately placed the business end of the Uzi just below Rush's right ear. "Hey," he said. "Just think. Now I might even be able to sleep at night."

"I'm sorry, Rush." said Rica, stroking his cheek with long, delicate fingers before she walked away.

Rush felt spasms of fear grip his bowels as he rolled around inside the boot of the vehicle. He kicked out at the lid in furious desperation but it refused to budge.

He might have expected to be executed outside the club right there and then. Instead, Forrester marched him at gunpoint to where the Range Rover was parked and ordered him to climb into the boot.

Panic struck him when he realised that he would soon be dead and no one would ever know what had happened to him or why. He would just disappear. What had started as a scam, an adventure, had led here, to this. What a fucking stupid way to die, he thought, tears springing into his eyes at the thought of Aprilia.

If only he hadn't got fired from his job. Then he would've gone straight home after work instead of having a drink with Johnny Too Bad. Then he wouldn't have been blamed for Harry Randall's motor getting torched. Then he wouldn't have met the guy who gave him that bag at the tube station. Funny, he thought, how one wrong decision could fuck up your whole life, or maybe end it.

The hiss of rubber on tarmac eventually gave way to the crunch of gravel. He heard the crackle of gunfire; a series of violent jolts rolled him around and his head cracked against the wheel arch. The vehicle plunged suddenly downward at a right angle, jerking to a sudden halt. Glass shattered and metal crumpled in the darkness. The engine idled for a while and then was silent.

The boot swung open and a torch beam shone directly into his eyes, blinding him. Dazzled, he stiffly climbed out of the boot, disorientated and bruised but otherwise unhurt. His head throbbed. He blinked and rubbed his eyes, shocked to see standing in front of him the same figure in the photo Rica had showed him earlier, still cocky, still self-assured. His twin. The doppelganger. Jooksie looked on, arms folded, dispassionate and expressionless. "Get out," he said.

The vehicle had plunged into a ditch at the side of the road, half-filled with rainwater, coming to rest at the bottom. The driver's door swung drunkenly on its hinges and Forrester was leaning forward out of the seat, bent over the dashboard, head pressed against the windscreen at a strange angle. Rush looked closer. The windscreen was spattered with a fine crimson mist, the dashboard and upholstery blasted with blood, bone and brain matter. Feeling suddenly nauseous, Rush looked away. In the front passenger seat, pattered with Forrester's blood, Rica sat shakily, a small calibre silver handgun in her hand. Small calibre but big enough to do the job, especially at close quarters. Blood streamed down her face from a deep cut above her left eyebrow.

"Rica? Rica? Yuh hear me? Easy, now. Give me the gun, Rica." She stared vacantly through him into the middle distance. He reached in through the shattered window, tried to snatch the gun from her. A shot rang out and a flock of nesting birds fluttered into the indigo sky. Blasted backward into the long grass at the side of the road, it was a few moments before he realised he'd actually been shot. A crimson stain rapidly spread across his shirt and the top of his jeans, leaking from under his jacket. Curiously he felt no pain at all. He watched with mounting horror as Jooksie gently took the dainty silver revolver from Rica's hand and pressed the muzzle against the back of her head. Rush slumped back into the wet grass and screwed his eyes shut as another shot reverberated into the early morning air. When he finally opened his eyes, he saw the clouds had briefly parted, bathing the deserted country lane in pale moonlight. He was sure the next bullet would be for him.

The drizzle had stopped. Jooksie rummaged around in the back seat of the Range Rover, emerging with a brown leather case. Rush was paralysed, lying frozen in the glare of the Range Rover's headlights. Completely helpless, he felt his remaining strength draining away as Jooksie crouched over him, rifling through his jacket, finding the brick of notes in the inside pocket as well as the wallet containing his driving licence. Jooksie watched him, shaking his head, smiling. "Pay day," he said.

Rush knew he was losing a lot of blood; in the moonlight he could see black liquid spreading in pools, seeping into the grass from the exit wound in his back. His sight blurred and his eyelids suddenly weighed a ton. He felt overwhelmed by a deep calm. None of it mattered now, not the drugs, not the money. None of it seemed very important anymore and even dying didn't seem so bad now. He stared up into the inky darkness of the starless night sky, watching the slanting needles of rain being blown around like tiny fireflies. As his vision faded and the grey mist covering his vision darkened to black, he felt warm, rusty-tasting liquid fill his throat. He panicked for a moment as he realised he was blacking out. Then he thought of Aprilia, and, feeling an urge to fight the curtain of darkness overwhelming him, he finally understood his part in it all.

Aprilia woke to the sound of a key in the lock of her front door. Drowsy, she reached out a hand, touching the empty space in the bed next to her. The indentation was still warm. He hadn't been gone too long, then. Stiffly, she turned over, stretched her aching limbs and peered at her alarm clock. Five o'clock. Yawning, she ruffled her dark shoulder length hair, stretching again. She climbed out of bed, gathering the duvet around her and shuffled over to the bedroom window. Naked under the quilt, she shivered in the cold morning air, her pale skin dimpling with goose pimples, the camisole she'd worn to bed in shreds on the bedroom floor. God knows she'd never felt so exhausted;

no wonder her body still felt bruised and ached. But she also glowed with pleasure. Outside, the drizzle had stopped and a watery sun made a half-hearted attempt to poke through the grey sky. A milk float whirred through deserted streets, the clink of empty milk bottles echoing in the early morning air. The flat was in darkness, weak shards of light struggling to infiltrate the gloom through the living room blinds.

Aprilia padded into the lounge. He stood there, grinning mischievously, dapper in a dark suit and a black silk shirt she was sure she had never seen him in before. He looked good, though. An open brown leather case containing neatly packaged banknotes was on the coffee table. Her eyes flickered from her man to the money and back again. He unbuttoned his jacket, removed it and hung it on the back of a chair. "Told you I wouldn't be long. Just had to take care of a little business."

"You're worth waiting for," she said, dropping the quilt to the floor. She wondered what had happened to make Rush so attentive and caring all of a sudden. Apart from the new outfit, he looked pretty much the same, but something intangible about him had changed. He was sharper, somehow, more vibrant and focused. She slipped an arm round him, inadvertently brushing the small silver handgun tucked into the back of the waistband of his expensively tailored trousers. They drifted towards the bedroom, the money forgotten, arranged in neat and tidy identical piles on the lounge coffee table.

Black Jack and the Blitz
KIERON HUMPHREY

The war was beginning to take its toll on Black Jack. He'd shifted so much gear, hooky, for the most part, that his back seemed to lock up ever more tightly every day. Crates of pilfered parts, leather coats, booze, antiques, petrol, cigs, the lot. He'd even been lumbered with a lorry load of mannequins. What a joke — there was only Simpson's which still had any glass in the windows and those had been barricaded for the last six months. So he spent a couple of evenings in the lock-up with a hacksaw and carted the lot down to King's.

Managed to persuade a junior doctor that the collection of mottled and chipped limbs in the back of his Thorneycroft was the latest in prosthetics, made by the Swedes. Salvaged from a cargo being sent to America which washed up in Gravesend a week last Tuesday. Wouldn't take anything for them, war effort, doing his bit, out of action due to an industrial accident. On the docks at Chatham loading midget submarines. Actually there was something the doctor could do. Just slip him a bit of morphine, helped ease the pain. Helped everything.

Sometimes the pain made Jack think about topping himself. Not out of cowardice, but just for the one blissful moment of release before the lights went out. No more nights when the devil twisted white hot rods into his joints. No bastard seizures while he was out delivering and collecting. He'd get a gun and do it.

He'd get a gun and take himself up West to the dearest knocking shop he could find and get himself sucked and then blow his head off while he was still hard.

What the hell the hooker would make of that he'd like to know.

Black Jack executed the first part of his masterplan on a regular basis, but his resolve ebbed away at the crucial moment. When the time was right, then he'd do it. He caught the bus back home to the Elephant, head full of missed opportunities. Got his head down if he could, or stood in the dingy kitchen, arms stretched out against the sides of the window frame, Samson-spent. The pigeons huddled on the ledge of the railway bridge opposite bobbed nervously for a moment when they clocked him, then settled back down. They'd know a real threat if they saw one.

Nights were Jack's favourite time. Always had been, ever since the time Dad hauled him out of a dream with these few gruff words, " Jackie, come on, Market waits for no man. Wrap up, it's cold." It had been cold, a November chill stalked the streets as they tramped towards

Bermondsey but Jack didn't mind.

He'd heard of the market from boys on his street. Not so much a market as a cave full of pirates' treasure – real pirates! Cutlasses, swords, golden jars and paintings of nudey women. As he stepped through the towering iron gates, the market sucked Jack in, taught him its language and rules and tricks and soon he was a Market Boy, 'Jack the Rat' they called him, running errands, sweeping up, earning coppers, then it sucked again and he was a Market Lad, in charge of setting up the stall and cleaning the great French table tops and blacking down the new bolts with pitch so no one would question the items' age – that's where he got his moniker: anyone needing a chest or a bureau aged would shout across, "Bring your black, Jack."

Then the market spat. Spat his Dad coughing and dying into the upstairs room. So Jack finally became a Market Man. Now he could savour for himself the moonlit mile.

With his Dad, before the soot in his lungs got too thick for him to breathe, the mile had been mapped out by references to the dead. Bert's place, used to be, 'til his heart packed in. Four doors further on was Reg. Fell off a ladder and skewered himself on his own ribs. Didn't die for a month. Kept him doped up at first but after a while they just locked him away with a mattress against the door so they couldn't hear the screams. At the junction with the Lane: Arthur's Lillian passed yesterday, God love her – Arthur never did.

Death, if Dad was right, was a jovial tradesman-type who went up and down the mile tap-tapping at doors and windows when the occupant had been foolish (mainly men) or a nag (women only). On days when he'd been told off for not being careful or for whining Jack pulled the covers right up over his head so Death couldn't spot him. If he did die, he hoped he'd get a proper funeral carriage with plumed black horses, not just a coffin carried by Dad and the Market Men like when Jess whose Mum and Dad had the grocers on the Causeway died.

On his own the journey was from a different world. He no longer thought of the estate as a giant mausoleum, each terrace housing more dead than living. It was transformed into a hive, a teeming rabbit warren. He heard the scuttling footsteps and rattling sashes, saw the guilty doorway two-steps and smelled cheap colognes, applied too liberally not to suggest other scents lurking beneath. It was as if Death had been pensioned off, replaced by a randy satyr who had ordered a threefold increase in the mile's nocturnal rubbing and rummaging, half-stifled gasps and grunts.

Most nights Jack headed resolutely towards the Lane with Barney the Bloodhound casting about for new intrigue on either side. He'd wanted a dog ever since he could remember but Dad would never have allowed it in the house. So the first thing he did after the funeral was track down a bloke whose name he'd had on a grimy piece of card under his mattress for a dozen years. Luckily he was a regular in his local because the house whose address was also scrawled on the card was a flame-blackened carcass. Jack picked out the first dog who took an interest. Traded a lovely French console for him and named him

Barney, like his old man. Ever since then the two had been glued together.

Already he could see the glimmer of lights from the Market. The curve of the parapet beckoned him on. Although too far off to be read, Jack mentally traced over the shapes of the letters painted onto the frontage. He had spent hours up there as a boy, leaning over with his nose up against the flaking paint to chuck pieces of bitumen at the deliverymen's nags nodding in their traces below. The sign said FINE ANTIQUES AND SILVERWARE. Some finer than others. That was what Dad used to say as they approached.

By half past three he was hard at it. Hauling covers off the big items, sweating with a dresser that had to be brought out from the warehouse, getting the place set right. No good clustering all your good stuff at one end of the pitch. Vary your quality, then they think it's all decent. If it's French say it's Italian and if it's Italian say it's a masterpiece. If they can't tell the difference, it can't hurt them. Anything you came by in the dark, check thoroughly for identifying marks. George and his lad got nabbed for a bleeding four-poster once. They'd given it a good going over, but they didn't spot that every inch of the drapes was covered in the family crest. Three years they got, bloody idiots.

The Market was Jack's family, had always been, even before Dad died. It had provided him with an education, friends, a sanctuary and a purpose. Not forgetting the livelihood. A very good one at that, because Jack, miraculously, had the nous, the grease, the nose, the touch, the gift. The first time he forked out for some dusty-looking bureau or a chaise longue with the stuffing hanging out, the peals of laughter of the other Market Men could be heard in Wapping. A week later he was offered five times what he'd parted with by a sharp-eyed dealer from St James and the laughter ceased. "What I always say," he said when questioned, "is that if I don't get double, there'd have been trouble." For a while the phrase became famous, everyone using it, even as far away as the Lane. Then the war came, the Market was closed and Jack was all at sea. He had cash, that wasn't it – what he missed was that smell first thing in the morning- like sacks of potatoes. Tea in enamel mugs for tuppence bought from the café next door and eyeing up the buyers: you could spot trade a mile off, then agents with their patent shoes and notebooks and finally the public, all podgy fingers and ripe purses.

It was a sod, the war. Malcolm from next door's boy had joined up right away, or more likely been bullied into it. Went missing at Dunkirk and that was it. He had gone round to pay his respects when he'd heard. Malcolm was out but his Maureen was there, half-choked and the sourness of gin on her breath. She asked him in for a cuppa and he'd not paused for a moment. Putting the kettle on the hob she staggered a little and he stepped nearer to support her. She half-turned and let herself be cradled between his arms, shoulders convulsing in time with her sobs. It didn't cross his mind that there would be grief, barring the bereavement kind, but he hadn't counted on Malcolm barreling in, pissed, and primed like a UXB. "Turn my back and you've got the neighbours pawing all over you," he'd hissed at her. To Jack: "Get out, you fuckin' gravedigger." After that they never spoke, never so much as glanced next door. But Jack felt eyes burning into him whenever he left the house.

The wireless kept on serving up Important Information: conserve fuel; avoid careless talk; be prepared to fight. "What, with my back half-screwed and them using live ammunition, not on your Nelly!" said Jack, to an appreciative huddle of former Market Men. "There's being useful, and there's being on the wrong side of the Channel. I'll be a help when the time comes."

And Jack did help – helped himself to every 'spare' shipment which came in at Rotherhithe, truckloads of 'surplus' which the army wasn't keeping a close enough eye on (and therefore could manage without) and, when the raids started, 'salvage' from bomb-damaged buildings. On occasion, the building may have yet to be bomb-damaged, but the risk was increasing every day as the raids grew steadily heavier.

Jack quickly embraced his new life. But one thing he never missed was his stroll down the mile. Strictly speaking, there was a curfew and he had no business being out and about at that hour. Not with the Heinkels forever missing the docks and turning the Elephant into a landscape like a bare-knuckle fighter's face after six rounds with 'Masher' McGannon. So far the bombs had

missed him and he didn't catch any from the wardens —
they knew him well enough. He'd take his usual route
(except to circumnavigate the giant crater halfway along
the Lane which chewed off the entire front of Morley's
fishmongers one night) then carry out an inspection of the
Market. Gates padlocked, windows boarded up, no lights,
snug and safe like a pope in a barrel.

War chugged on, Christmas, New Year, almost Easter
and it was his birthday, April 10th 1941. Jack was awake.
The raid had begun earlier than usual, heavier too. Great
booming explosions which he felt squeeze down on his
chest like a piston, rattling frantically at the window panes.
He slipped outside and scanned the trapezoid slice of sky
between the squat terraces. Uneven orange stains spread
into the night to the West, maybe Westminster itself, which
was off his patch as far as being on friendly terms with the
ARPs was concerned. Even then they weren't all he had to
worry about. The night the Guildhall took a hit he'd
decided to take a look. Left Barney howling in the yard and
got across the river on a milk float then it was a piece of
cake to get in the back of the Mayor's private residence. As
expected, everyone had been evacuated or was helping
with the fires on the other side of the building. He was just
admiring a canteen of very good cutlery when he heard a
movement behind him. He turned but he wasn't ready and
took a slug on his eye. They had his own duffel bag over
his head in a second. "Fucking git. Thieving gypsy bastard.
Any nicking goes on round here is by special permission.
Now fuck off." He expected another blow but when he

pulled the bag off and looked around with the good eye, he was alone. He left the cutlery though.

Bath Terrace was empty and Jack set off, whistling quietly to himself. Barney cocked his leg against next door's boot-scraper and bounded off to terrorize the shadows. On the corner Jessop's Brushes and Household Products was sagging a little more, like an old woman who has dropped her keys but the arthritis in her knees won't quite let her stoop down to reach them. There was a pram outside No.73, where the Gordons lived. Seemed daft, what if it rained? Up Brockham Street, straight towards the high smooth back wall of Trinity Church, shepherd to the fine flock of town houses around the square. Not a single hit in any raid and the joke went that was fine as long as they kept the vicar in whiskey, but if he sobered up he might start asking for money.

When he rounded the side of the church, Jack noticed a glow above the rooftops over in the direction of the Market and he knew. He started to run and he knew it was a bad idea because his back would get its revenge later but he ran all the same. As he dashed out into the Lane he was nearly brained by a fire engine coming from the Borough, he hadn't heard the bell with his heart drumming in his ears. It was too late anyway. Half the roof was gone and the adjacent warehouse was an inferno so no amount of water could put it out. Some of the letters on the parapet were still visible:

'FIN ANTIQ S AN', it read, in between oily trails of smoke. Jack stood some way off, staring at the wicked red blades of flame which appeared now and again in a window space. His face was bloodless and he felt like throwing up. He knew it was just bricks, he'd seen others, places he knew, friends' houses, but he'd never felt like this. How could things get back to normal now? Barney ran backwards and forwards and jerked out little, muted barks. What was the point of keeping going? He sank to his haunches and brought his clenched fists together pressing them hard against his mouth.

He stayed like that until his back made a noise like a rat's neck breaking, jawlocked by a ferret. Fortunately he had some morphine — for emergencies — nestling in an old Capstan tin in the pocket of his reefer jacket. He hurriedly snapped the teat end of the ampoule and tilted his head right back to let the bitter contents drop into his throat. Just as his eyes closed, he registered two things. The first was the wail of the air raid siren which must have just started up again. The second was a small dark cross above him, far above – the searchlights probing the sky from their pontoons on the river could not reach so high. Waves of calm rippled across Jack's mind. When he opened his eyes the cross had moved away, down towards Peckham now. Probably lost. He watched it, closing his left eye, as if aiming, and wished it gone, softly expelling the air from his mouth. The cross in the sky became a ball of fire. Jack let his head loll back. That would make them think twice about bombing his Market.

After he had slept Jack thought about the plane. It had evaporated in an instant, like a bulb blowing, the outline of its filament imprinted on the underside of his eyelid but nothing else. He hadn't heard, much less seen what hit it. Normally an anti-aircraft barrage was as noisy as fireworks at the fair, filling the sky with explosions. And there hadn't been any tracer fire from ground or air. Mechanical malfunction he decided.

The following night Jack couldn't face seeing the charred ribs of the market again so he headed for the river and the raid came as he was loitering by a warehouse on Blackfriars Road. A grim phalanx of aircraft stretched across the skyscape punctuated at intervals by the soft mushrooms of smoke from the ack-ack shells. Jack almost left them to it. But a guilty curiosity took hold of him and he repeated what he'd done the night before. Singling out a cluster of planes almost directly overhead, he held his breath, shut one eye and this time extended the forefinger of his right hand towards them. A crimson rose bloomed in the sky, and then emptiness. Kiss a lizard on the nose, it was him! He did it again, aiming carefully as the last of the enemy planes droned by. Same result.

Like having a ray gun from a kid's comic. Except there was no gun, just him.

After that Jack was a changed man. He had a weapon and he was going to use it to revenge the market, the borough, the dead. Often he didn't bother going out.

He'd wait for the sound of the engines then shove open the window and sow destruction from the bedroom. Dozens of them glowing for an instant like fireflies. Or he'd take Barney out into the yard to enjoy the spectacle.

Once he thought he had spied a bulky silhouette behind the nets next door and he'd hurried inside – anyone who saw him would get him carted off to a mental institute double quick.

Strange that none of the papers mentioned any increase in downed enemy planes, but perhaps the War Office was still trying to work out what was going on. Well let them try! A month after his birthday he was still pondering on this, on his way outside to the lav. As he dropped his pyjamas the sirens came again like banshees.

He hauled up his johns with one hand and swung open the door. The planes were tiny crosses creeping across the sky. He closed his left eye and locked the right onto the aircraft. Tracked it slowly with his outstretched figure and tensed his balls. The tight formation seemed to spill untidily to one side and hesitate slightly. Jack tried again and this time there was a bright flare like before, then in quick succession a whole line of aircraft was engulfed, as if they were rockets positioned at intervals along a length of fuse.

He waited expectantly. His back began to ache from craning and he swiveled his neck to ease it. From the corner of his eye he saw the face at the window next door. The familiar beetle-brow of Malcolm Dowell, eyes fixed on him, then slowly lifting in the direction of where the aircraft had been until a second before.

Jack stumbled wordlessly towards the sanctuary of the kitchen. Inside he managed to make a cup of tea and felt a little more in control once he'd gulped it down.

What the fuck was he going to do now? It'd be all round the estate in a flash:

"You'll never guess – Jack, you know, the bastard who was messing about with my missus, took out a squadron of German planes just by pointing at them. From his back yard, in his sodding pyjamas!" There'd be all sorts of questions. Maybe they'd say he was a witch. In the stories Jack knew, witches got burned.

He'd have to leave – take the van and head up to Birmingham where his sister was. As soon as it was dark he'd slip out the back, just a change of clothes in his duffel and the wad of notes from the cistern.

He waited at the window. On the ledge opposite the pigeons jostled closer together. He pursed his lips, but something must have alarmed them, an owl perhaps: they were gone in a flurry. The moon was full. Bomber's moon. Nothing stirred out the backs and he slipped downstairs, his movements eased by the last phial of morphine from his tin. Barney alongside.

By the time he got to the lock-up where he kept the van he was almost looking forward to the journey. He had it all worked out: the valuable hospital supplies story to feed to any over-eager johnnies in uniform. A couple of fivers for anyone who looked like they might need a bit more persuading.

They were waiting for him outside the lock-up. Not many, about seven, Malcolm, Malcolm's brother and some of the other boys he'd seen in the pub with them.

There was no point trying to make run for it. Malcolm's

brother took a step towards him, "Jack, we were wondering when you'd show your face — Malcolm's been telling us about your little talent and none of us believe a word he said." He was carrying a metal can in one hand but Jack couldn't see the label, hidden by the man's mac. "But he says he saw what he saw with his own eyes and any of us who calls him a liar gets themselves a kicking. That's bollocks, of course.

There's enough of us getting blown apart by the Huns without turning on each other. So we arranged a little bet instead. Malcolm's fifty says you can, Trevor's here says you can't. We're all witnesses." "What, the business in the yard? Look Malcolm, that was just a... it was an accident. I mean, I'm just a normal bloke."

"That's what we thought you'd say."

The man nodded and Jack was grabbed from behind, he hadn't heard them slip from the shadows, pinned his arms before he could move. At the same time he heard a sharp yelp. "Leave the dog you cunts. Lay a finger on him and I'll kill...." Pain ripped through him as a heavy blow from a bar landed across his kidneys. "Don't be silly Jack; it'll all be sorted in a shake." Malcolm had taken hold of the can now and he walked over to where the dog was being held – two loops of cord over his head and the ends yanked sharply in opposite directions. Whichever way he tried to lash out, the ropes bit deeper into his neck. When Malcolm unscrewed the cap of the can, Jack smelled kerosene. He wrenched his arms free but the bar came down on his back and he fell onto his knees. Barney stopped whimpering and began to screech like a bird as the burning liquid streamed into his eyes and nose, over his back. Malcolm tossed the can onto the ground and fished about in his pocket for a box of matches: "The first one which comes over. You do your pointing thing or we'll torch the dog." He found the matches and brandished them theatrically.

Jack waited. He could hear the murmur of voices but the pain in his back made it hard to decipher what they were saying. Barney was still keening, but more quietly than before, and occasionally he was seized by strange rattling coughs.

The sirens echoed up from the WAF Headquarters at the old asylum.

"Time for your party piece, Jack. Look lively!"

For a moment everyone froze. All ears straining to hear the throb of engines over the sound of the siren. Their shadows stiff on the tinder. Dogs continued howling in the distance, but Barney had fallen silent. Sometimes it took minutes, sometimes an hour. Never at all, if they were lucky. Not tonight though, tonight it was swift. They all turned as one, facing the oncoming drone of the engines. Then the planes came into view over the roof of the sheds and Jack saw the flare of a flame, Malcolm's piggy features illuminated as it fizzed. "Do it now Jack, or the dog'll be bacon."

He forced his head up, saw the moon and the dark silhouettes etched onto it. He raised one arm and pointed towards them. Malcolm and the rest gazed up like kids during a high wire act, fists balled with excitement. Jack willed the leading plane gone. It glowed red and was gone. No one spoke. They were mesmerised by the show. Again he pointed and more of the shapes vanished. He was drained, shaking now, wracked with the pain from his crippled back. Around him the buildings seemed to shift, crabwalking this way and that. Loud, harsh voices. He lurched forward towards the sound, stumbled on something in his path. The bloodhound was on its side with legs stretched out straight. Raw patches glistened around the neck, the eye swollen and lacerated where the cords had raked the skin. Not moving, even when he touched the slick fur along his jaw. It hadn't felt like this when his Dad died, no hatred, no murderous surge in his blood.

Malcolm was still standing there, hands wide in a gesture of posed innocence, still clutching the matches.

"Let's forget about it, Jack. Nothing ever happened. Right?"

But Jack was already on his feet, eyes alight with reflections of the blazing city, arms outstretched. Now he would walk the mile one last time with his hound alongside. Crowds on every corner and every window crammed. So many! Where would they all go, five, ten, fifty years from now? This was what he mused on as London burned. And with a final, colossal wrench, he drew the last lumbering steel albatross out of the sky; it came down at them like a stone. And he looked at Malcolm and smiled to think that his wife would instantly think of Jack when the thunder of the explosion startled her in the shelter. Jack would be the one to inhabit this place in her memory.

The Angus Sword
JARED LOUCHE

When I first moved to London, I ended up in a tiny one-room apartment above a gay bar on Old Compton Street, the kind of place that made your car seem roomy. The four-storey building seemed full of these little cubicles, but I only ever saw one other occupied after dark — the rest all seemed to be offices for dodgy Greek and Japanese shipping firms and grimy sex shops. I can't remember now how I got there, but I liked living in the thick of the noise and chaos of Soho in the summertime.

Angus was from the Bronx, had been in London for almost six years, and lived in the room directly opposite mine at the end of a rather dark and grim hallway. He was generally a pain in the ass but he had a great sense of humour and I was new in town. I spent many low-glow evenings that stretched to deep blue night hanging out with him, smoking reefer and listening to him talk all manner of shit. He talked a lot about music and we compared our favourite all-time records and what they meant to us. He could talk the legs off a chair but when I was smoking his dope, that was just fine with me. Sometimes I just liked to hear another New York accent — didn't much matter what the hell he was talking about. If I tuned out what he was actually saying and blurred my eyes against my surroundings, it almost felt like home.

The problem was that he was one of those cats who didn't know when to shut the fuck up. He'd pop out of his room as I was rushing out to meet my agent or late for a studio session, and just launch in on one topic or another. It didn't seem to matter whether I was listening, or even if I stopped — he'd just follow me downstairs, talking and talking and talking, then wave good bye as I walked out the front door as though that were the most natural thing in the world. He was so hungry for conversation and was so irritatingly sweet with it that sometimes I just had to stand there and listen to him, whether I wanted to or not.

He would usually start with something like, "Hey, dude, you got time for some coffee? I got you some of that fancy shit you like, but when I got it home, it turned out there's nothing but beans in the fucking bag. I mean, what the hell am I supposed to do with a bag of beans? I got a hammer, that's about it. You got a grinder? Because if you've got a grinder, you can bring it over and we can make some coffee. I think I've got some filters somewhere, leftover from the guy who lived here before me, I think — I was using them to line the bottom of the cat box but I haven't seen the cat in weeks so I stopped using them, but I think there's a few left under the sink. What? You're on the way out? Oh. Sure you don't want a coffee first? Hey, I scored some killer dope last night from some guy on Denmark Street — it's a real black eye.

It was a friendly routine but a routine none the less and definitely a tricky snare. Once he asked me if I wanted to come in and listen to the first Lynard Skynard record which he'd just found at Reckless Records — "Vinyl, of course, and in excellent condition. It's not mint, you know, but who can afford that, right? I mean, it's gonna get scratched anyway, so what the hell are you paying for? Right?" We'd been talking about the manic collector mentality and that very record only a few nights earlier. Fuck me, the guy definitely had too much time on his hands.

His classic line though was a real bear trap. "Hey, you splitting? Hold on a second. I'm heading out too. Just let me grab my stuff and I'll walk out with you." For the next fifteen minutes I'd be stuck twitching at the door, watching him putz around his joint in search of one thing or another, mumbling to himself over and over, "keys, fees, IDs" amongst a steady stream of disconnected sentences tossed in my general direction.

There seemed to be a direct correlation between how pressed for time I was and how much he needed company, but I could never figure out how he knew. Problem was, when he pulled his cuckoo clock number on me, I could no more bark at him to fuck off than he would understand me if I did. Angus just wasn't wired like that. "Hey, man, don't sweat it, I'll catch you later." I'd groan, he'd wave. Once I even tried to psyche out his perverse radar for my urgency by strolling in a ridiculously forced fashion out the door and down the hall. It worked too — I got out the front door just fine. Unfortunately, I was feigning nonchalance so hard that I forgot to lock my own damn door and had to come sauntering back like a laissez-faire jack-ass. By the time I got back to the stairs, he'd was at his door, cheerfully asking me if I wanted to come in and listen to some music.

Angus was one hell of a dope smoker, a real chimney, but he wasn't much of a drinker. There were times when I'd come home from a club and find him lying dead drunk just in front of his door, crumpled into a sweaty heap, like a bunch of wet rags. Our hallway actually closed into a wedge, one edge of it was my door and on the other was his, so when he was crashed out like that, I'd have to climb over him to get in. Not to say that I didn't try to wake him up, at least occasionally. It's not that I wanted to leave him out in the hallway but I was never able to actually manoeuvre him into his room and so he'd stay where he collapsed. I remember one time, he was snoring up a storm sitting on the top step of the stairway. His smile was delicate but drawn clearly across his face and he had his keys clutched in his hand, his room key pointing straight out, determined and ready to penetrate the lock, if only the lock wasn't at least a dozen feet away. His response that time, as I shook his shoulders in my neighbourly attempt to rouse him, was that I was a great guy and did I want to come in for a cup of coffee?

Angus used to sleep in the nude. Now, this was far

252

more than I really wanted to know about the guy, but it's not like I found out the regular way. I'd spent the evening painting the town black and blue, and crashed hard as soon as I came in. It must've been at least an hour later when the intercom buzzer sawed into my dreams and shook me awake. It took a while to unwind the whole story, but it seemed to start with two kids, junkie-types either looking for some quick cash or a place to settle down their sirening nerves for the night.

In my drunky stupor, I guess I left the street door open, and Angus was just as stupid as I was careless — he hardly ever locked his door back then. These two characters had cruised through the whole building, desperately turning doorknobs until they hit our floor. My door was locked but Jabberjaws' wasn't and, as they creaked it open, Angus jacked awake, all bug-eyed and flailing-limbed. He saw two twitchy figures outlined in hazy silhouette against the hallway light. In recounting the story he was never really sure what he thought he saw but he knew it wasn't good.

I have no idea why Angus kept a scimitar next to his bed, but he did. Who knows, maybe it was his grandfather's or he'd won it in a bet, but in any case, it was in his hand as he sprang out of bed and raced, headlong and bellowing, towards the two horrified kids who were now cowering in the doorway. He held the scimitar above his head, two-handed, like a bizarre manifestation of the spirit of an ancient Persian warrior prince. He let out a terrifying war-whoop and fearlessly swung the curved and heavy sword down towards them. At that same moment, the two guys unfroze long enough to turn and crash into each other as they headed for the stairwell.

Fortunately for them, the scimitar slammed into the wooden moulding at the top of the door frame. The blade was sharp and the wood was old — it bit deep and stuck there. With a shriek of rising rage mixed now with frustration, Angus twisted and yanked until the sword came free, then rocketed down the stairwell in hot pursuit of the ricocheting kids. Although it was four tight flights of stairs, Angus closed the distance relentlessly, screaming bloody murder and slashing the sword in front of him. At the bottom of the stairs, the kids managed to put just enough distance between them and the dark blade to race madly out the street door and disappear into the night just as Angus hit the sidewalk, scimitar in hand, baying like a madman.

And that was the moment Angus found himself in the midst of a roiling, 2am club-letting-out crowd on Old Compton Street. The next sound he heard was the combined shriek of a dozen drunken and slightly dog-eared girls on a hen-night, followed closely by the disturbingly solid slamming of the front door. Forget the intruders — now he had a new and much more pressing problem: what the hell do you do when you're locked out of your apartment in the middle of the night, you're armed with a large lethal weapon and you're buck naked? Same as anyone would do — show the world your ass while chuckling like you meant to be there and casually press the buzzer for the only other joint in the building you know is occupied.

"Hey, man, it's Angus — am I waking you up? Yeah, um... sorry man, but I'm kinda in a jam down here. Can you buzz me in? Jared? It's me, Angus, from across the hall. You gotta help me out, dude, there's cops down the street and I'm kinda conspicuous here — can you just buzz me in already? You won't believe what just happened to me, man.

I thought about it just long enough to sweat him a bit, then pressed the transmit button. " Angus... hmm... oh, riiight, Angus... Angus, Angus, Angus... don't you owe me money?"

West, London
PATRICK NEATE

The appointment was for 4.30. It was a spring afternoon. At least that's what the weatherman claimed though the sun might have had a word or two to say about it. I was dressed for the occasion; woollen slacks and a kashmir jacket over a beige roll neck. Nothing remarkable. But no one pays a show off in my line of work.

I flicked through the notes I'd made from the phone call with this new client. I realised I knew nothing about this cat. He sounded youngish, tenseish, coolish.

Not much to go on. But in my experience preconceptions can be more trouble than they're worth.

I opened The Times. It was Bashan's copy from the office downstairs. The racing pages were covered in ballpoint circles, arrows and stars. God knows what Bashan was doing buying The Times. He should have stuck to the red tops.

I thumbed idly through. My eye was caught by an inside headline: 'Hanso Low.'

Real Funny. I couldn't believe this case was still in the news.

There was a statement from the chief executive: 'The employee was dismissed for breach of contract, as simple as that. Our regulations clearly state that every employee. when asked their well-being, will reply 'I am Hanso good'. Our brand is an essential asset and our workforce understand they are a key feature of brand identity. Frankly, the fact that he was not in the workplace and addressing someone he thought was a member of the public only compounds the breach. He was, you might say, bootlegging the Hanso brand.'

Personally I liked the comment from the cat's barrister. Asked how his client was holding up, he said, 'Not Hanso good.' Wryly. That's how they put it. 'He said wryly.' I liked that and I made a mental note.

The intercom buzzed at 435 precisely. My appointment was late. The kind of late that feels like fashion.

'Come on up,'l said, as friendly as I could muster for a Monday. 'Second floor,'

I added. If he was as young and tense and cool as he sounded, I didn't want him bothering the drivers in the office or Mrs P downstairs.

He entered without knocking. But I'd heard his footsteps and I was ready for him and my expression was sombre like the weather. He was scruffily dressed in track pants, T shirt and sneakers (without a stripe or swoosh to be seen). But his nails were clean and sharpened and his haircut could have paid my rent three times over. He checked me up and down like a disapproving District Commissioner.

Hell, if I'd wanted to go back into uniform I'd have joined the boys in blue.

I could tell he was surprised by my complexion. People often are which is something I can never figure. There aren't many Asian dicks, for sure, but check out my card for yourself: 'Javed Khan. Private investigations and Oasis Cabs.

Specialist in business, private and marital work. Flat rates to Gatwick and Heathrow.' So you can see what I'm saying, right? One look at my name and he can't have been expecting a snowdrop.

'Mr ...?' I said and offered him my hand. He took the shake but ignored the question. It was hardly an interrogation technique but I'd had him right from the first: this cool cat was as nervous as a redhead in the Thar.

'Terrible day,' I began.

'What's that?'

'The day. Terrible weather. You found it easy enough?'

He shrugged. This cat's guts were wound tight like a tennis racket.

'You Hanso good?' I said. I was messing with him. His face rinsed confusion so I indicated my desk where the paper lay open at the story.

'Right,' he said. 'Yeah, right.'

'Tea? Coffee?'

'Cappuccino.'

I poured him a mug of instant black and he was happy

with it.

The tannoy on my desk crackled with an irritated voice. Bashan had gone awol again. Joy, my controller, figured he was moonlighting and she was calling him every name under the sun. She has a foul tongue that woman. I turned down the volume without meeting the client's eye.

I'd dusted down the black leather armchair but he preferred to stand. He scoped my office. Not much to look at. There's the book shelf that holds Himes, Chandler, Hammet and Leonard (What? You think a newsagent doesn't read the papers?) and a dictionary, an atlas and a Bible (just my little joke). There's the mirror above the three bar electric fire, a couple of cheap prints and a bedraggled pot plant (an unwanted gift from an unwanted job). His eyes homed in on the photograph of Musharraf and me that sat on the mantelpiece. I'd meant to take it down.

'A client?' he said.

But I wouldn't give him the satisfaction.

'What can I do for you Mr...?' I asked again.

'No names.'

'So long as I get paid that's okay by me.'

'You'll get paid.'

'Then that's okay by me.'

I tried a smile. The look on his face told me not to bother.

He outlined the job for me. It was the kind of bread and butter work that puts bread and butter on the table. It was the usual caper; surveillance of some broad who lives on

259

Hammersmith Grove. Ashley Cope, 182, Apartment 4. A real classy piece if the curl of his lip was anything to go by. I noticed his use of the word 'apartment'. Not 'flat'. I wondered about the easy Americanism.

'What's your interest?' I asked.

'I think she fucked me over.'

'You don't say?'

Jilted husbands are my forte. But this cat had never married. There was no ring on his finger and his face looked like he was sucking a lemon.

He didn't want the usual service; no pictures to make him wince, no faxed timetables of her latest trysts. He wanted to come by once a week and I was to tell him how she was doing.

'How she's doing?'I asked.

'Yeah. Is she happy? Does she smile when she walks down the street? Does she feel secure.'

'I'm an investigator,' l said. 'I'm no shrink.'

'So investigate.'

'And you'll come here once a week for the lowdown?'

'That's right. Once a week. Monday convenient? About this time?'

'Sure,' I said. So I'd have to rearrange my tea break? When the fat lady clears her throat, it's all about the queen's head in blue or brown or purple and it was a slow time of year.

I leaned back in my chair and heard the wood creak. I needed some new office furniture. I checked him over with my eyes like he was past his sell by date and it made him feel uncomfortable, not because I didn't want the job but because I wanted to return the compliment. I licked my lips. Bad coffee leaves your mouth feeling gummy and unclean and that's why I usually stick to tea. Or maybe there was something in the air.

'So how many others did you see before coming here?' I asked.

'None,' he said. 'You're the first.'

They're bad liars these Englishers and that loosened me up.

'Why me?'

'You're local.'

'The best dicks are always local,' I said. But his mouth didn't flicker. Either he didn't catch my drift or he had no mind for backchat.

'Two fifty a day,' I said. 'Plus expenses.'

This was 50 per cent over the odds. But my gut told me not to trust him and I wanted to see how desperate he was.

'That will be satisfactory,' he said and I knew that he was real desperate and real untrustworthy. But I needed the money.

The cat decided the interview was over so I got no more chance to quiz him. He handed me a photograph and said a cold farewell. I crossed my legs and contemplated my subject. It could have been a whole lot worse. She was a sweet broad all right; a real city girl in a severe black suit that looked part office and part fetish; long dark hair, kissing lips and eyes that could kindle tinder.

Watching her for a month or two could sure bring out

the voyeur in me. I flipped the photo and found pencil scribbles on the back. It was dated the previous day.

Clearly the cat had been doing some detective work of his own. And now... Maybe he wanted a professional. Maybe the broad had clocked him. Maybe he had better things to do with his time.

The next morning I was up with the ambitious. It was a bright morning; the kind that would make a better man feel good to be alive. Seven thirty on the dot and I was sitting on the low wall of 182 Hammersmith Grove waiting for the appearance of Ms Cope. Sitting on her wall? Of course I was. Take it from me, play the private eye and you'll be spotted in a flash but step up to their face and you may as well be invisible.

It helps to be Asian too. Black cats are potential muggers, whites are potential rapists and Arabs are potential terrorists. But Pakistanis? We sell you your newspaper and give the correct change. It's what I call the 'Stani double consciousness', because we're 'of' but not 'in'. Look at it like this: I'd fail Tebbit's cricket test but at least I still watch the damn game. That's more than can be said for the Englishers. You don't like my attitude? So tell it to the judge.

She was out of the door at twenty-three minutes to eight and she was already stopping traffic. This broad had the type of legs that look good in a skirt and better out of it. I followed her at that 'just so' distance; close enough to narrow the angle so that she'd have to turn full circle to see me. And no one ever does that.

We got on the subway at Shepherd's Bush and headed into the city. I boarded first and took the last seat. I offered her my space before we reached Notting Hill. She accepted and smiled straight through me. She read a book. 'What I know' by Dr Lesley Peace. It looked like one of those self-help manuals. I wondered if she was reading it in an ironic way. I wondered if Dr Lesley Peace was a man or a woman. I wondered If Dr Lesley Peace had bought her title from one of those online degree shops. But I knew one thing: within an hour Ms Cope wouldn't even remember our brief dance around the seat.

We walked through the courtyard of St Paul's and down onto Peddler's Way. She strode through the doors of Hixton Smith, a city law firm, and smiled at a bald man by the elevator. He wasn't relevant.

I couldn't follow her so I sat in Mario's Italian Coffee House opposite and ordered a tea. Mario — he looked like a plausible Mario — glared at me and poured me a stewed, filmy cuppa thick enough to stand a spoon in. I made some notes in my Filofax: the clothes she was wearing, the shade of lipstick (whisky peach), the name of the book. I didn't know what details my client would want.

How was his ex? She was in gainful employment and looked none too happy about it. Just like the rest of us.

At 12.43pm, Ms Cope emerged from Hixton Smith. She turned left and walked about a block before entering Munchkins, an upmarket sandwich bar that will serve you three types of pig on half a dozen different breads and charge you a lady for the privilege. She bought low fat cream cheese and roasted vegetables on granary, a diet soda and an individual portion of blueberry cheesecake which comes with an individual aluminium foil tray and a plastic spoon. A broad and her diet is one thing I'll never understand.

She returned to her office at eight minutes to one and I left her to it. I didn't figure No Name would be so interested in her work so there was nothing else for me to do.

In the subway I went to the far end of the platform where there was room to breathe, away from the sheep flocking the exit. I must have been deep in thought because I snagged my toe in a crack in the tarmac and landed on my hands and knees. I looked up and some cat practically ran me over.

I said, 'Sorry friend.'

He was a non descript black man dressed in white man's clothes; snug jeans, polo shirt and sports jacket. For a moment his face played an uncertain tune then it relaxed into a smile and he offered me his hand up: 'You okay?'

'Yeah,' I said.

'You sure you're okay?'

'Yeah,' I said. 'I'm fine.'

No choc-ice had ever been so friendly.

The following Monday No Name was in my office at 4.25pm. I'd expected as much.

He was tense and desperate. Coolish? Sure. But a real cool cat has no need of a dick; beading temples and sweat stains are our currency, As I talked, he licked his fingertips and pulled a strand of fringe down in front of his eyes.

I had a report printed up but he waved it away carelessly. So I told him about the broad's schedule; five days of work (late home on Thursday; 10pm), a drink with a girlfriend at The Stonemasons on Friday night (Emily Miller. Blonde, chubby and jealous. One bottle of Becks. Two glasses of white wine), a pilates class on Saturday afternoon (electric blue lycra top, leggings, Adidas sneakers and Sunday brunch with Emily Miller at a local brasserie (smoked chicken caesar with balsamic vinegar and a side order of fries). On Tuesday evening she went to visit a shrink in that Hammersmith sprawl estate agents call 'Brackenbury Village'. June Price, her name was. She was nudging 60, wore spectacles on a cord and suffered some sickening alopecia. When the broad left, she looked bored; like she needed a drink. Time was when this information would be the substance of a case. But everyone's a bleeding heart these days. Everyone's a patient.

No Name listened without interest. Every now and then he licked his fingers again and twisted the strand of hair a little tighter. He asked about the book she was reading. I'd checked out 'What I know' by Dr Lesley Peace — Male.

Psychologist. Doctorate from Berkeley. But I still had my doubts. I'd noted down the opening paragraph:

'Life is a series of questions, petty and meaningful. I have devoted my life to answering one question and, now that I have the answer, I pray that you are in a quiet room when you read this. I know who I am.'

I looked up at No Name and tried a hollow laugh I'd been practising. 'And they pay for this kind of crap,' I said. But the cat wasn't the joining kind and his lips didn't twitch.

'How does a Paki get into this line of work?' he asked.

You think the question caught me off guard? You don't know me so well.

'That's real friendly,' I said. 'That's a swell attitude.'

He pulled a tight bankroll from the packet of his track pants and paid me in crisp fifties. More than a grand for a week's work. This cat could cough his racist guts over me any time. Hell, for that kind of money I'd play the damn char-woller.

'I want to know how she's doing,' he said finally. And he didn't shut the door behind him.

The next couple of meetings with the cat followed the same kind of pattern. I told him the dull facts and he stared at me blankly while he fidgeted with his hair or filed his nails or untied and retied the laces of his pristine white sneakers (without a stripe or a swoosh to be seen). I knew more about this broad than any man's right. I knew more about her than she knew about herself, sub-conscious little traits that will only ever be spotted by a third party. Her toiletry shopping for example. You can tell a lot about someone from their personal hygiene.

This broad was quite a piece of work. She spent at least thirty notes a week on make-up. She bought dental floss weekly and always carried moisturised tissues in her

266

purse. She bought own brand smokers' toothpaste and the most expensive mouthwash available. She bought the cheapest toilet paper; the kind that's like sandpaper on your backside. I only saw her buy tampons on one occasion and she bought a supply for a year. So you can guess where I'm coming from. This broad had an organised mind. She pampered herself because she knew she had to look and smell just so. Otherwise it was pure functionality. Like I say, she was quite a piece of work.

No Name showed no interest in these minor details which, to my way of thinking, was a sure sign of a lazy brain. But I figured that wasn't my call to make so I spent hours drinking Mario's tea and buried in a newspaper on the wall of 182. I kept up with the Hanso case. Most days there was something new — an affidavit from an ex employee, righteous indignation from a competitor or some bleeding heart knicker-twisting about the super brands and personal freedom. Turned out they'd sent an undercover hack to the sweatshops in the free trade zones outside Islamabad. The workers there were 'Hanso good', on message. Of course they were.

I found myself shaking my head and allowed myself a smile. These Englishers were always surprised by a conspiracy where as nothing surprises you when you come from the Empire's arse. So I flipped to the funnies.

No Name's frustration with my reports grew. After a month, he stood up and threw my fee at my chest, fifty by fifty, each note punctuated with a word like a bullet.

'This. Is Not. Good. Enough. I. Want. To. Know. How.

She. Is. Doing.'

I needed to make a plan of action.

The next morning I decided not to follow her into work but allowed myself a lie in. I didn't shake sleep till around nine and even then I got up slowly. I shaved with unusual care and ate breakfast for the first time since I was a kid. The UHT milk, tepid frorn the cupboard, made the cereal taste of better times.

I was out of the door at 9.30. On the stairs I nearly flattened a motorcycle courier. Lucky for him he was wearing a helmet.

'What you got there friend?' I asked. If it was for me, why hadn't Joy signed for it downstairs?

'A package.'

'I'll take it.'

The courier looked uncertain. Or as uncertain as a man can manage while wearing a helmet.

'Who's it for?' I asked. 'I'm the only cat on the top floor. Oasis Cabs administration office and Javed Khan Investigations.'

The man examined his package.

'Mrs Poster,' he said.

'Next floor down,' I said and hurried on my way.

My first stop was Irish Polly's. Irish Polly was well known in this neck of the woods; a beetroot faced obese woman who had a taste for fancy liquors and the flexible morality of a life of struggle. She cleaned all the yuppie flats in the area (Ms Cope's included) and had a reputation with the Selfridges set for her unshakeable honesty (which just goes to show the naivety of the modern middle class. Now there's a change from the age of empire).

Irish Polly was no more Irish than me but her first husband was a Mulligan and the name had Stuck. The latest I'd heard was that she was knocking about with Paddy, the Jamaican sort who used to knock Lily Fletcher around before she got a place in a refuge. Irish Polly had been Lily's best friend. It was the kind of incestuous arrangement that can only ever happen in a one pub village or the big big city; the kind of arrangement that has you reaching for the toothbrush.

Irish Polly opened the door with a cigarette stuck to her bottom lip. She dangled the keys to Ms Cope's in front of me and I slipped an Ayrton into her sweaty palm.

'Half an hour,' she said.

Her voice sounded like an industrial power tool. Her breath smelled of ashtrays and sweet spirits. Her breasts were like two babies fighting for freedom. Whatever you thought about Paddy, you had to give the man some respect.

I was in and out of that flat in less than 20 minutes. The place was nothing out of the ordinary , decorated with the eye of someone who knows what good taste is but doesn't get the reasons; functional carpet smothered in ethnic rugs, apple white walls hidden beneath bold prints of Van Gogh and Klimt and Rivera. Her work blouses were neatly ironed and carefully hung in the small pine wardrobe. Her tatty underwear was stuffed haphazardly in a matching chest of drawers. She had a condom box by the sink. She was using it to hold cotton buds. I picked up a hardback from the bedside table: 'The Popcorn Report' by Faith Popcorn. I scanned the jacket. 'If we are to be successful in the new economy, all of us must self-incorporate into our very own brand.'

'Right on sister,' I thought. And, 'Javed Khan, Private Eye.' I still liked the sound of it.

If this broad had a taste for American gurus, it was nothing unusual for an Englisher and nothing I didn't know already. How was she doing? There were no easy answers. There never are.

Before I left I noticed that the ansaphone held a message. I pushed the button. It was from the previous day. 9pm.

'Ash? You there? Pick it up. Shit. Pick it up. You ... shit ... look. Don't take it hard but you're either in or you're out, yeah? Look. Whatever. I just wanted to see how you were doing.'

The message clicked and rewound. I'd found something I wasn't looking for and my blood was icy. So it was a message from her ex-boyfriend? One thing was for sure, I didn't know the voice. The pining puppy on the ansaphone wasn't No Name.

I was back in my office by 10am. I had some figuring to do — like who was this No Name cat, why was he having the broad tailed and how had I let myself make such dangerous assumptions? But the figuring would have to wait.

Someone had been in my office and through my desk

and they'd done a good job.

Everything, was just as I'd left it but the General's eyes caught me right as I walked in the room, a subtle change in angle that pricked my attention. Let me tell you something about being a professional outsider. You don't notice what is — any ordinary Joe can do that — you notice what is different. My mind flicked back to the courier on the stairs. Damn! I was getting complacent.

I scoured my office for some sign of what the intruder was after. Nothing was missing and, to my eye, my papers were untouched. Maybe they were bugging the joint? I checked the light socket, books, mirror and telephone. Nothing. This wasn't a break in. More like a practical joke.

I got on my hands and knees and checked under the desk. There was a polarold sticky-taped to the wooden slats. It was a picture of me entering 182 that morning, maybe 40 minutes ago. I was looking over my left shoulder, furtively. I looked like a private dick. I laughed like somebody was listening. So the courier broke in, then followed me out, took my picture and carne back? It didn't seem so likely. This was a joke all right.

I sat back in my chair and juggled all kinds of possibilities in my head. To the questions of who No Name was and his interest in Ms Cope, I had to add another; where did I fit into this crazy game? It was a difficult one to call. Since when does a jigsaw puzzle assemble itself. This stuff could have driven me to drink if I'd trusted the chauffeur so I shot an arrow to Allah (praise be his name). Because whichever way I arranged the questions, there were no easy answers. And to come to such a helpless conclusion took me two hours of simmering like mutton for gravy. Eventually, I stood up and stretched my hands above my head, a drowning man.

'Maybe the cat's just a city freak,' I said aloud. 'Maybe he's after this broad just because. Maybe I'm tied in like a street on a street atlas.'

When I said this I felt sick to my stomach like the words were a bad Brick Lane curry. Because whatever road you're on in this city, you're always on the way to everywhere else. It can be a good route or a bad route but you're still on the map. Motive means nothing in a city where the city is motive enough. And it's that random plan that sinks a person. Even a London street cat like me.

I had two choices. Because you've always got choices. I could sit back and wait for No Name's next visit a week away or I could continue my investigation of the broad. What's a guy to do? Sit like a lap dog or be led by the leash? I figured I had to get to know Ms Cope and fast. To get to know how she was doing.

I slipped into my one suit — non-descript gray wool with unfashionable detail on the lapel — and I hurried out. I passed Irish Polly's and she was on her doorstep alongside some middle-aged cancer-fodder scribbling in a notebook. He was such an obvious cop that he had to be something else. When she glanced my way, I ducked my head and quickened my pace. I didn't feel like such a professional outsider any more. I wasn't even an invisible Stani.

I was at Hixton Smith by 4pm. This was no time for a cat to be pussyfooting. I looked through the towering glass facade at the list of partners on the wall. The first name was Anthony Abel. Next to it was written 'Basing Street. 1401'. Basing Street was two blocks down on the left. This would be easy.

I called the firm from my cellphone and asked to speak to Ms Cope.

'This is Tony Abel,' I said. 'I wondered if it would be possible to have a word? Now. If that's convenient. 1401. Basing Street.'

She bought it. Why shouldn't she? She said she'd be right there. She'd never spoken to me before. Her voice was viscous and sweet like lassi.

I waited until I saw the broad appear from the elevator to make my move. Then I was through the doors in quick time. I knocked her with my shoulder as she went by and apologised profusely in an Asian way and got that vicarious thrill that will land me in trouble some day. The security was a white knucklehead and he stopped me before I reached the elevator. I stayed frosty.

'Pass,' he said.

'I've come to see Ms Cope.'

'You need a pass. I'll call up.'

'Cope,' I said and smiled dimly. C. 0. P.E.'

The security looked at me and laughed. Then he peeled a sticker from his pad and slapped it to my chest in a patronising manner. He looked at the file in front of him.

'Ashley Cope,' he said. 'Fourth floor. 416. Turn left out

of the lift.'

'Thank you,' I said. 'Most kind. Most kind indeed.'

He bent over his register and asked me my name.

'You must fuck butts,' I said, smiling. 'Spell it as it sounds.'

It was a childish joke and I'd used it before. But I got off on watching him scribble officiously. His sort annoy you after a while and, when you spend a life playing an unthreatening Paki, you take the small victories.

I took a left out of the lift. There was hardly anyone around and those that were had no interest in me. I found room 416 without any trouble and entered without knocking. Sitting at the desk was a white middle aged man in a suit, a city gent to his button down collar. His shirt was a gift from his wife but he'd chosen the tie himself. He looked surprised to see me. The feeling was mutual.

'You're looking for Ashley?' he asked.

'Ms Cope,' I said. 'Yes.'

'What's your name?'

'Fukbutz. Yumuz Fukbutz'

The suit got to his feet and offered me his hand like it was a gift to the initiated.

'Bill Giles,' he said. 'Ashley's boss. Ashley's told me a lot about you Mr Fukbutz.'

I smiled, enjoying the easy lies of the suited Englisher.

'Ms Cope's not here?'

'I was looking for her myself. But I can't wait. As you know, Mr Fukbutz, time is money. Time is i money. You must know that in your line of work.'

'Of course,' I said.

The suit walked round the desk and shook my hand again. Unnecessary. The toes of his shoes were scuffed and he had a fresh earring hole in his left lobe. Maybe he wore a stud at weekends; a nod to a fading past.

'You mind if I wait here?' I asked.

'Make yourself at home,' he said. And he shut the door on his way out.

With the suit out of the way, I headed straight for the broad's desk and began to flick through her papers and the like. I had light fingers and a clear conscience. On the left of her desk was a regulation issue desk tidy. It contained a box of staples and four red ballpoints, all chewed to splinters. On the right were three stacked plastic trays that fitted together uncomfortably. The top tray overflowed with one sizeable loose leaf document. I picked it up and looked over the cover sheet. It said 'Anon Vs Hanso: Initial disclosure'. So she was caught up in this shit? I shouldn't have been surprised. I said to myself. 'Life's a street atlas, Javed. So you're always on the map.' But which side was she on? Something caught in my throat as I thought of No Name and my breath came out with a whistle.

I replaced the document but not before I'd noticed the three sticky Post its in Ms Cope's handwriting that labelled each tray. The top one read 'In Tray'. Then 'Out Tray', which was empty. The bottom tray read 'Shake It All About Tray!!' with that double exclamation mark at the end. It contained only an empty photo frame. This was one funny broad. Real funny.

On the front of her desk, I noticed a small cactus hiding behind the telephone. It sat in a tiny earthenware pot Filled with bone dry soil; one of those cacti that's topped with an ugly red 'flower' that looks like a scab with spines to tell you that it doesn't want company. If you'd sliced its body, you'd have made a five pointed star. Otherwise it was an ugly little thing , but the only sign of life — me excepted — in the whole office.

So you see what I'm saying? The broad's office gave you little personal to work with and what there was told me more about the workings of my own mind than 'how she was doing'. The whole damn case was beginning to make me feel claustrophobic and I unfastened my collar button. When a case tells you more about yourself than you're comfortable knowing, you can bet you're in the wrong profession. Because, for a private dick, a sense of self is only one step away from a conscience and damn Dr Lesley Peace and his smug assertions.

I have to get out of here, I thought.

At that moment, the door opened and Ms Cope walked in. It took me less than a second to regain my composure. I've been doing this a long time.

She didn't seem surprised to see me. Of course we hadn't stood face to face before so maybe I was just confused by something I saw in her eyes: a melancholy, a shallow emptiness, like they were two pools just made for paddling. I licked my lips. I figured she needed a man and I figured she wasn't planning on a Pakistani.

'Who are you?' she asked.

I smiled back at her — white teeth look good against brown skin and I said nothing for a moment. Then I couldn't resist it: 'How are you doing?'

'Fine,' she said quickly. 'Who are you?'

'I am looking for Mr Giles.'

'Mr who?'

'Giles. Bill Giles.'

The broad looked at me blankly. Suddenly I knew what she was going to say but it still caught me like all Aluam bouncer; in swinging and right to the kisser.

'Never heard of him,' she said.

That was it. I lost my cool and there's no other way of saying it. My breathing came short and fast like No Name himself was pinching my lungs.

'I'm ...' I said. And I stumbled to the door like a drunken bum. Ms Cope backed away and her face was now a collage of confusion and fear with a little panic thrown in for good measure. I was riding my luck. Her uncertainty gave me the second I needed and I was out of that office and away down the corridor before you could say 'Javed Khan's lost his nerve'. Behind me I knew she was calling security so I didn't bother with the lift. I made straight for the emergency exit and took the stairs three at a time. My ears were keen for banging doors and angry voices but I didn't hear a thing. By the time I reached ground level, I was sweating like a guilty man. I wiped my brow on my sleeve, took a deep breath and strolled into the foyer looking as bored and preoccupied as the rest of the city suits. I was almost at the door when the knucklehead security called to me.

'Mr Fukbutz,' he said. 'You've got to sign yourself out.'

'Oh yes!' I said. 'Oh yes indeed.'

And I smiled my Paki smile again.

I picked up the knucklehead's clipboard and I signed with a flourish. Four words. 'You must fuck butts.' I quit the building without looking back. I knew I'd out-stayed my welcome.

In the street I glanced left and right before heading up Peddlers Way to the St Paul's subway. It was coming up to 5pm and the day had gone bad, wind howling through the scrapers like a mourning mother. I turned up my collar and plunged my hands deep into my pockets. My brain was giving the wind a run for its money. What the hell was going on? Who was No Name? What was his interest in the broad? Where did I fit into this crazy game?' The questions were the same as before but they'd sharpened their teeth. There were two things I knew for sure: she was fine and I was off the case. But these thoughts were squashed by another that stuck to my mind like molasses. I couldn't see where I ended and the fucking case began. Excuse my French.

At St Paul's I was stopped by a bum who thought I could use the experience.

'Twenty pence.'

'Sorry friend,' I said and didn't meet his eye.

'Butt fuck,' he said.

I span round but he'd melted into the rest of the city fodder.

On the platform, I sat down on a bench. There was a discarded newspaper next to me, open at the business section. The headline sang 'HANSO TRIUMPHANT'. But before I could read on, a young suit was pointing at the paper.

'This yours?' he asked. He looked like he should still be in school. But the crow's feet at his eyes gave the game away.

'No.'

'You reading it?'

'No. It's fine.'

'You sure? You sure you're not reading it?'

'Friend,' I said. 'It's fine. I said it's fine.'

'I should take it.'

'Sure,' I said. 'Pick it up.'

'I should pick it up?' he asked and his hand reached for the paper. An eerie smile peeled his face. When he said those words — 'pick it up' — the bells started ringing in the hollow of my gut. Pick it up. Shit. Pick it up. Lose an ounce of self confidence, add a year's pining and run the whole lot through an ansaphone and who was I left with?

Instinctively I caught the young suit by the hand and I had his index finger ready for breaking in a split second (a useful trick I'd learned from a Nigerian who used to drive for me).

'It's you,' I said. He yelped with pain and people began to stare. I let him go and he shook the ache out of his hand.

'Shit!' he said. 'It's only a paper.'

He hurried away. People were staring. At me. They

were staring at me. So I hid behind the paper like a bullied kid in the school yard. 'HANSO TRIUMPHANT'. Beneath the headline there was a picture that stopped my heart. It was No Name at a press conference. The caption read 'St. John James, ex Hanso VP, has dropped his claim of wrongful dismissal against his former employers.' He looked broken. I should have known. Because no-one stays anonymous for ever in this city. I scanned the page and quickly found what I was looking for. 'James announced that he had agreed to settle on the advice of his solicitors, Hixton Smith.' So the broad was on message all along. A real piece of work.

When I got on the subway people were still staring so I closed my eyes, marking each station with the synthetic voice on the tannoy. I knew I had to get out of London. The way I had it figured, there was just me and this city and one of us was crazy and it didn't matter which way round. If I was crazy then the city had made me that way. If the city was crazy then I'd made it that way. So that meant I had to get out. I still had some friends in the Ministry of the Interior and I needed to pull a few strings.

'The next station is Shepherd's Bush,' the tannoy announced and I opened my eyes. 'Shepherd's Bush.' And I didn't like what I saw.

The carriage was empty bar a dozen figures. I scoped their faces and I knew them all: the rude bum, the choc ice, the young suit, the would be cop, even Basilan the moonlighter … I don't need to go on. Standing by the door was the cat called Bill Giles. He was talking quietly into a

280

cell phone. He walked towards me and I began to hear what he was saying.

'Yeah. We've got him,' he said. I'll ask him.'

He looked at me and his eyes were playful.

'So how's she doing?' he said and my mind cleared like Karachi under fire. So this was the deal. I knew her better than she knew herself and I felt like I owed her something. But I didn't. I didn't owe her shit.

'She's fine,' I said wryly. Then he broke my nose.

They marched me out of Shepherd's Bush station and onto the green. They stuffed my mouth full of paper so that I could barely breath, let alone cry out. The green was deserted apart from the usual bums and nobody was in the mood for looking anyway. They took me behind the dilapidated, padlocked toilets and they didn't say anything. But the attack was uncontrolled. Twelve to one? They could have killed me with a little planning. I guess Englishers aren't so good at that these days. They smashed my eye socket and left me with double vision that's never going to unify. They knocked out most of my Pakistani white teeth. They kicked me in the guts so many times that the quacks removed my spleen. They left me licking tarmac and wishing I could close my eyes.

It's funny what you think about when you're in too much pain to pass out. I recalled a story they used to tell in the Mujahidin; the real tough nuts who knew jail cells like pop stars know airports. When are we talking? Early nineties, I guess.

'The Russians,' they said, 'break your fingers before

they ask their first question. The Americans break your toes. But the English? They think they know all the answers so they just give you a cup of tea.'

'A cup of tea?' I remember us youngsters were goggle-eyed.

'Sure. And then they break your fingers, break your toes and cut off your dick.'

Real funny. But I would have done anything for a cup of tea right then.

From my position I could see scores of feet crossing the road, quick timing their way home. I spotted a pair of legs times two; the kind that look good in a skirt and better out of it. The legs walked away from me with just enough hip movement to remind me I was still alive. How was the broad doing? I'll tell you something for nothing; she wasn't 'fine'. She was Hanso good and a whole lot better than me. It was a West, London joke all right. And I'd got it.

King of Kings
DOTUN ADEBAYO

"Er... excuse me gentlemen, may I have a look in your luggage?" a uniformed official requested as the three Africans made their way through the green 'nothing to declare' exit. He had seen a lot of things in his time, but this was the first time he had witnessed a tribal dance in the Arrivals lounge. There was clearly something suspicious about them. And why were they only carrying a rucksack each? Nobody travelled that light from Africa.

Shaka, the king of the Zulus turned to Asha, the Ashanti king, with a quizzical look on his face. Asha turned to Odumare, the oba of the Yorubas. They shrugged their shoulders and allowed the official to rummage through their personal belongings.

"Hello-hello..." the customs guy quipped. He pulled an opaque bottle out of one of the rucksacks.

The African kings looked at each other, but said nothing. Their silence made the official even more suspicious. He pulled out the cork from the bottle and sniffed. The bitter, sweet scent of incense rushed up his nostrils.

"Phuuouh!" The official grimaced. "That's a bit strong isn't it? What d'you call that then?"

Shaka spoke first.

"Frankincense", he said forcefully, his jaw muscles tensing as he spoke. "...From Africa."

Unimpressed the official turned his attentions to Odumare's rucksack.

"And what's this," he said, pulling out another dark bottle and sniffing its content.

"Myrrh," answered the oba, his flesh trembling with rage. Like Shaka he couldn't believe that this peasant dared to look him in the eye and address him — king of all his people — disrespectfully. But they had come from the East and were guests in a strange land where the customs were different. He would ignore it for now, but he would remember it in the event that the man ever came to his country.

"And what's all this then?" the custom's man asked, pulling a handful of freshly-mined gold nuggets out of Asha's rucksack.

"Oh just rocks," the Ashanti king replied calmly. Just rocks, he thought. Yes, at one time it really was just like rocks to his people. In those days people called his country the Gold Coast and there was more than enough for everyone. But all that was a long time ago. Pirates came and hustled them and laughed all the way back to Europe with their 'rocks'. Today, not even the most remote tribesman considered gold nuggets to be rocks. Gold was gold and that was all there was to it.

The customs man was curious. He couldn't figure out why this African was coming to England with a rucksack full of rocks, still encrusted with the dirt from the ground they had been dug out of. Oh well, mine is not to question why, he decided after giving the Africans a long hard look. As far as he was concerned, Africans were a funny lot.

Horace couldn't believe it. He had lost his job. It was Christmas Eve, his wife had just given birth to their first baby and here he was driving home to announce that he was unemployed. As he pulled away from the traffic lights, all he saw on the road ahead was doom and gloom. It was going to be a terrible Christmas.

It couldn't be helped, the boss had said. It was unfortunate, but he had to let him go. He blamed the recession and how, despite what the government was saying about a recovery, the housing market was just not picking up. The office could only expect to carry two estate agents, which meant Horace had to go. It was nothing to do with Horace being black either, the boss insisted unprompted. It was a simple case of "last in first out." The boss had paid him one month's salary in cash there and then as a gesture of good will, but told him not to show his face again in the New Year.

Horace's anger guided his driving as he jerked the Escort forward in fits and starts, headlights on full beam, in the early evening traffic of Lewisham High Street. What was he going to do? He had a newborn kid and all he had in his pocket was a grand until he got another job. That could take forever.

Even as he was thinking about it, he knew what he was going to do. It had been on his mind anyway, even before he lost the job. In fact, since Bigsy first introduced him to Robert. It was the only way. The only way to make sure that little Junior's first Christmas wasn't going to be an austere one. And to make sure that Taiwo wouldn't be worried about how they were going to work it out.

Instead of continuing straight down the High Street towards his home in Catford, Horace took a right at the swimming baths, down Ladywell Road, to Robert's apartment on Adelaide Avenue. He parked the Escort in a space in front of the four-storey Edwardian house overlooking Hilly Fields. He looked up through the windscreen at the second floor apartment where he knew Robert was staying. There was a light on. That was a good sign. He switched off the ignition and climbed out.

After ringing the middle bell a second time, Horace heard the sound of footsteps skipping down the stairs two at a time. The front door opened. From behind it, Robert's smiling face welcomed him.

"Horace, nice to see you. And merry christmas!"

"Merry christmas," Horace replied, stepping in out of the cold and closing the door behind him. He followed Robert up the stairs.

Horace looked around the spacious apartment as he entered. It was the first time he had been there since he came with Bigsy. It looked like it had been completely furnished by Ikea. On top of the television was a photograph of Robert's girlfriend and their daughter, a mixed race cherub of about six-years-old.

"What brings you about these parts?" Robert asked. "I thought you weren't interested in our little business proposition?"

Horace felt slightly embarrassed. It was one thing to have to ask a white guy for help, but he didn't need to be reminded of his initial reluctance.

"Yeah, well…" Horace said, "I changed my mind."

Robert smiled. "Fancied a bit of extra cash for the Christmas did we?"

Horace blushed.

"Well, old chap," Robert continued, "this is your lucky day. I'm going to see my friend from the Exchange later on this evening. The markets will still be open tomorrow. People aren't going to stop making money just because it's Christmas Eve!" Robert laughed. Horace smiled nervously. "So, how much money do you want me to put in on your behalf?"

Horace took a moment to think about it. He didn't need to. His mind was already made up.

"A grand," he replied firmly.

Robert's eyes lit up. "You really mean business, don't you? Well that's good. That's the same amount that Bigsy is in for." He put his arm around Hector reassuringly. "Don't worry, you'll see that it'll all be okay. By tomorrow, that one thousand pounds will be two. You'll see. I'll come by tomorrow evening with your profits. If I was you, I would let my stake ride, through into next year and you'll see how much you'll be picking up every week."

Horace pulled out the wad of notes from his back pocket. He counted out the twenty fifties, slowly, then handed Robert the whole lot.

"I'll be by about seven tomorrow evening," Robert said, showing Horace out the door.

They weren't going to buy a christmas tree. Horace felt that the reusable tree in the attic would do fine. But Taiwo wanted to make this Christmas special. They had every reason to celebrate with their week-old son.

She had the tree delivered while Horace was out at work and paid for it on credit. And she had found time to decorate it because her twin sister Shola who lived next door with her husband and also had a new-born baby, was only too willing to look after Junior.

The tree looked magnificent. Three years at art college hadn't gone to waste, Taiwo had an eye for the beautiful.

Horace returned home with his worries still on his mind. What if things never turned out right? Supposing he lost his money? Even though Robert assured him otherwise, there was always a possibility wasn't there? It was a gamble, he was taking a risk. If anything happened to that money he would be in some dire financial straits.

He had resolved not to say anything to his wife about being laid off. He would do the worrying for the two of them. And he definitely wouldn't say anything about his little visit to Robert's place either. She wouldn't have approved. She had been against it from the start.

He parked the car and made his way up to their two-bedroom 17th floor flat in Catford. He noticed the bright lights of the Christmas tree as soon as he opened the door. It made him warm inside. But the tree was much larger than their usual.

"Surprise!" Taiwo called out as her husband entered. She walked over cradling her sleeping baby in her arms and kissed her husband on the cheek and then on the lips.

Horace caressed his wife gently then bent down low and kissed his baby on the forehead.

"Where did you get that from?" he asked miserably.

"I got the greengrocer to deliver it. It was the biggest in the shop."

"And the most expensive?"

It wasn't the only thing she had bought on credit that day. At the foot of the tree were wrapped an assortment of large packages wrapped in festive paper.

"Oh no, oh no, oh no..." Horace repeated, holding his head in anguish. They couldn't afford to keep spending money like this, they had just had a baby. they had to be saving every penny. Taiwo couldn't understand why Horace was so upset. They weren't desperate for money, were they? Horace's salary would tie them over until she returned to work in a few months time.

"Oh no, oh no, oh no..." Horace groaned some more.

Horace was up early on Christmas Eve morning. He was

unable to sleep for most of the night. He stayed at home all day, but was restless and unable to concentrate his thoughts on being a loving husband and father. Taiwo was just glad to have him home for an extra day. By evening time, Horace was sweating and hyperventilating. Seven o'clock came, but there was no sign of Robert. Horace gave it some time. Eight o'clock came and went but still no sign of Robert. By this time Horace couldn't take it anymore. He picked up his One 2 One and dialled Bigsy's number.

"Yaow, what's up Big? You hear from the white boy yet…? What the hell's happening, man? No man, I'm not taking it easy. Let's go to his house right now. I'll meet you outside. In fifteen minutes."

Horace told Taiwo that he needed to sort out a couple of things, that he wouldn't be long. Outside in his car, he was fuming. His mind told him that no news was bad news and he had begun to wish that he hadn't given Robert the money.

It had seemed so easy. About a month before, his best friend Bigsy met this white guy Robert, who claimed that he had friends in the City who made stacks of money doing bits and pieces of insider trading. These friends were going to do Robert a favour and let him invest some of his money. They couldn't lose. With their insider information, they would be able to buy shares cheap one day and sell them for double the next.

Bigsy, whose attitude was "why should white guys have all the fun?" urged Horace to join them on the money-go-round. Horace was thinking of investing a couple of hundred pounds, just to see what would happen, but Taiwo wouldn't allow him. She told him that his avarice was making him blind. He would have probably agreed with her, if it wasn't for losing his job. That had put everything in a different perspective.

"I swear, I'll kill him if I get hold of him!" Bigsy threatened.

Horace merely stared ahead, a blank expression in his eyes. They had been sitting for hours in Bigsy's Suzuki jeep outside the flat where Robert lived. It was now after midnight on Christmas morning.

When first they arrived, they had rung the bell and Robert's woman Wendy, had answered. She said that she hadn't seen him all day, she didn't know where he was. And anyway, he didn't really live there, she did. He had only been staying there a while to see his daughter while he was in England. Ordinarily he lived in Paris with his mother.

Bigsy was unwilling to believe her, but it was clear to Horace that Wendy was telling the truth. She had a weary look on her face as if she had been through this all before.

After another hour sitting and waiting, Horace said he was going home, there was no point in sitting, waiting for Robert. The guy had clearly done a runner. Bigsy insisted that he was staying put. He was going to sit in that car waiting, until Robert came by. The man wouldn't just disappear without saying goodbye to his daughter would he?

"Suit yourself," said Horace as he stepped out of the

jeep feeling sick to the bone.

The sound of the front doorbell ringing woke Taiwo from her slumber. She had put Junior to bed earlier and then fallen asleep in front of the television, waiting for her husband to come home.

"You're not going to believe this," Shola was saying with a wry smile as Taiwo opened the front door, "but these men have come all the way from Africa and say they're looking for a new-born baby."

Startled, Taiwo looked at her twin sister, her spitting image, then at the three African men dressed in traditional outfits with Shola on the doorstep.

"Wait a minute," Taiwo said, "take it from the beginning, what's all this about?"

Odumare spoke up. He explained that they had travelled all the way from Africa following a certain star in the sky, which the wise men of their countries had declared was a sign that a child was born who would one day lead his people out of mental slavery, out of economic bondage and out of self-destruction. A child who would save the endangered species and one day unite the peoples throughout the diaspora. They had followed the star all the way to London to offer their gifts to the new born child. And the star had come to rest directly above their block of flats. The Yoruba oba pointed to a particular star in the Christmas sky. Taiwo's eyes followed his gaze out the window and she had to admit that it did seem to be shining brighter than all the other stars. But she wasn't convinced. This sort of thing really didn't happen. Shaka smiled impressed. "You are right to question, my child," he said. "The one who asks questions doesn't lose her way."

Shola said that they had already been in her house and had taken a look at her baby son Daniel, but he wasn't the child they were looking for. She had suggested that maybe they could take a look at little Junior. Taiwo was reluctant, but her sister pressed on:

"You never know, do you? Remember how Daddy always used to say that he had seen things happen in Africa that no amount of reason could explain? Wouldn't it be great, if Junior really was going to become a great man?"

Finally, Taiwo agreed. She invited her sister and the Africans in. After seating them in the living room, she went to the kitchen to fix up some refreshments. Then she went to fetch the sleeping Junior from the nursery room. The moment she came in with her son wrapped in blankets, cradled on her arm, the Africans knew their journey had come to an end. They fell down to their knees, each with his head bowed and holding the palms of their outstretched hands upwards in praise.

At that moment, Horace stepped in the door. He almost fell back at the sight of the three Africans kneeling on the floor in his living room dressed in tribal regalia. One of them even carried a spear!

"What the hell's going on?" Horace said, turning to his wife.

"These...these men... I'm sorry, I didn't even get your

names…"

The Africans stood up one by one and presented themselves. Asha, king of the Ashantis. Shaka the Zulu king and Odumare the Yoruba oba. They explained their mission once again. Horace looked miffed. He didn't believe it for one minute. He had had enough of con men for one night and wasn't about to get bitten again. He wanted them out of his home, straight away.

The Africans obeyed him with a bow.

"At least," said Asha as they were about to depart, "let us give you the gifts we have brought for the child."

They reached in their rucksacks and each one pulled out a gift from Africa. Shaka placed his bottle of frankincense on the ground carefully. Odumare followed with his bottle of myrrh. Taiwo thanked them sincerely as she saw the gifts.

Odumare said it was their honour. "What you give you get, ten times over."

Unimpressed, Horace told them to hurry up. Asha asked for a sheet of paper to place his gift on. Taiwo produced the front page of that week's copy of The Voice. Asha laid it flat on the ground and poured out his gift of gold nuggets.

Despite the dullness of colour, Horace's eyebrows raised as he saw a slight glitter amongst the rocks that fell out of the African's rucksack. Curiosity had the better of him and he couldn't resist walking over and picking up a rock.

"Is this gold?" he asked urgently.

"Some people call it that," Asha answered.

Horace's mind was in a state of panic, he examined another piece, and another and another... He couldn't believe it. If his mind wasn't playing tricks on him, he had thousands of pounds of raw gold on his living room floor, which this African guy was saying was a gift.

"Look, maybe I was being a bit hasty. Maybe you guys need somewhere to kip tonight? You're welcome to stay. I mean, it's Christmas Day now, you can't be walking around in the middle of the night dressed like that."

Taiwo was embarrassed at her husband's sudden change of heart. She mentioned it to him later that night in bed. She felt that his hospitality had something to do with the gold. Horace admitted that it probably did, but he had had so many money worries lately, what with the new baby and all. He revealed that he had been made redundant. He hadn't wanted to tell her, he hadn't known how to tell her. Seeing all that gold had taken a load off his mind. Now at least, they wouldn't have to struggle to make ends meet with their new baby. They had been given a new lease of life. There had to be thousands of pounds worth of gold there. He thought it best however, not to mention how he had lost his redundancy pay.

Taiwo suspected that the gold was affecting Horace more than he would care to admit. She wanted to hand the gifts back to the African kings, but Horace wouldn't hear of it.

"We're not stealing it from anybody," he insisted, "they're giving it all to us. I never asked for nothing. It's for the baby, right? People give new born babies gifts all the time."

The Africans stayed the whole of Christmas Day also. Despite their royalty, they were only too happy to sleep on the living room floor, if it meant that they could spend just a little more time with Junior. It was one of the happiest Christmases that Taiwo could remember and Shola had brought her son Daniel and her husband Carl over to hear the stories of Africa from their guests.

On Boxing Day, the three kings said they had to depart, to return to their peoples. They took their farewells and promised that they would return every Christmas with gifts.

"Remember," said Odumare as they were going, "your failures in life come from not realising your nearness to success when you give up."

Taiwo smiled and thanked him for his words of wisdom she seemed to understand. Horace stood on the doorstep with a puzzled look on his face.

"Remember also," said Shaka, "there are four rungs on the ladder of success: Plan purposefully, Prepare Prayerfully, Proceed Positively and Pursue Persistently."

Taiwo smiled, thanked him. Horace still looked puzzled.

"And finally," said King Asha, "if you want to know the end, look to the beginning."

With these final words the three African kings made their way. From his window in the high rise, Horace watched them finally disappearing in the distance.

It took a few days before Horace could trade the gold for cash. He got hold of Bigsy who was still keeping watch outside Robert's house. Bigsy gave Horace the number of a guy who would hook him up no questions asked. Horace was there at the weigh in. The gold fetched £20,000. He got paid in cash, the way he liked it. From the gold merchant, he made his way to the bank and deposited the money in his account. He didn't care about losing his job anymore. He was considering doing a spot of property speculation himself now. This cash would see them through for a year, and if the Africans kept their word, there would be more next year.

The New Year came and went. Horace soon got used to staying at home with Taiwo and the baby. There was no rush. He could take his time about his next move. He was reading the property pages of the local papers. If the right property came up, he would put down an offer with the money in the bank. Taiwo suggested that they should give half of the money to her sister and Carl next door. After all, if it wasn't for Shola telling the African kings that her twin sister next door had just had a kid, they wouldn't have had any money at all.

Horace insisted that that wasn't a good idea. It was only £20,000 after all, it wasn't like they had won the Lottery or anything. The money was hardly enough to pay for the extra cost of having a kid. And after all that was what the Africans had said it was for.

By Easter, Taiwo was tired of sitting at home with Horace, doing nothing in particular, decided to go back to her job at the Tate Gallery, where she worked restoring faded paintings by old masters to their former glory. Horace would stay at home and look after the kid instead.

Junior was growing at what seemed like an incredible rate. He was already sitting up by himself and his first teeth had come through. By the summer, he seemed to be half the size again as most kids his age. He was a precocious child, who always seemed to be happy and giggling.

Horace found the house he was looking for in the autumn. It was already November and the £20,000 had dwindled to £5,000, but it was still enough to put down as a deposit. The house was good value, he was sure of it. He was simply going to exchange contracts for the house one day and put it up for sale the next day at a few grand higher.

The house had only been on the market for a week, when the Chancellor of the Exchequer tripled the interest rates and killed his business venture in one swoop. Horace lost his deposit. He was a desperate man again.

The in-laws met up at Shola and Carl's house next door to celebrate their sons' joint birthday a week before Christmas. Junior and Daniel each had a cake with a single candle on top. They didn't quite know what was going on, but their mothers' insisted that they probably had a feeling that this was a special day. After all, they didn't get to pick their way through a cake every day.

Shola had been looking at Junior strangely all day. The

deep dimples on the little boy's cheeks, that lopsided smile and that big round bottom. Finally, she said what was on her mind.

"That boy is the spitting image of Carl," she said to her sister.

Taiwo agreed. She had noticed it also. And she had noticed how Daniel was looking more and more like Horace every day. It was his lazy left eye and the stubby little fingers, they reminded her more of her husband than anything. Carl agreed. He hadn't wanted to say anything, but now that the air had been cleared, he was willing to admit his own misgivings. Horace looked up at this point and stated quite firmly that he didn't agree in the least. His son looked nothing like Carl and he couldn't see any resemblance between himself and Daniel.

But Shola would not be put off so easily. Seeing the two families together in the same room had confirmed her suspicions. The next day, she convinced Taiwo and Carl to take the babies and follow her to the hospital where both she and her sister shared a room in the maternity ward. They had to wait an extra day, before the results of the blood tests came through, but the doctor was in no doubt. There was no way Carl was Daniel's father and there was a 99.99999999% likelihood that Carl fathered Junior. Shola collapsed. It took several minutes to revive her. There had to be some explanation, Taiwo insisted. It took another twenty-four hours before the mix-up was traced to a nurse who had mistakenly swapped the babies around in each other's cots. It was a mistake anybody could have made, the hospital insisted.

Horace still refused to believe the fact when his wife came home to tell him the story. Junior was his son and that was all there was to it. But he couldn't argue with the authorities who immediately took steps to rectify the situation and return the children to their rightful parents. There were only a few days to Christmas and everything had to be done in great haste. An extraordinary court session was quickly set up to right the situation. Taiwo definitely wanted her proper child. She had grown to love Junior, but there was nothing like your own baby, the one you gave birth to. Carl and Shola also wanted their rightful son. But Horace pleaded in court that even though Junior was not his by blood, he had more rights to the child having been a father to him for the past year. The judge ignored him and ordered that the families swap babies immediately.

Horace had been expecting the knock on the door all day. It was early evening on Christmas Eve and, true to their word, the three African kings returned, with their rucksacks filled with gifts.

"Welcome back," Horace said, inviting them in with a friendly gesture.

Taiwo was playing with Daniel in the living room when the three men, dressed in their traditional outfits, stepped in. She smiled happily and said how good it was to see them again. The little boy looked up at the guests, wide-eyed.

"Oh he has grown a lot since you were last here," Horace said, pointing at the child. Taiwo shot him an angry glare.

"This isn't the boy," Shaka said, studying Daniel closely.

"Oh yeah, I was going to tell you," Horace said sheepishly, averting his wife's gaze, "you see this is really our son. Not the other kid. It doesn't matter does it? The star was shining above our house. This is the kid you should have come to see in the first place. This is the right boy."

The African kings looked at each other, puzzled.

"So where is the other boy?" King Asha asked.

"He's next door," Taiwo said quickly, before Horace could say anything. "There was a mix-up you see, and my sister's son is the boy you came to see last year."

"Well then we must bid you good night," Odumare said apologetically.

The three kings turned and left. Horace watched as they went next door with their gifts. He sighed dejectedly.

"You shouldn't have tried to lie to them," Taiwo said. "They're not fools, you know. Three wise men... you think you're cleverer than them. Serves you right for being so greedy. All you were thinking about was the money."

Horace held his head. Yes, she was right. He wanted that gold. He needed it. He needed it a lot more than Carl and Shola. Why should they have it? For a moment, he had to check what he was saying. Had he really become consumed by the gold that much? Was he now so obsessed with it that he wasn't prepared to wish his in-laws well on their good fortune? He felt guilty about what he had thought. He felt ashamed of his greed and of how he had hated his son, his first born child Daniel, for costing him his windfall. He may be broke he thought, but surely he had riches greater than any amount of money. He had a beautiful wife, a healthy child and good people around him. What more could he want?

A moment later, the doorbell rang. Taiwo went to answer it. Shola and Carl stepped in.

"It's really incredible they just came and gave us all this incense and all this gold. Just like they did for you last Christmas."

Carl handed Taiwo and Horace the parcel he was carrying.

"It's half of the gold," he said. "We thought you should have it."